DEATH ASSEMBLAGE

Death Assemblage

Susan Cummins Miller

Texas Tech University Press

This book is dedicated to my parents, Marj and Jim, who took me along as they explored the West; and to Mike and Jon, who introduced me to the Paleozoic rocks of Nevada.

The paper used in this book meets the minimum requirements of ANSI/NISO Z39.48-1992 (R1997). ∞

Book design by Brandi Price

Printed in the United States of America

Library of Congress Cataloging-in-Publication Data
Miller, Susan Cummins, 1949–
    Death assemblage / by Susan Cummins Miller.
        p.   cm.
    ISBN 0-89672-481-6 (cloth : alk. paper)
    ISBN 0-89672-517-0 (pbk : alk. paper)
Geologists—Fiction. 2. Graduate students—Fiction. I. Title.
PS3613.I555 D43 2002
813.'6—dc21

                                    2001006279

03 04 05 06 07 06 07 08 09 10 / 9 8 7 6 5 4 3 2 1

Texas Tech University Press
Box 41037
Lubbock, TX 79409-1037 USA
800.832.4042
ttup@ttu.edu
www.ttup.ttu.edu

DEATH ASSEMBLAGE

Death assemblage (thanatocoenosis): In paleontology, a group of fossils brought together after death.

PROLOGUE

THE GREAT BASIN
FRIDAY, AUGUST 4, 3 A.M.

The dream percolated up from his subconscious, seeping like oil through permeable rock. Images broke over, crept around, slid under the barriers he'd erected to hold the ugliness at bay, until the night scene filled the corners and crevices of his mind.

In the dream, a woman bent over a cookfire. With a two-pronged fork she turned bacon in a cast-iron skillet. Her long black dress brushed the dirt. A shawl lay across slim shoulders, crossed over her breast, tied in back. Her dark skin was smooth, fitting tightly over the high cheekbones and elegant nose. In profile, hair gathered high on her head under a dark scarf, she resembled the statues of Nefertiti he'd seen in Egypt. Her lips moved; she swayed slightly. She seemed to be singing.

He could almost smell the wood smoke mixing with the heavy scent of pork. She pulled the lid off a Dutch oven buried in the coals. Wrapping a white cloth around the handle, she lifted the heavy pot and set it nearby.

She was alone. At the edge of the clearing, half-hidden by the shadows and the piñon pines, a flatbed wagon sat, its hubs reflecting the reddish glow of the fire. Household goods—stove, satchels, washtub, blankets, and shovel—were piled in the wagon bed. The woman lifted her head and stared into the darkness, face alert, listening. A gentle smile creased her cheeks. Behind her, a tall figure in dark pants, white

3

shirt, and flat-heeled boots moved around a tree. Pale eyes glittered from beneath his western hat. He stood poised, the hunter sensing prey.

The dreamer hugged the ground, fingernails clawing the dirt. He knew what happened next and wanted desperately to crawl away into consciousness. But he couldn't desert the woman, separated from him by an invisible barrier. He watched the stranger steal up behind her, yank her back against his body, push her to the ground. A flash of white. The stranger's smile turned to a grimace of pain as the woman sank her teeth into his hand. He hit her then, once, twice, a third time, snapping her head from side to side. The dreamer felt his own body quiver from the force of the blows. Finally she lay still—unconscious, dead, the dreamer couldn't tell. The stranger didn't care. The rape took less time than the beating.

The man stood, straightened his clothes, and started for the trees. Something stopped him. He went back and broke her neck with one swift jerk of his hands. The dreamer screamed soundlessly. The murderer turned, scanning the clearing. For a moment, their eyes met. Then he was gone.

The fire flared as a log collapsed and the frying pan tilted, spilling grease. The flickering glow showed a plank across two logs, a table set for three. An enameled mug in the center held wildflowers. In the shadow of a sagebrush, light reflected from a small brown face shiny with tears . . . slowly the face metamorphosed into a wrinkled old man with haunted eyes. The light died. Smoke rose in a billowing plume to meet the stars.

The dreamer woke to the frantic yelping of coyotes, the hunting cry that signals death. He barely heard the sound above the beating of his heart. Sweat mingled with tears on his cheeks. Around him, the air sucked moisture from his skin and grew heavy, reminding him of home. He drank in the smell of dew-damp earth beside his sleeping bag. Above him, the drinking gourd poured out Polaris. There were no city lights, no lights at all, to dim the Milky Way or light a path to his sleeping place.

He was safe . . . for now. And close. In that second he believed—no, knew—that she lay under the same night sky. He'd find her. And when his work was done, he'd bury her. And say the words.

4

ONE

At one o'clock, the first clouds had appeared on the horizon. By three-thirty, they'd coalesced into towering, mutating bodies that marched implacably up the range from the south. I started down the mountain, alternately sliding and schussing in a talus chute, trying to beat the storm.

I didn't. Fifteen minutes later, while I was still above 7000 feet, the hail started. Violent winds and rain pummeled the hillside. Crouched in the shelter of a ledge of black chert, I stripped my body of metal objects, anything that would attract lightning. Canteen, Brunton compass, rock pick, knife, mechanical pencils, hand lens, and watch went into my worn field hat. But I drew the line at my earrings and class ring. My great-grandmother had given me the tiny silver bells from Taxco on my sixth birthday. The ring had my initials engraved inside: F. C. M. Francisca Coltrane MacFarlane. Sentimental value aside, if I were struck by lightning, the ring would help identify my body.

Something moved two thousand feet below me. I retrieved the binoculars. Through them I watched as two men hopped out of a baby-blue Ford pickup and hot-wired my Jeep.

"Stop," I yelled. My voice echoed off the ochre-and-black-striped cliffs to be swallowed by a swell of thunder. The men didn't look up. Impotent, I watched the rain-softened outlines of the two vehicles slide on the dirt track toward the tiny distant town of Pair-a-Dice.

5

The northern Nevada desert spread out below me, steaming gently where sunlight sifted between thunderheads.

"Damn you, Anderson." I cursed the practical jokers who'd taken my Jeep. I cursed the rain. I cursed myself for working solo. It was stupid and dangerous. Nobody'd look for me until tomorrow.

I plucked my watch from the pile. The foggy crystal showed 4:15. Lightning torched a scarred old juniper two hundred feet away. Simultaneous thunder vibrated the rock beneath me. The hairs on my body stood up, the silver bells tinkled softly at my ears as if pulled by the force of the lightning. The watch seemed to burn. I tossed it back into the hat and shrank deeper into the meager shelter of the rough rock wall, praying the next strike would be miles away.

Water dripped off the ledge overhead, dotted my forearm. After three months of fieldwork, my skin was as dark as my great-grandmother's had been. I'd also inherited her Lipan Apache cheekbones, black mane, and name. I was at least a foot taller, but like her I needed the solitude and expanse of desert and mountain. I felt claustrophobic in the city. Geoff, my ex-fiancé, had felt the same . . . or so I thought. I looked at my hands. The white band on my left ring finger had faded, but time hadn't dented the pain, protected as it was by layers of emotional scar tissue.

A gust of wind drove rain under my poncho, delivering the smells of Hell—sulfur, damp wood, and hot, petroliferous limestone. Not that I believed in Hell, unless it was the emotional limbo, the gray in-between world I'd inhabited since our break-up. Three months after Geoff's betrayal, I still harbored an instinctive distrust of the male of the species.

Five minutes later, the storm passed. Water ran in rills down the hillside. The breeze carried the scent of wet clay. I collected my gear, tightened my bootlaces, tucked my black braid under my hat, and started for town, fifteen miles away. I kicked a chunk of dolomite, pretending it was Bill Anderson's head. It landed in a juniper ten feet away. A piñon jay squawked. "Sorry," I said, booting the next rock straight down the mountain. I'd be lucky if I got back before they stopped serving dinner at the Pair-a-Dice Bar. Saturday night's special was barbecued ribs. My stomach rumbled.

———

At the base of the mountain, in a hollow screened from the damp road by a low curving hill, I sat for a short rest and a swig of water.

6

The cooler air of the summit poured down the mountainside, rustling the pine needles in the tree above me, whining in the sparse grass, giving the place a melancholy air. I'd never been to this secluded spot. I doubted anyone else had either, at least since the turn of the century. . . .

I was wrong. Beside my boot lay a small, curled-up, leather sole with a pointed toe and sturdy heel. Left shoe. I dragged myself upright and poked around. Six feet away, half-buried in the sandy topsoil, lay the rusty black, ancient buttontop. Nearby, trapped by the roots of a piñon, an olivine-colored glass button caught a stray beam of light. Flowers and leaves scored its convex, rectangular surface. Blowing sand had pitted its finish, but the pattern was still clear. And beside the button was a human tooth—upper right second molar.

"Jesus H. Christ!" I hesitated, unsure whether to leave the tooth in place or take it to the sheriff. Above, on the mountainside, light flashed for an instant, a reflection off glass or metal. Suddenly I felt vulnerable, exposed in that empty clearing. I quickly wrapped tooth and button in tissues and tucked them into a pocket of my red Filson field vest. I'd come back, but not alone.

The sun slipped behind the mountains as I started over the sloping surface of older gravel that dipped toward the valley floor. In the golden light of late afternoon, the distant buildings glowed like amber. Above me, a common nighthawk dove straight for the ground, then swooped sharply upward with a whirring sound. I ate raw almonds to stem the hunger, sipped water, and chewed gum. Imagined what I'd do to Bill Anderson. I couldn't even sic the law on him right away. The closest sheriff's office was in Elko, two hours by car. I'd have to call when I got to Pair-a-Dice.

I was halfway to town when I heard the growl of a truck in first gear coming down the road behind me. I moved to the side as the truck pulled even and stopped.

Luck, or fate, is a quirky thing. If I'd been injured, desperate for help, I wouldn't have found it for days. But here I was, going at a good clip, settled into my stride, and a savior happened along. I looked at the driver, a stranger. On the highway, I might have kept walking, but out here in sagebrush country, people relied on each other.

He wore faded fatigues, had a face like Caliban and the bulk of a refrigerator—the 30 cubic-foot model. Judging by the size of his wrists and neck, the weight was muscle. He looked like he could bench-press five hundred pounds. His tightly curled hair was the rusty color of sard. Black eyes, old eyes, stared from a well-traveled face. The dark, coarse-textured skin covered a broad, flat plane with heavy cheekbones; the lumpy nose appeared to have been broken at least twice. When he smiled, the teeth were straight, unlike those of most of the local population who seemed to have avoided a dentist's chair for thirty years or more.

"What ya waitin' for? Get in," he said. "I won't bite."

I walked around the truck, looked in the window. He covered two-thirds of the seat. On the shelf below the dash was a binocular case. He followed my gaze. "I saw you from the ridge," he said. "Wondered why you were afoot. Car trouble?"

He looked at me, waiting for me to decide. The skin in front of his right ear was puckered and discolored, as if from an old burn. The scar extended down and around the side of his neck. The lobe of his ear was gone.

"Sort of. A couple of friends liberated my Jeep."

"Friends?"

"I used to think so."

He extended his hand. "Name's Killeen. E. J. Killeen."

That matched the tag over his right breast pocket. Reassured, I tossed my daypack into the truck bed and climbed in beside him.

"Frankie MacFarlane," I said. He had a grip like a pair of specialty pliers, the kind they hype around Father's Day. Gently flexing my right hand to restore the circulation, I opened my canteen and drank the last of my water. There wasn't any point in saving it now.

"Do I call you E. J.? Killeen?"

"Killeen'll do."

"You own land around here?"

"Nope. Just prospecting. It's a hobby." He started the truck down the track at a fast fifteen miles per hour. "Noticed your gear . . . you with a mining company?"

"Grad student. Finishing up my field work."

"You don't mind working alone?" he asked.

Yes, I did. I'd gotten used to having Geoff around. Sharing discoveries over dinner and a beer was one of the joys of geology. But it wasn't my fault Geoff had "borrowed" some of my work without permission. It would have been so easy for him to quote me.

"I do what I have to do," I said.

"You from around here?"

"Tucson." I'd been away twelve years, but my roots were there.

"I was stationed at Fort Huachuca awhile back. You're a long way from home."

8

"I thought about that when they took my Jeep."

"Why'd they do it?"

"Bill doesn't deal well with rejection." I yawned, the rhythm of the truck massaging my muscles. It felt good to sit.

"He oughtta be strung up," said Killeen. "What if you'd broken your leg or been bit by a rattler?"

"I doubt he was sober enough to consider those possibilities."

"You don't seem too upset."

"Wouldn't change anything."

"Don't get mad, get even?"

"Something like that."

Glancing at his watch, he turned up the radio. "Wonder if they caught that Utah killer."

"Utah killer?" I sat up straight, no longer sleepy.

"Where you been hidin'?"

"I wasn't hiding."

He gave me one of those looks my mother used to give me when, covered with mud, I nevertheless denied taking part in my brothers' misadventures.

"Until two days ago, I was using Lon Bovey's line shack back in the hills," I said. "No electricity. No newspapers. It was heaven."

"Well, somebody killed a woman near Salt Lake. Dumped her next to I-80. They found another body today—not far from Wendover. Heard it on the noon news."

"You could have told me that before I got into the truck." I craned my neck to stare southeast, as if my eyes could pierce the mountains and valleys that lay between the truck and Interstate 80. Wendover was fifty miles away, next door in this country.

"Figured you knew. Figured that was why you took so long to size me up."

"There's a lot of you to size up."

Killeen didn't answer. His eyes were fixed on the winding dirt road as we listened to the headlines. The two unidentified women had been strangled.

We passed the carcass of a cow. In the side mirror, I watched a turkey vulture land gently on the bloated stomach. Somehow I knew that was how they'd found the last victim. A rancher or poacher, drawn by the downward-spiraling birds, investigated. I felt a wrenching pity for those two women. I wondered how long they'd lain there, uncovered, food for scavengers and insects. I wondered if, at the end, they'd gone gently, or had fought the mists. I wondered how it would feel to die with a stranger's hands around my neck. . . .

Killeen's lips pressed together, straight and taut; his huge hands tightened on the steering wheel for a moment before he switched off the radio.

"Didn't tell us much," he said.

I thought they'd told us a lot. It would be easy to hide murder among the broken hills, but the killer had left his victims near the interstate, unburied. He, or she, had wanted them to be found. Relatively few roads funnel traffic through the vastness of the Great Basin, and strangers are easy to spot—strangers like E. J. Killeen, with his remarkable physique and unlikely reason for visiting Pair-a-Dice. Killeen, who'd watched me from the mountainside when I found the tooth. I wiped sweaty palms on my vest pockets, reassuring myself the tooth and button were still there.

With what I hoped was a nonchalant gesture, I took the puny pocketknife from my belt, using the two-inch blade to clean under my short fingernails. It's amazing how dirty a geologist's nails can get. "You staying in Pair-a-Dice, Killeen?"

"Yeah. Got in yesterday. Pete's rentin' me a place. I like to do my own cookin'." He said the right words, but a frown compressed his forehead and his mind seemed to be somewhere else. I let a silence grow, staring at his profile and the tightness that came and went like stream eddies across his temples. After five minutes or so, he glanced at the rearview mirror, gave a little shrug, and mentally reentered the truck.

"Silence makes most people uncomfortable," he said, looking anything but uncomfortable. When I didn't say anything, he began to talk about himself.

He spoke easily, but I had no confidence he was telling the truth. Geoff's legacy, again. Lies are easy. Truth is as hard as diorite.

Killeen had retired from the Army at forty-three, starting off in Southeast Asia and ending up in Eastern Europe. He'd specialized in machines—claimed he could build, rebuild, or fix any machine I could name. That much I believed. I watched his right hand on the wheel. The blunt fingers were deft, unhurried. He led the truck around ruts and boulders without jerking the wheel. It was the smoothest off-road ride I'd had in a long time. But I noticed his down-home accent seemed to come and go, as if adopted for the occasion. I doubted he was just the simple mechanic he claimed to be.

When we reached town, he stopped in front of the Pair-a-Dice Motel. My home away from home had six units under the limited shade of an old cottonwood. Over the past three years I'd spent time in most of them. I suspected that the same room key fit all the locks. Each room had a television that showed snow on all thirteen channels. The penuche-colored walls were the thickness of corrugated cardboard. So were the doors, but they had two layers with a dead space in between. Most of them had boot-size holes somewhere in the lower half; the fist-size holes were at eye-level.

The motel beds resembled the Appalachians—old, rolling, worn-out mountains interspersed with low, bowl-shaped valleys. I would have slept on the floor if it hadn't been for the ticks. Last night I'd listened to the civil war being waged next door under faded brown blankets and spreads, the rhythmical creaking and thunking of the cavalry charges culminated in the moans of the dying. The scene had been repeated every night I'd spent here over the years. The participants changed, but the night sounds stayed the same.

"Interesting place," Killeen said, smiling.

"The decor is early functional." Clambering out, I hefted my pack. "I owe you one, Killeen." I hesitated. I didn't know this guy, but I figured I'd be safe enough in a restaurant full of people. "Can I buy you dinner?"

"I never turn down free food."

"Meet you at the Pair-a-Dice Bar at seven-thirty."

My Jeep was parked in front of Room 6—my room. The windshield wiper anchored an unsigned note. The neatly printed block letters asked: "HOW ABOUT TONIGHT?"

I ripped out the paper, jabbed my key in the room lock, and kicked open the door.

Two

Pair-a-Dice was a thirty-truck town, an hour's drive from anywhere. One truck for every five people, and the head count included all the itinerant cowboys within a forty-mile radius. Probably included a few cows and coyotes, too.

The town sat on the western edge of a long, linear basin that separated two north-trending mountain ranges. Perennial springs back in Mustang Canyon provided water through an unsophisticated system of aboveground pipes. Enough water for ice cubes, even in times of drought. The townsfolk had their priorities straight.

Pair-a-Dice fronted on a blue highway that headed northeast in a big graceful curve until it ended somewhere beyond the Idaho border. Nobody I talked to had been to the end . . . or planned to go. The train tracks paralleled the road on the valley side, where the sagebrush-and-saltbush flats shimmered in the summer heat. There was no "other side of the tracks" in Pair-a-Dice.

The buildings were a hodgepodge of weathered clapboard, brick, tarpaper, and old railroad ties. Pair-a-Dice boasted two restaurants, three bars, seven pool tables, and twenty-one slot machines. The restaurants were in the bars, which was handy.

I'd based out of Pair-a-Dice the first two summers I did field work, long enough to meet most of the citizens. The town cooks, Fern and Opal, switched places every three months or so, after fighting with the restaurant/bar owners, Pete and Alf. When I stayed in town and wasn't cooking for myself, I ate breakfast at one place, dinner at the other. I didn't want to alienate anyone. After dinner, I'd walk over to

Freda's bar for a nightcap and a game of pool. Whether I'd been with Geoff or by myself, this nightly ritual culminated in a proposition from Bill Anderson, a descendant of old Bloody Bill. Proud of his connection with the man who rode with William Quantrill, the Younger brothers and the James brothers, Bill claimed the Anderson family still ran true to form. He couldn't understand why that might make me uncomfortable.

Pair-a-Dice had a grocery store that also served as an antique shop, post office, video arcade, and laundromat. It was open five afternoons a week, after Isabel Elorrio finished cleaning her motel. The antiques were thirty years old, the lettuce moldy, the tomatoes bruised, and the milk turning. But the soft drinks were cold and there was a big freezer-chest stocked with ice cream bars. Two long pine benches, weathered to a soft dove-gray, flanked the entrance to the store. If you sat on one end, you landed on the floor. I found that out the first day.

The Pair-a-Dice Bar was a rectangular log structure built next to the highway. I opened the screen door and entered the gloom. At the bar extending the length of the building on the right, a couple of regulars stared into their glasses. They seemed to grow out of the duct-tape-mended barstools like withered carrots on top of toadstools. I got a beer from Alf, the rheumy-eyed bartender, and went to find Killeen.

The restaurant side had two pool tables, quarter a game. A woman in a low-cut, ribbed tank top tucked into denim cut-offs was perched on the edge of one table. Her bleached-blonde hair looked as if a dull X-acto knife had layered it; a braided rat-tail trailed down from the nape. A silver religious medal dangled from one hoop earring, her Phi Beta Kappa key from the other. The cut-offs rode high on her cheeks, and the scarlet top exposed most of an exquisite tattoo that covered her back: Our Lady of Sorrows, straight off a Catholic holy card.

The woman was attempting a tricky behind-the-back shot that made her breasts jut into the next county. The effect was not lost on the five young men gathered around the jukebox. I could tell by the line of bottles under the table that they'd been there awhile. One of them pressed button E6, "If You Got the Money, Honey, I Got the Time"—appropriate for this Saturday-night ritualized foreplay. One by one, the brown-faced men played a game of pool with Diane Laterans, the schoolteacher. It didn't matter who won. When the game was over, she escorted her partner into the summer night. Twenty minutes later they were back, she took a trip to the restroom, and a new game began. It had been a long time since Pair-a-Dice had insisted their schoolteacher be above reproach. Good teachers were

13

too hard to come by, and Diane had a graduate degree in comparative literature from Berkeley.

At a table near the back, Lon Bovey, owner of the Paradise Ranch and would-be congressman, dawdled over his peach cobbler, pushing the last bite around on his plate. Lon always reminded me of a mica flake—shiny, sheet-like, and flexible. In my opinion, most politicians are mica-people because constituents want to see their own views reflected back at them. Voters don't care what lies behind the mirror. The problem with a mineral that has perfect basal cleavage is that only two dimensions are strongly developed; depth is rarely an issue. But I wasn't sure about Lon—that shiny surface might just hide a very complex personality.

Tonight, Lon's high-browed, sun-weathered face wore a pensive expression, as if he were trying to remember the square root of three. The familiar broad smile and controlled energy were absent. Thick silver hair showed a crease where his fawn-colored Stetson, now covering one post of an empty chair, had perched. Lon must have felt my look. Glancing up, he motioned to the empty chair. I shook my head, and pointed to where Killeen sat. I saw Lon's interest sharpen as he studied the unknown male who'd invaded his territory.

"Evening, Diane," I said, as I moved around the pool table. She missed the shot.

"Howdy, Frankie."

As she handed the pool cue to her partner, a skinny, jug-eared young cowboy barreled through the screen door. He stood there, chin thrust out, legs apart, thumbs hooked into the front pockets of his jeans, waiting for Diane to notice him.

"Go home, Milo," she said.

"I got just as much right as the rest of 'em."

"They don't have a wife and baby at home."

"Junior screams all the time. Night and day. I can't take it." He sounded on the verge of a tantrum himself.

"All the more reason for you to go home." She straightened up, leaned on her cue. "Nancy must be climbing the walls."

"She can wait an hour."

"No." The word was final. She resumed her game.

Milo paused a minute, face flushed, glaring first at Diane and then at the others. Suddenly Lon was there, six-two in his polished cowboy boots, towering over Milo. He draped a friendly arm around his foreman's shoulder. Milo jerked away and stumped to the door, pausing on the threshold. "You're nothin' but a two-bit whore," he said loudly enough for the entire restaurant to hear.

The screen door slammed shut behind him. The song ended. High-desert melodrama. Somebody laughed. Lon looked indecisive for a moment before following Milo out.

"Another quiet Saturday night in Pair-a-Dice," I said into the silence.

"Ain't it just," said Diane, chalking her cue stick. "But I did resent the 'two-bit' touch."

"A bit clichéd."

"Uh-huh. And I've never accepted donations of less than twenty bucks . . . except from the occasional charity case, of course."

"Of course."

Her partner fed another quarter into the jukebox, and "Drop Kick Me, Jesus, Through the Goalposts of Life" filled the void. Somebody had a sense of humor.

I crossed to where Killeen, still dressed in fatigues with his name on the left breast pocket, sat alone at a table for four. He was studying the decor which consisted of mounted deer heads, their antlers trailing faded crepe-paper flowers; dusty Remington reproductions; decoupage signs with cute western sayings; beer advertisements. This was Bud country, and Killeen was a quick study. His hands cradled a glass of draft.

I pulled out a wooden chair and sat down, resting my elbows and my beer on the Formica tabletop. "Well?" I said.

"It's not what I expected."

I looked around at the patrons. "Typical small Western town. At least the ones I've worked in."

Opal came to take our order, the Saturday-night special. We got the last three servings. Killeen needed two of them.

"I've spent my life on and around Army bases. Here, I thought I'd stand out, be the only black face within a hundred miles."

"Disappointed?" I asked, as we watched Alf draw a beer for Joe Tucker.

"Are you kidding?"

"Alf Small, the bartender, has been here only ten years or so, but the Tuckers have lived here almost as long as the Boveys. A Tucker came West after the Civil War and worked as a cowboy on some of the bigger spreads before settling in Pair-a-Dice. You're staying in the oldest Tucker home."

"I thought Pete owned the place I'm renting."

"Dan Tucker sold it to Pete last year because the kids wanted to build something new out on the ranch. Pete rents out the house—to miners, mostly."

Opal brought the food. We tucked in like starving refugees.

"Get you anything else?" Opal asked.

"Another beer for him." I gestured toward Killeen. "Coffee for me."

"Anybody written the history of this place?" Killeen asked.

"I don't know. Diane might. She handles the school library—in her spare time. You interested in history?"

"Black history. Took a few courses."

"Then you might want to try the Tuckers. Or the historical society in Elko."

Opal brought our desserts and poured me a cup of coffee. As she left, a deputy sheriff ducked through the doorway. He was thirty-something, bow-legged, and lean as a slat-backed rocker. When he swept off his hat, the neon beer ads reflected off the top of his head. He paused next to Diane, curved his hand around her flank.

"You need a little charity tonight, Buddy?" she said, not lifting her eyes from the green felt.

"Is that what you call it? One day you'll push the envelope a tad too far—even for Pair-a-Dice," he said. But he removed his hand.

"Your decision, deputy," she said, leaning far over the table and pointing toward a corner pocket. With a soft bank shot she sank the 8-ball, then laid the cue on the table. "But arresting me will cost you your badge."

He held his hands above his head. "You win, Diane."

He watched her escort a cowboy outside. I couldn't read Buddy's expression. Anger? Humor? Wistfulness? I was a whole lot better at deciphering rocks. I waved him over to the table.

"Howdy, stranger," he said. "Heard you'd moved back to town."

"Lon needed the shack, and I got tired of my own company. Buddy Montana, meet E. J. Killeen."

He shook hands with Killeen, then turned a chair around and straddled it. "The station relayed your message, Frankie. What's up?"

"Bill Anderson." I explained about the stolen Jeep. "It was a prank, Buddy, but something could have happened to me out there. Tell him to lay off."

"Beggin' your pardon, ma'am," Buddy said in his best Broderick Crawford voice, "but you're about as defenseless as a . . . as a . . . "

"As a sheep at shearing time?"

"No. As Isabel." Everyone in town knew that Isabel Elorrio kept a shotgun under the counter at the grocery store, a big old Webley pistol at the motel desk, and a .357 Magnum at the gas station. *Nobody* tangled with Isabel—not even testosterone-laden high-school boys. "What you *really* want is for me to kick some official butt. Right?"

"Affirmatory, good Buddy."

He took out his official-looking black leather notebook and his official-looking black-and-silver Parker T-ball Jotter and dutifully jotted down the date, time, place and note: KICK BILLYS BUTT. He stretched, cracked his knuckles, and signaled Opal for a cup of coffee. After she filled the heavy white crockery, he turned patient brown eyes on me. "Anything else? I'm here to serve."

"You forgot the apostrophe." I tried not to smile as he jabbed the paper. "And, yes . . . well, there is just one other little thing."

"Oh, goody. I can hardly wait." He turned over a fresh page, waited, pen poised like a waiter in a French restaurant. "Kick Randy's Butt?" he prompted.

In answer, I drew two folded tissues from my pocket and laid them on the table. My hand hovered protectively, unsure if stirring up ghosts was the right thing to do. Buddy took the decision out of my hands by pulling the tissues toward him. Raising one graying eyebrow, he gently opened the papers, whistling softly. "Where'd you get these?"

"Up on the hill this afternoon. The site must be eighty, ninety years old—at least. I found pieces of a high-buttoned leather shoe, too."

Killeen was staring, his beer glass poised halfway to his mouth. "Is that a human tooth?"

"Yes," I said.

"You sure?"

"Yes."

"Can I touch it?" Killeen reached toward the fragile, ivory-colored tooth, but hesitated, waiting for permission.

"Better not," said Buddy. "Man or woman?" he asked me.

"I'm not sure. Either a small man or a woman. The button and shoe suggest the latter, but she might not have been alone."

"God Almighty," Killeen said. "I need another beer."

"Buddy, are there any old stories of people disappearing from Pair-a-Dice?" I asked.

"There was Shelley Gates, Milo's sister—but that was only ten, eleven years back."

"I didn't know. Poor Milo."

"Yeah. Shelley was seventeen, and kinda wild. She's still listed as a runaway. Now, let me think . . . older stories . . . I don't know. That's long before my family moved to this part of the country. Easy Thomasson would've known, but he died years ago. You might ask Lon Bovey, though. His family's been here since before the Flood. Hundred and forty years or so." He swallowed some coffee. "Anyway, I'll have someone look through the files. See if they can come up with anything. Can you find the place again, Frankie?"

"I marked it on my map. I could take you there tomorrow."

"Can't. We're all on alert in case that Utah killer crosses the line."

"What's the story? I didn't know anything until Killeen mentioned it this afternoon."

"Don't you listen to the news?"

"Not if I can help it."

Buddy shook his head but repeated the information we'd heard on the radio. The time of death was still unknown.

"How do you know the same person killed 'em both?" Killeen asked.

"Same M.O."

"Which is?" I asked.

"You know better than to ask. Word gets out, we'll have every wacko in four states confessing."

Killeen stood up and rummaged in his pocket for change. I wasn't sure if it was for the jukebox or a game of pool with Diane. He'd rolled up his shirtsleeves, and his left forearm showed four fresh scratches. I looked at my blunt fingernails and wondered if the murdered women's nails were longer, sharper. Buddy's eyes followed mine.

"How'd you get those scratches, Killeen?" I could hear the suspicion in Buddy's voice.

"Tangled with some barbed wire back in the hills."

"Where?" I asked.

Killeen didn't react to the sharpness of my tone. "Near a tumbledown shack."

"That narrows it down quite a bit." Was Killeen being purposefully obtuse? If he'd been driving around for the last day or so, he knew there were half a dozen ruins in the range.

"When did you say you got into town?" Buddy asked.

"Didn't say. But it was yesterday noon. Slept in the back of my truck last night. Rented the old Tucker place from Pete this mornin'."

"You staying?" Buddy sounded skeptical.

"For a while. I'm looking for a place to roost."

"In Pair-a-Dice?"

"Why not?"

"I'll have to check you out, Killeen."

"You do that, Montana. I ain't goin' no place." Killeen sauntered over to the bar for another beer, then put a quarter in the jukebox. There was something odd about his gait: at each step his foot rolled from the outside edge to the flat plane. Not heel-toe like most people. And his step was silent on the plank floor. I'd seen that same, deliberate walk before, a long time ago—my brothers' judo instructor. If Killeen were to come after me in the dark . . . I shivered. I'd never hear him coming.

Unlike Lon Bovey, Killeen was adding crystal faces by the minute. I wasn't dealing with a simple cube, soft and transparent, like halite. He struck me as a far more complex person. A stubby prism of black tourmaline, maybe—intriguing, opaque, and a little frightening.

"Frankie, what do you know about Killeen?" Buddy asked.

"Nothing much. He gave me a ride back to town today." I related what Killeen had told me on the drive.

"Well, be careful. I don't want to collect your body from some ditch next to the highway."

"Cheerful thought."

"I mean it. Don't work alone. This may be a serial killer. If so, he'll kill again."

"It's not a choice, Buddy. I have to work alone. But I promise to stay as far away from the highway as I can. Good enough?"

"No."

"Then tell me what I'm up against."

"Same tire tracks lead up to and away from the bodies." Buddy swirled the dregs around in his cup. "The victims were strangled. Their clothes and shoes were taken, but their feet are clean."

"So they didn't walk anywhere."

"Right. Their hands looked like they'd tried to claw their way out of some box, maybe the trunk of a car. And the bodies had multiple bites—like bull's-eyes."

"Insect bites?" My whole body started to itch, and I scratched my neck.

"Insect or spider. We aren't sure yet."

"Were they raped?"

"No, thank God. They were spared that. I suspect the killer wants power, wants to terrorize. But not sexually. Revenge, maybe. It's possible he knew the victims."

"But you think it's a man?" I asked.

"Has to be—or an awfully strong woman." He studied me for a minute. "You could manage it. You're taller than I am, and probably strong enough. But I don't see this as a woman's job."

"We keep our distance? Arsenic in coffee? Rat poison? That's sexist, Buddy."

"Yeah." He grinned. "I know. The statistics back me up, though, so don't expect an apology. And since you insist . . . what were you doing last night, Frankie?"

"Moved into town. I had dinner here, then stopped by Diane's. After that, I played two games of pool at Freda's place with Bill and Randy, worked on my map until 10:30, went to bed. No witnesses to the last two activities."

"Not for want of trying."

I wrinkled my nose at him. "You'd think Bill had never been shut down before."

"I'm not sure he has—since sixth grade, anyway. And this is the third summer he's been pushing you."

"There was Geoff . . . " Too late. I couldn't call back the words.

"That never stopped him before. Kinda added to the thrill of the chase." When he raised his hand, Opal hurried over to refill his cup. "What's Geoff up to these days?"

I'd known I couldn't avoid the subject forever. "I don't know where he is . . . We split up in May." I tried to hide behind an expressionless face. I don't know what he saw in my eyes.

"Oh." He grimaced, then lifted his right foot and tried to stuff the black boot tip in his mouth. He was pretty limber—almost made it. The boot thudded back against the floor. "I'm sorry, Frankie. I didn't know."

"I haven't felt like talking about it."

Killeen's return prevented me from having to answer any more questions. He smiled and straddled a chair, facing Buddy.

"Army?" Buddy resumed the casual interrogation.

"Yeah. Career."

Buddy'd been a Marine. I listened for awhile as the two men reminisced. They'd seen a lot of the same places, shared experiences.

The weariness I'd pushed aside for the past few hours descended like a tule fog. I paid for dinner and excused myself. Buddy stood up. "I gotta get going, too. Got a two-hour drive ahead of me."

"Thanks for coming, Buddy," I said. "I appreciate it."

"Anytime. I'll talk to Billy tonight, but if you have any more trouble, let me know."

I nodded. "But I just hope this is the end of it."

"I'll be keepin' an eye on things, just in case," Killeen said.

"Better not get involved. Those guys can make your life miserable," Buddy said.

"I've seen misery before."

"Your funeral. See you around, Killeen." Buddy strode out the door.

"What's there to do on a Saturday night in Pair-a-Dice?" Killeen asked.

"You mean, besides Diane?" He nodded. "You can pick up a game of pool over at Pete's, too, or at the new bar—Freda's place."

"The Black-Light Bar?"

"Is that what she's calling it?"

"Sign went up today. Guess I'll check it out. See you tomorrow, Frankie. Thanks for dinner."

"Ditto for the ride."

Outside, Diane perched on the porch railing, sucking on a cigarette. She massaged her neck with her free hand.

"Had a chance to read my manuscript, Frankie?" She'd handed me a thick sheaf of papers in a battered brown folder the night before, insisting I was the only one in Pair-a-Dice qualified to critique a novel.

"No. I was going to start it tonight, but I'm bushed. Had to walk most of the way home."

"Engine trouble?"

"In a manner of speaking. The Andersons borrowed the Jeep."

She exhaled soft blue smoke through her pug nose. "Punks. You'd think they'd have something better to do with their time." She ground out the cigarette on the heel of her hand-stitched boot, then tucked the butt in her pocket. "Speaking of which, I'd better get back to work."

I said goodnight and started back to the motel. Behind me, someone stepped into the darkness at the other end of the porch. Diane murmured, "Later—wait for me," before she went back inside. There was no reply.

Walking beside the highway back to the motel, I heard rustling and scrabbling off to the right in the shadows thrown by the store. Then silence. Probably a dog. But I hurried now, distrusting my instincts, watching over my shoulder. In the distance a coyote sang to the slowly rising moon. Behind me, a figure in plaid shirt, dark pants, and straw cowboy hat detached itself from the greater blackness of the buildings. Geoff wore his battered hat canted at just that angle.

21

"Geoff?" It seemed as if I'd been looking for him all day, all summer—waiting for . . . what? Not reconciliation. Closure. Had he been here all that time?

The figure touched his hat brim and took a step towards me before turning abruptly and hurrying around the corner. I still wasn't sure. Was it Geoff, or Walker, the local eccentric? Or Bill, waiting for a showdown? Still looking behind me, I stumbled into a moving wall. I yelped in surprise, and struggled against the hands that closed around my upper arms.

"You okay, Frankie?" It was Lon.

"Yes," I said, pulling back, away from his touch. "You just startled me, that's all. I'm a little jumpy tonight."

"I was looking for Ruth. She was supposed to meet me after she stopped by Milo's. You seen her?" He leaned forward as he spoke, invading my space. I took another step back.

"Not tonight," I said.

"You're jumpy as a jackrabbit. Want me to walk the rest of the way with you?"

"No thanks, Lon. It's not far." I started walking.

"Well, if you're sure . . . good-night, then."

The night was quiet again but for the restless wind traveling unimpeded down the long valley, carrying the rolling call of a poor-will. Uneasy fingers goose-stepped down my spine. Glancing back, I found him staring after me. I gave a little wave, and nearly ran the short distance to my room. Turning to shut my door, I noticed the right front tire on the Jeep was flat. Hell. Bill Anderson was determined to provoke a confrontation tonight. Well, I was damned if I'd give him the satisfaction. I was damned if I'd change that tire, either. He could do it in the morning.

I locked the door of my room, for what it was worth, and crashed on my wretched bed.

But restful sleep eluded me—Geoff invaded dream after dream. I woke to the pounding of fists on the thin wall by my head. "Shut up in there, will ya!" a voice yelled from Room 5.

I didn't answer. My cheeks and pillow were wet, my hands clenched the coarse top sheet. My throat ached as the muscles slowly relaxed. It was two in the morning. I didn't want to go back to sleep, back to a nightmare fight with Geoff. Instead, I got a drink of water and picked up Diane's manuscript.

EASYTOWN—A NOVEL
by Diane Laterans.

CHAPTER 1

I've loved only two men in my life: my priest, and my half-brother. I couldn't live with the first; thought I couldn't live without the second.

When I was sixteen, I had a child by one of them. I called her Anna, which means "grace" in Hebrew. She lives now in some far-off place with strangers who said they'd love her. She and I will never meet. I couldn't bear to see the embodiment of what I lost.

This is the story of how Anna came to be, and what happened to me after I gave her away.

———

Two hours and one hundred pages later, I switched off the light. Only later would I learn that in the short time before dawn, while I slept, a third voice was silenced. But this time, the killer struck in Nevada, not fifty miles from Pair-a-Dice.

THREE

The funny thing about boundaries, state or national, is that they're imaginary, arbitrary. One can't see them or touch them. The lines and planes traverse mountains and valleys, bisect rivers and lakes, divide the constantly moving oceans. They're redefined as money changes hands, wars are won or lost, technology advances, and meandering rivers change course. We feel safe within these imaginary borders, threatened when the lines are breached.

The last two murders were the same distance away from Pair-a-Dice, but illogically I didn't feel threatened until the murderer shifted from Utah into Nevada.

I dragged myself awake at five. By five-twenty, I'd showered, dressed, and braided my hip-length damp hair. The world that greeted me as I stepped outside was sharp, clear. Yesterday's rain and the overnight dew had settled the dust. Doves mourned and scrub jays called raucously from the cottonwoods. A meadowlark trilled in the black-eyed Susans across the tracks. The air smelled of sage and clover . . . and cinnamon.

Fern was cooking at Pete's bar/restaurant. She made the world's best cinnamon rolls, the size of a saucer and as tall as a mug of coffee. She was just pulling a pan from the oven when I opened the door to the single-wide mobile home fitted out with a long counter and stools. No tables, no decor to speak of except last year's feedstore calendar showing Aberdeen Angus belly-deep in a field of grass. A sign above

24

the grill read: "GET US OUT OF THE UNITED NATIONS." Reminded me of road signs back home in Arizona.

Pete had built a plywood addition on the back to house the bar, pool tables, slot machines, and card tables. The mobile home was temporary, he said. He was building a real restaurant on the adjacent lot—but the cinder-block foundation and part of the front wall had lain untouched for at least three summers. That was not unusual in Pair-a-Dice. The current of life here was slow, temporary turned into permanent.

Pete sat on a stool, resting his beefy, hairy forearms on the counter. By tradition, he passed judgment on the first batch of rolls every morning. The tradition had settled at his waist, which folded around the edge of the counter as he leaned into the task. Fern waited for his nod before giving me a roll and coffee. I ordered two-eggs-over-easy with ham, refusing to worry about fat and cholesterol while I was in the field.

Pete and Fern seemed quiet this morning. "Anything wrong?" I asked Pete.

"That bastard's—excuse my French—done it again. Just heard it on the radio."

Pete summarized while Fern dealt with the eggs. Buddy Montana had found a woman's body late last night. She was lying next to her car under an I-80 overpass. It was Emmajean Rogers from the service station in Wells, murdered on her way home from work.

"Emmajean—" Pete stopped, cleared his throat, swirled the dregs of coffee in his cup. "She was local. Raised right here in Pair-a-Dice. God, what a charmer. And full of the devil. She worked for me when she was in high school, maybe ten, eleven, years back. Would've stayed on, too, 'cept she and Billy broke up. She married some guy from Wells."

I remembered Emmajean from fleeting conversations at the service station. A petite honey-blond with an earthy sense of humor, freckled skin and a cheerleader's energy. She'd found it funny that I liked climbing around in the mountains. "I used to eat dirt myself," she said one time. "I grew out of it."

I felt the strangler's fingers twist in my hair. He was miles away, but our paths had intersected at Emmajean's body. Why had she stopped under that overpass at eleven at night? To help with a broken-down vehicle? To talk to a friend?

"Do you have to go out today, Frankie?" asked Fern, bringing me back to the too-bright lights of Pete's restaurant. I blinked. She reminded me of a sparrow standing there, tiny, with moist dark eyes. "Can't you put off work until they catch this guy? Emmajean was no older than you."

Emmajean was my age. I hadn't thought in terms that linked us; somehow that made it personal. But I couldn't allow anything to interrupt my last few days. There wasn't enough time as it was. I felt the tension growing in my stomach. "My teaching job starts a week from tomorrow, Fern. It's contingent on my having a degree by the end of the year."

"There are other jobs, Frankie."

"Not teaching jobs. And not in Tucson. There are hundreds of applicants for every position these days, most of them more qualified than I am." When she gave me one of those things-can't-be-that-bad sniffs, I let loose with both barrels. "The major oil companies and mineral-exploration companies downsized in the eighties. In the nineties, certain congressional representatives decided to close down the U.S. Geological Survey. The Survey responded by reducing its geologic force by roughly thirty percent. It won't be hiring for a long time—if it survives. The situation at the public universities is just as critical. Geology departments are being scaled down, merged with other disciplines, or closed. And there's no one to blame but the earth scientists who've had their heads in the sand and their tails in ivory towers for one hundred years. When they weren't looking, the gap between the scientists and the public widened—but the public wields the money club."

"Oh." Fern's eyes were glazed. She almost dumped my breakfast in my lap.

"The upshot is I won't have time or resources to come back here. It's finish now, or kiss the job good-bye." I relented, softening my tone. "But I'm not stupid, Fern—I'll be safe enough back in the hills."

"Well, you could take Billy with you. He's good with rocks."

Pete choked on his second roll, face going from pink to purple. Fern reached across and slapped him twice between the shoulder blades while I mentally reviewed the Heimlich maneuver. Luckily he started breathing again before I had to find out if my arms were long enough to surround his girth.

"Bill thinks limestone beds are good for only one thing," I said.

Fern caught the gist. "Then you just be careful, honey," she said, echoing Buddy's advice the night before. "Real careful."

"I'm always careful." Well, almost always, I amended silently, thinking about my upcoming meeting with the Anderson brothers.

Killeen came in as I finished my breakfast. He'd already met Fern—probably followed his nose the first morning.

"I thought you were cooking for yourself," I said.

"I was. But there's too much going on in this town. Afraid I might miss something."

"I'm sure your decision had nothing to do with the rolls."

"Guilty as charged." He accepted a pastry and a mug of coffee from Fern. "You got a flat tire on your Cherokee, Frankie."

"I noticed." I took a sip of coffee. "Last night. But I was too tired to deal with it."

"Help you after I finish this."

"Thanks, but I'll get Bill and Randy to fix it."

Pete found this hysterically funny. "Good luck," he wheezed. "Billy never gets up before ten when he's not workin'. Wake him any earlier, and he's mean as a springtime rattler."

"Ask me if I care." But I did care. I dawdled over my coffee, postponing the confrontation, feeling anger and frustration build with my procrastination. The acid churned in my stomach. "I thought Bill was working on the summer road crew?"

"Got fired last week for drinkin' on the job. Picked a fight with the boss' son."

"We played pool Friday night. I asked him about the bruises on his cheek—he just said he'd had a difference of opinion with somebody."

"It was a tad bit more than that, Frankie. Randy had to wade in after him. Wish he'd cut loose of his brother and make his own way. He's a good kid."

Somebody tripped on the stairs, crashing into the railing. Bill stumbled through the screen door. Using the wall for support, he attempted to focus on the silent group. He wore ragged jeans, pistol tucked into the waistband, unbuttoned red-plaid shirt, boots and cowboy hat. He looked as if he hadn't been to bed. He certainly couldn't lift a tire iron.

"You expecting trouble, Billy?" Pete asked.

Bill ignored him. "Ah," he said, seeing me. "The mountancomestamommed."

"Can you sober him up, Pete?"

Pete shook his head while Fern poured coffee. Bill plopped down on a stool, drained the cup in one gulp. Fern refilled it. Damn. At this rate, he'd be a wide-awake drunk.

Bill separated his mouth from the mug long enough to fix me with a bleary stare. "If this is how you look in the morning, Frankie, it's no wonder Geoff cut out."

Nobody moved. Nobody spoke. I forced my fingers to unclench from the haft of the butter knife I didn't remember picking up. Scary. "Is that offer still good?" I asked Killeen.

"Lead on, Macduff."

"MacFarlane."

"Whatever you say."

I tossed a ten on the counter. Didn't wait for change, didn't check to see if Killeen followed as I marched down the stairs and started across the dirt parking lot.

"Hold your fuckin' horses," Bill yelled from the doorway.

I kept walking. Behind me there was a soft *thunk,* then the whisper of boots running in the dust. Bill grabbed my shoulder from behind.

I didn't think, I swear I didn't. My left hand crossed to trap his wrist while I pivoted, swung my right arm around his waist, bent my knees, rolled him over my hip, dropped him in the dust. It took two seconds, maybe less.

"Don't manhandle me, Bill. I don't like it." I picked up his hat, dusted it off with trembling fingers. I'd never thrown a man before.

"No shit, Frankie. You made your point." He rolled to the side, vomiting into the dust. Blood tinged the mixture. I almost lost my breakfast.

There was a flicker of movement from the steps. Killeen held Bill's pistol, pointed at the ground. Pete and Fern were halfway down the steps, passive spectators, letting me fight my own battles. Some friends. Well, what had I expected? I didn't belong to Pair-a-Dice.

Randy rounded the corner and surveyed the scene. He walked slowly to stand over his brother. He had Bill's lean build, sun-streaked brown hair, and gentian-blue eyes. But he was ten years younger, no more than nineteen, and his eyes were clear.

"Maybe I should just let him shoot you, Billy—save you the trouble of killin' yourself."

"The way I feel, he'd be doin' me a favor."

Randy shook his head and looked beyond me to Killeen. "Who's the stranger, Frankie?"

"E. J. Killeen. He gave me a ride into town after you guys put my Jeep out of commission."

"That was Billy."

"But you were along for the ride."

"Just to make sure he didn't total it. I drove the Jeep . . . he was drunk." His eyes held mine for a long moment. "Even drunk or hung over, Billy wouldn't hurt you, Frankie. Neither would I."

I relaxed a bit. "Maybe not on purpose," I said, rubbing my sore shoulder. "But the effect's the same." I nodded at the figure lying still in the dust. Old bruises showed mottled yellow-green on his left cheek. I could see more dotting his lower rib cage where his shirt hung open. There were fresh gashes on his right wrist and forehead, just scabbing over. They hadn't been there Friday night. "Has he been in another fight?"

"Looks like it," Randy said. "He went to Wells last night. Didn't come home—that's why I was out looking for him."

"Did he see a doctor?"

"Nope." He shrugged helplessly. "I tried to convince him before, right after we got fired. He says we don't have the money."

Bill dragged himself to a sitting position. It must have hurt, but the only signs were the tightening of his jaw muscle and the lines around his eyes. "I won't go to a doctor, Frankie."

"Don't be silly. The county will pay for it."

"Don't mother-hen me. You're as bad as Randy. I've been taking care of myself for a long time."

"Right," Randy said. "And a good job you've done, too. How long's it been since you ate?"

"Yesterday, sometime. Day before. Christ, I don't remember." His voice trailed off.

"Then go finish your breakfast," I said. "Can't have you fainting while you fix my tire."

"Fix your own damn tire."

"I'll help you soon as I get some food into him," said Randy. "Come on, you jackass." He pulled Bill up and half-lifted him up the stairs. Killeen handed Randy the gun as he went by.

"Woman, you have a short fuse. You mad at Bill, or this Geoff guy?" Killeen's eyes twinkled.

"Both, I think. Bill hit the target."

"So did you. You a black belt?"

I took a deep breath, trying to steady my nerves. "Hardly. My brothers took jujitsu and practiced on me. You saw the sum total of my experience."

"I take it you forgot about the gun?"

Damn. "I won't make a habit of it."

"Good. A body could get killed around you."

29

"I hope not. But thanks for taking the gun away from Bill."

"Child's play."

When Bill and Randy drove up thirty minutes later, Killeen and I had the Jeep jacked up and the tire off. Randy got out looking a little white around the gills; his eyes were bloodshot. He must have heard about Emmajean.

"Billy's too sick to help," he said, as the truck peeled out of the courtyard and headed up the highway. Randy rolled the tire to the gas station next door. It was only six-forty-five.

"This place is like an ant colony," said Killeen. "Lots going on under the surface."

Was it a coincidence that so much had happened since his arrival? His face looked placid in the soft morning shadows of the doorway, but the slightly protuberant black eyes probed, studied the courtyard, followed the Andersons' progress.

"Somebody know where you're gonna be—in case you get stuck again?" he asked.

I treated it as an innocent question. "I leave a topographic map in my room. Circle and date the area I'm mapping. A square mile or two. If I don't come home, Isabel can send out a search party the next day. I carry survival gear with me so I can make it through a night or two. The only predators I worry about are the two-legged variety."

"Sounds foolproof, unless you're unconscious—or Isabel's gone."

"Best I can do."

"Can I take a look at that map?"

Why would he want to know where I'd be? Natural curiosity, or something else? That uneasy feeling was back. "No offense, but I feel safer if only Isabel knows exactly where I'll be."

"You don't trust me." There was an underlying note of humor in his voice, but the eyes met mine squarely.

"Right now, I don't trust anybody."

"Keep it that way," was the surprising response. "You'll live longer. What time did you tell Isabel to start worrying?"

"If I'm not back by dark, there's something wrong. What will you be doing?"

"Prospecting—like I said yesterday. Stay out of trouble." Before I could ask any more questions, he started off in the direction of the Pair-a-Dice Bar.

I washed my clothes in the motel sink and hung them to dry in the shower stall. Pair-a-Dice had a laundromat at the side of the store—a dollar for the washer, a quarter for the dryer. But it took two hours and four dollars to dry one load. I think it was Isabel's way of saving for retirement.

Thirty minutes later Randy handed me my keys. "Isabel talked Billy into seein' the doctor. Need anything from Elko?"

"No. Tell Bill I'm sorry about Emmajean."

He looked down, kicked a pebble with the toe of his boot. "I will. They had their differences . . . but she was always good to me. And she didn't deserve to die like that."

He turned to go, stopping before he'd gone two steps. "Frankie?"

"Hmm?" I was halfway into the Jeep, my mind on the day ahead.

"About yesterday? I had to make a choice, you know?" He was staring at the mountains, not at me.

"I know."

"It's always been like that—Billy and me against everybody else. The old Billy was . . . I don't know . . . Something happened after Ma died, after Emmajean left. But when I look at him, I see the old Billy, not some angry, stupid ass. I wish you'd met him before. He was . . . somethin'."

I wondered when the hero worship had died. "So are you," I said.

His face reddened. "Thanks. It's been a long time since anybody said that. If I'd been with Billy last night, the flat tire wouldn't have happened."

"I know. People change, Randy—even people we love."

"Not Billy . . . not inside." He squinted at the sky. "It's gonna be hot today, Frankie. Take lots of water." I watched him walk away, a sad, lonely rescuer facing a dismal future in Pair-a-Dice.

———

At eight-thirty-one I parked the Jeep in a broad, northeast-trending depression. On my left, a red-and-tan mountain of Triassic rock rose gently at first, then steeply to its crest seventeen hundred feet above. From this distance, the top looked flat. It wasn't.

On my right were lower hills of older, gray-weathering, Permian rock. I stood on the contact between two geologic eras: the Paleozoic and the Mesozoic. The extinction of the dinosaurs at the end of the Mesozoic hogs the limelight these days. That event was peanuts compared to the mass extinctions that occurred at the end of the Paleozoic when more than ninety percent of the Permian species died out in a relatively short time, a few million years. Someday I wanted to bring students to this range. I wanted them to walk upwards through the rock section and examine the ancient marine environments teeming with fossil animals. I wanted them to feel the same sense of awe that I felt as I crossed that time/rock boundary and saw the paucity of species on the other side. To me, standing on an old seabed 240 million years after catastrophe, life appeared fragile, finite, random, impersonal, survival a matter of chance and adaptation. Like life in any urban environment today—or along I-80, for that matter.

I stared at Red Mountain. Not enough time. I had to be back in Tucson to teach introductory geology in nine days. Before I headed home, I needed to search the scree-covered mountainside one last time, ridge by spiny ridge, for a death assemblage—what paleontologists call a thanatocoenosis—fossils concentrated after death by gravity and the winnowing action of paleocurrents, frozen in place by the slowly crystallizing fabric of rock.

The geologic map, the basis for my dissertation, was essentially complete. I'd measured rock unit thickness at different localities, collected samples for further description and age dates. I'd established, at least to my satisfaction, that the Paleozoic and Mesozoic sediments that formed the rocks of this range had not been deposited *in situ,* but in a basin somewhere to the northwest. Then, in the late Mesozoic, the Earth's crustal plates had pressed against each other, crumpling this part of North America and thrusting these folded and broken rock slices southeast to their present geographic position. The interleaved rock units weren't exposed during thrust-faulting, but only later, in Tertiary time, after plate movements caused the crust to thin and break, creating the block-faulted topography so characteristic of this Basin-and-Range region.

It was an elegant and complex story. Only two pieces of data eluded me. The first was a limestone marker bed chock-full of fossil ammonoids. I needed that marker to tie down in time the base of my uppermost rock unit, to link it with other Triassic exposures throughout the world. Last year, I'd searched for the bed among the shifting limestone talus. My measured sections had been pieced together from outcrops at various points along the mountainside, but those partial sections were younger or older than the fabled marker bed. If I didn't find it now, either because it had never been deposited with this package of rocks, or because it was covered, my dating would be less precise. More importantly, I wouldn't be able to establish *when* the huge slices of rock had moved.

The second problem was more difficult. Geologic mapping of the Permian strata proved that the uppermost Permian beds, including the contact between the Paleozoic and Mesozoic eras, were missing from the northern part of the range. I needed to prove whether the Permian rocks had been eroded *before* the Triassic beds were deposited, or whether a huge low-angle fault cut across the boundary. Unfortunately, the Triassic beds were so friable that they slumped down to cover the contact in most places. If I'd had money and a backhoe, I'd have trenched across the contact in several places. I had neither. But maybe I'd missed something. I remembered one day in particular when Geoff and I'd had other things on our minds; afterwards, my notes were incomprehensible scribbles. Sex has a tendency to interfere with left-brained activities.

So I would walk the contact one last time. Taking a deep breath, I shouldered into my neon orange daypack and started up the slope.

———

Just before noon, I startled a mule deer from its daybed. It darted north along the faint suggestion of a trail screened from below by intermittent clumps of piñon pine and juniper. The sun poured through the weave of my faded-blue work shirt. The cool shadows beckoned. Curious, I followed the deer. The way was old, very old. It hugged the contours of the hillside, the path of least resistance, and it led where I wanted to go. I moved from sunlight to shadow and back again, smelling sage and dust and pine, scents that had filled the air here for thousands of years. When I stepped on a pink wild-onion flower, the rich garlicky smell clung to my boot. The Indians and immigrants used the plant to flavor soups and stews.

Antelope squirrels, tails saluting, stopped their foraging as I passed, then quickly resumed their search for piñon nuts. I saw no sign that humans had been here for eons. But I could feel a presence, friendly and watchful, as if those who had gone before had left something behind, a bruise on the atmosphere. In the past, whenever I'd felt that awareness, I'd found physical traces of earlier people. The sensitivity was inherited from both sides of the family. Sometimes I wondered if I should have gone into anthropology, where such sensitivity would have been useful.

The trail entered a hollow between the mountain and an old landslide, then turned up a canyon. Looking for the perfect lunch spot, I climbed to the top of the landslide, fifty feet above the trail. The red-gray, silty limestone blocks were broken and tilted back toward the mountain. Trees grew out of fissures, creating pools of shade and cooling the rocks. I could see Pair-a-Dice sweltering in the valley, heat waves dimming the outlines. I savored the view and the moment, knowing I'd be leaving soon.

I sat down and pulled out the lunch Fern had fixed this morning. A breeze ruffled the branches above me, and sunlight reflected off something shiny and black at my feet—obsidian flakes. The closest rock source I knew of was sixty miles away. I picked up the two unfinished arrow points, one at a time, stroking the smooth, glassy texture before replacing them gently.

I was stuffed before I'd made a dent in the massive lunch. Using my daypack for a pillow, I lay back and watched the afternoon clouds start to build over the town. From this distance, Pair-a-Dice looked innocent. Innocence is relative, I thought, remembering Diane's novel.

Lack of sleep the last two nights, coupled with fresh air and exercise, had left me drowsy. I fought the weariness for a few minutes before giving in. A twenty-minute snooze, I rationalized. Just twenty minutes . . . I could afford that . . . As easily as the sun slid across the sky, I drifted off to sleep. . . .

A twig snapped. I started from sleep into wakefulness, heart racing like a hunted rabbit. Slowly, I adjusted to the bright, white daylight. The fingers of my right hand were clenched, buried in the soft dirt under the pine needles. Something hard scored my palm. At the periphery of my vision a shape loomed, black against the sun.

"Don't move," Killeen said. He held a gun that seemed to be aimed at the middle of my forehead. He wasn't smiling.

I obeyed.

FOUR

"What now?" I tried to ask. Only a croak came out.

"There's a rattler coiled above your head." A sound like a stick beating dry brush accompanied his words. "No, don't look. Just take my hand—slowly, now—and I'll pull you out of the way. Ready?"

In answer, I inched my left hand into his huge palm and waited, muscles taut, for the tug. He nearly yanked my arm out of its socket; I landed five feet from my daypack. The dry buzzing was silenced by a shot. The ricochet whined off among the boulders. We were lucky it didn't come back to nick us.

He slid the gun back into its holster, grinned, studying my hot face. "Thought you were choosier about who you slept with."

"I draw the line at snakes . . . usually." I frowned down at the still-twitching, headless carcass.

He saw my look. "I got no use for snakes. Was bitten once, at Huachuca. You a snake-lover?" The tone of his voice implied that tree-huggers and desert pupfish-defenders were the scourge of the earth.

"Do you know what happens if we kill all the snakes that are courteous enough to buzz when we get too close?"

"We make the world safe for children and geologists?"

"Just the opposite. We genetically select for snakes that don't rattle—a relatively small segment of the population. I read that in parts of California, where young men prove their masculinity by taking pot shots at anything that moves, the silent rattlers are taking over."

"Ouch."

"I'm sorry. You thought you were saving my life. Thank you."

"You're welcome—I think. Maybe next time I'll let you fend for yourself."

I deserved that. I watched him, ugly face impassive, toss the carcass down the hill and kick sand over the bloody ground. "Why are you here, Killeen?"

"In Pair-a-Dice?"

"In Nevada, in Pair-a-Dice, in my mountains—take your pick."

"Your mountains?" He looked up at Red Mountain, not at me.

"You always answer a question with another question."

"Do I?"

"Yes. God, it's irritating. And you still haven't answered my question."

"How about . . . I'm here to serve and protect? It's what a soldier's trained to do."

"I don't need protecting."

"Tell that to the snake."

"Touché." He'd managed to deflect my question again. "How did you find me?"

"Tracked your Jeep. Easy enough. Only two sets of tire prints since the rain. And by the way, your tires need rotating."

"Thanks. I'll do it when I get home." I lifted a hand to rub my shoulder, but stopped, arm half-raised, and stared at the object in my hand—a dirt-encrusted, mud-brown point.

"Sorry if I hurt you." His voice sharpened. "What's that?"

I opened my hand, palm upward. "Projectile point. It was in the dirt." I let him hold it. Watched him brush the dirt off and examine the tan-flecked waxy surface, the laurel-leaf shape, and the beautifully worked edges.

"Pretty sharp." He handed it back. "You could kill someone with that." This time he met my eyes squarely.

"Not likely I'll have to." But my skin prickled at the thought. "You said there were two sets of tire tracks. Whose were the others?"

"Looked like a passenger car. No clearance. You can see the scrape marks where it bottomed out on the road."

There weren't many passenger cars in Pair-a-Dice. You needed clearance to tackle the rutted dirt roads. "Where'd the tracks go?"

"Headed due west across the range. But I didn't follow 'em to see if they turned off or not."

"Maybe it was a sucker from back East who bought one of those parcels out on the flats." Whole sections were marked off into little one-acre squares: no water, no electricity, no shade trees, no privacy.

Lon Bovey had sold them to Pete to help finance the Bovey-for-Congress campaign. I'd run into three elderly couples this summer staring with forlorn disbelief at their future retirement plots in this "lovely, forest-rimmed valley."

"Maybe. But I think I'll mosey over and check it out. Want to come?"

"I've got to get back to work."

Killeen, camouflage clothes blending in with the scenery, started off down the hill toward a cluster of trees. I could just make out the vague shape of a truck parked behind them. A careful man. His voice floated back over his shoulder.

"Watch out for those quiet snakes—reptilian and otherwise." He chuckled at his own humor.

"Are you a betting man, Killeen?"

"Sometimes."

"Then you can make book on it."

I kept pushing for three more hours. Starting at a break in slope where the marker bed should have cropped out, I crisscrossed a hillside awash with limestone debris. No outcrops to speak of: a few fossil clams in the float, but not a decent ammonoid in sight. Maybe the unit was faulted out after all. Maybe it had been eroded away millions of years ago. Maybe it had never been deposited where the rest of these rocks were laid down. It didn't help that I couldn't seem to shake off the encounter with Killeen and the snake. I kept wondering what he was doing, if he had binoculars pressed to his eyes, watching me work. I gave up and went back to town.

The Anderson truck wasn't parked in their yard. Music blared through the screen door of Diane's mobile home, and her cherry-red Harley-Davidson was beside the front steps. Killeen's truck wasn't in the driveway of the Tucker house next door . . . Should I, or shouldn't I? If Killeen could invade my work space two days in a row, couldn't I invade his living space? Okay, two wrongs don't make a right, but . . .

I gave in to temptation, turned down the alley between Pete's house and the Tucker place, and parked behind the schoolhouse, half a block away. The rear yard of the Tucker place abutted the schoolyard. I was through the gate in the back fence before I could change my mind.

The main part of the Tucker house was constructed of railroad ties, weathered black, nailed together with rusty spikes. At one time the kitchen had been a separate building, but now crude walls with screened doors joined the buildings, making a room large enough to hold a picnic table. I remembered it well. Two mining geologists had served me dinner there in June. The doors could be opened during hot summer days to allow breezes to cool the eating area. Today, Mr. I-don't-have-anything-to-hide Killeen had left the closer door unlocked. I knocked gently, listened for an answering call that didn't come, and slipped inside.

I don't know what I expected to find—maybe insight into his personality, prospecting samples, or a clue to his reasons for choosing Pair-a-Dice over any other place. But Killeen was stingy with clues. There weren't any rock specimens piled in corners. In the kitchen, the uncluttered counters, stove, and floor sparkled, dry dishes rested in a strainer. He'd taken out the garbage. The refrigerator contained a twelve-pack of Bud in bottles, a half-gallon of skim milk, green apples, carrots, salad makings, margarine, and a loaf of stone-ground wheat bread (not Hannibal Lector's repast). The living room had been dusted (definitely not Pete's work); the toilet seat was down in the bathroom (the man was a paragon); the bedroom contained a footlocker (locked) and a book on the bedside table.

I expected Cussler or Grisham, but found *The American West* by Malone and Etulain. A cottonwood leaf marked page 66, and someone had underlined a passage: "Indeed, one of the most sordid episodes of the entire era occurred at Brownsville, Texas, in 1906. Following a ten-minute shoot-out there involving black troops, President Roosevelt discharged all 167 black soldiers in the three companies involved, without any proof as to which of them were or were not involved."

A truck turned onto the street, approaching slowly. I dropped the book on the bedside table and scooted toward the door, stopping on the threshold. On the wall beside the door, hanging from a hook where someone could study it while lying in bed, two pieces of framed glass held an ancient canned-food label. It hadn't been there when I'd visited before. I made out the faded word "SPINACH."

I heard the truck pull up down the street. Not Killeen, then. I quickly took down the label to check the reverse side. The faint, spidery writing of the note was difficult to decipher, gone completely where someone had written over the dried glue that had held the paper to a tin can. "To whom . . . concern . . . is Johnny, age 5. His parents

. . . Pair-a-Dice, Nevada, 6 June 1907. He cant stay here . . . home to Texas. Treat him nice." Ezekial Thomasson's signature looked as if it had been written yesterday.

I heard the truck engine start up again, coming toward the house. I fumbled, trying to get the wire at the back of the glass to slide over the wall hook. One swipe, two, three. My fingers cramped and I almost dropped the glass. Damn. On the fourth try the frame stayed on the wall. Heavy footsteps sounded on the porch. The frame was crooked, but I didn't have time to straighten it. Maybe Killeen wouldn't notice. I went out the side door as Killeen stepped into the front room.

Thirty seconds later, back at the Jeep, I crouched in the shadow of the driver's door, breathing hard. I'd escaped. My pulse seemed to think I'd just run three miles, my brain was high on endorphins. I hadn't had this much fun since I "borrowed" a rival hall's mascot my freshman year in college. Maybe I'd missed my calling. Maybe I should be investigating humans instead of rocks.

I peeked over the hood. Killeen stayed in the house, but the screened room was so dark a platoon could be watching and I wouldn't know. So I took a chance, hopped into the Jeep, circled around the schoolhouse, and drove nonchalantly by the Tucker place to the highway. A pile of cement blocks had been transferred from the storage area to Pete's building site. Randy'd managed to lay one row of blocks. It looked almost level.

"Pete hired Billy and me this morning," Randy said when I stopped to watch.

"About time. How'd it go in Elko?"

"They're gonna keep Billy in overnight. Want to run some tests. Isabel gave me a ride back." He slapped down mortar, settled a brick, tapped it into place, scraped off the extra mortar. Repeated the sequence, while late afternoon light gilded his sweaty torso. Slap, settle, tap, scrape, wipe brow. His rhythmically moving hands, encased in cotton work gloves, were covered with dried mortar.

"Looks pretty good," I said.

"Thanks. Pete's doin' the corners. He's broody as a sage hen. Comes out every fifteen minutes or so to see how it's goin'."

"Wouldn't you?"

"Yeah. I guess so." He started another row, eyes down, focused on the blocks.

"When will Bill get home?"

"Don't know. He'll call tomorrow."

"Well, tell him good luck from me." I drove on to the motel. Someone had left an old *Time Magazine* essay on my bed. Isabel, I supposed, until I saw the subject: passive-aggressive behavior as a result of stress. Very funny. I ripped it into little pieces and dropped them in the wastebasket. But while I showered off the dust and sweat, I puzzled over who'd invaded my space. Killeen? Diane? Pete? Bill? They all shared a warped sense of humor. But who had a key? I'd find out at dinner, no doubt. The whole town probably knew about this morning's scuffle. I changed into a coral tee-shirt and denim skirt, picked up Diane's manuscript, and made my way to the Pair-a-Dice Bar.

When I pushed open the screen door, the barstools were occupied by the same patrons as yesterday. They didn't look as though they'd moved an inch. I nodded to Alf and chose a table halfway back on the restaurant side. All the other tables were empty. Alf yelled to Opal that she had company; she trotted out of the kitchen with an expectant look on her triple-chinned face.

"Oh. It's only you, Frankie." She extracted a pencil from the pile of bottle-red curls on top of her head and fished a tablet from the pocket of the gravy-brown apron she wore over tight white jeans. "What can I get ya?"

"Nice to see you, too, Opal. What's the special?"

"Baked ham, baked potato, applesauce, dinner salad, dessert. Same as every Sunday."

"How could I have forgotten. Do you have any tomatoes?"

"A few. They're not too bad. Want a slice on your salad?"

"That'd be nice," I lied. The slice would be paper thin and granite-hard. "Thanks."

"To drink?"

"Iced tea. I need some caffeine."

"Don't we all," she muttered. She ambled back to the kitchen, broad hips swaying like a ship in strong swells.

The silence seemed heavy. I put a quarter in the jukebox, selected three old favorites. When I sat down again, the tea was on the table and Kenny Rogers and Kim Carnes crooned, "Don't Fall In Love With A Dreamer"—Geoff's favorite song. Apparently my subconscious was working overtime. This was where our relationship had started as we discussed geology problems and solutions over dinner one night. He hadn't minded "breathing the same air" back then. That was long before the verbal games started, the competition, the public put-downs . . . long before he'd copied sections of my dissertation from my computer file into his before "accidentally" trashing my files and erasing the two back-up disks. My work was in draft form. He thought I didn't have a paper copy. He hadn't counted on my retentive nature. A print-out and a back-up disk were stored in the departmental office safe....

It hurt to remember. When Opal thumped the special in front of me, my stomach lurched. I dashed for the restroom, splashed my face with cold water, and held my wrists under the stream until the world righted itself.

"What's the matter with the food?" Opal asked when I stepped out.

"Nothing. Something I had for lunch must have disagreed with me."

"Probably the mayo Fern put on your sandwich. Gotta watch that mayo in hot weather. I'll fix your lunch tomorrow, if you want."

"I don't think it was the mayo. I'll be okay, Opal. Just give me a few minutes." I had to get out of that room, away from the music and the memories. I picked up Diane's manuscript. "Would you mind keeping my dinner warm while I take a little walk?"

"No problem, honey. No problem at all. Take your time."

Outside, I gulped deep breaths of air that still retained the day's heat. Lon Bovey's green Suburban pulled up to the hitching rail and I escaped around the side of the bar. I wasn't in the mood for Sunday pleasantries.

Two unpaved streets cut through Pair-a-Dice at right angles to the highway. Every few years the county would send a crew to throw down a load of road metal on their dusty surfaces. The roads continued back of the place, crossing the slopes of older alluvium, and finally dropping down into the canyons that dissected the range. The roads were old. They followed immigrant wagon ruts that had erased ancient Indian footpaths.

The streets didn't have names. The locals called them "Easy Street" and "Not So Easy Street" after the town's founder, Ezekiel Thomasson. They didn't need real names because no one delivered mail to the houses. One either had a post office box or used general delivery. The system gave locals a chance to sit on the dusty store porch and gossip in the afternoon. And watch the cars go by, one every hour or so.

I heard the music from Diane's boombox long before I reached her place. I couldn't remember the vocalist's name, but the lyrics were ironic: "I've been to Paradise, but I've never been to me."

Diane lived in a single-wide mobile home under the cottonwoods on Easy Street. The home was at least thirty years old and had not aged gracefully. The white box squatted amidst a dented, rusting, corrugated skirt. Below and to the right of the front door, screws were missing and the skirt gaped open. I wondered how many generations of

41

cats or rattlesnakes had bred in that dark space. Curved aluminum poles hooked into the metal siding just below the roof, but only tattered canvas remnants, striped beige and faded green, clung to the frame, offering no shade. The pole closest to the road was bent at knee level, as if someone had backed a pickup into it.

Diane lay belly-down on a ratty plastic chaise lounge, elbows and pillow supporting her upper torso. The Hawaiian print bikini top was untied. The Madonna tattoo seemed almost alive as the shadows thrown by the cottonwood leaves flickered across her skin. I'd never asked her about the tattoo. It seemed an invasion of privacy, somehow. I realized she couldn't see her back as others saw it—only reflections in a mirror, the image reversed. As I stood there, she doodled a free-form Madonna and child at the margin of a green stenographer's notebook. The single black line looped around, suggesting sadness, but providing no facial detail. Was she drawing my thoughts? Or was this a common, garden-variety obsession? Obsession scared me. Obsession meant pain. Geoff had been obsessed with finishing his graduate work ahead of me. I didn't want to go down that road.

"Didn't know you were a fan of '70s music, Diane," I said instead, picking up the plastic tape box. "'The Adventures of Priscilla—Queen of the Desert'?"

She turned the volume down to a murmur. "A great movie. Terence Stamp deserved an Oscar."

"I'll have to rent it when I get home." I set down the box beside her on the chaise. A stray beam of sunlight showed puckered skin around one of the tattooed eyes. Nadia, the heroine in Diane's novel, had used a tattoo of the Virgin to cover a white slaver's brand. "Did you get that in the Middle East?"

She had no trouble following my tack. "Close enough."

"How long did it take?"

"Eighteen straight hours."

"A costly act of defiance."

"Cost is a relative term."

Like innocence, I thought again. "But why choose something so complicated, so time-consuming? Couldn't you have achieved the same results with a lot less pain?"

"Yes, and no. What do you think it does to a man's psyche to fuck a woman wearing a symbol like this? Makes them stop and think—at least, the first time."

"I've never heard you sound so angry."

"I hide it. And I'm not always angry. Sometimes, I'm just over-whelmed by . . . the French have a word for it . . . *tristesse*. You know it?"

"Sadness." The wide leather bracelets she usually wore were beside her on the chaise. Faint white scars blended with the creases in her wrists. Nadia had attempted suicide while being detained in a Central American prison. "Guatemala?"

"Two for two." She closed the notebook and stuck the pencil into the spiral.

"Just how much of this novel is autobiographical?" I placed the manila envelope containing the first hundred pages on the cooler beside her.

"I'll never tell." She stretched her long fingers. "God, I could use a break. I'm glad you came." She turned over and sat up, leaving her top behind. From one arm of the chaise she took a black tee-shirt and slowly pulled it over her head. The logo across her chest read 7th An-nual Hog Jamboree—Bridgeport, California. "Want a beer?" she asked.

"No, thanks."

She plucked one from the cooler, grabbing the manuscript as it slid toward the ground. "Well, what did you think?" She looked at me for the first time, her expression wary.

What did I think? The novel followed Nadia's adventures across the globe—stranded in the Australian Outback; arrested for spying in Guatemala; abducted from a yacht party in the Greek islands; sold into white slavery. The plot sounded like a bodice-ripper, but the physical evidence before me suggested that some of it was true.

As I'd flipped the pages, I'd found myself substituting Diane's name for the heroine's. Somehow, in her ironic voice, Nadia's adven-tures took on mythical proportions, as if Odysseus were trying to find his way home in the twentieth century. She had been torn loose from her moorings at four, when her parents divorced. Rootless, she'd been searching ever since, attempting to fill the voids in her life: fa-ther, mother, daughter, brother/lover, priest/lover. The search had led to dark places I would have run from. But I wasn't Nadia—or Di-ane, whose body was simply the housing around her intellect and spirit. It could suffer abuse while her mind observed and took notes, as if from a great distance. That was how some Jews survived the death camps—by segregating body from spirit. But Nadia/Diane, like other survivors, was scarred for life. And bitter.

I could empathize, to a certain extent, with Diane's predicament. Because of Geoff, I could no longer instinctively identify which men were trustworthy. But Diane had gone one step further—she'd lost faith in mankind.

"I think you may be the most complex person I've ever met," I said finally. "I think you have a bravado I don't possess . . . and I don't think you respect anyone or anything except your own intelligence."

I saw her neck muscles relax. She took another gulp of beer and lit a Marlboro, inhaling deeply. "If I don't respect you, then why did I give you the manuscript?" The smoke rolled out as she spoke. Her green eyes met mine for an instant before she focused on the glowing tip of her cigarette.

"I wish I knew. But that's beside the point. I think you could sell it, Diane. It's fast-paced, full of intrigue, has memorable characters and dark humor." I didn't tell her that it had no soul. I doubted anyone else would care.

"Thank you." Her shoulders slumped slightly, as if an invisible supporting rod had been removed. She drained the rest of her beer in one long pull. "Will you read the next section?"

"Of course. Nadia's just gotten to Pair-a-Dice—er, Easytown. You can't leave me hanging."

She paused as if to consider the notion, then set her empty beer bottle on the ground. "No. Let me get it for you." She winced, as she stood up, and stretched experimentally. She was five or six inches shorter than I—no more than five-seven. "The second day's the worst, you know. Tomorrow, that's when I'll really feel the aches and pains." Her laugh was throaty, warm, a self-aware sound. "And that's why I only work one night a week."

"Why do you—work nights, I mean?"

"You tell me."

I rolled my eyes. "C'mon, Diane."

"Humor me."

"Okay. It's not the money. You earn enough to keep body and soul together."

"Enough, yes. But I couldn't afford a Harley on a teacher's salary."

The answer was too glib. I sensed it was more complicated than that.

"We're a lot alike, you know," said Diane.

"Gasoline and water." And I wasn't the flammable one.

"We both have brothers, no sisters, attended Catholic schools, and went to college in California." She ticked them off on her fingers. "We like to be in charge, to control the world around us. It was our fate to be born into a male-dominated world. I control the male population by screwing ten or fifteen guys a week—on my terms, at my convenience. You control them by not screwing at all . . . Geoff excepted. You're up there on a pedestal."

"Not quite."

"All right, you're not the Virgin Mary. You still set yourself apart. So we use different approaches, with similar effects."

She'd touched a nerve. I wasn't sure I agreed with her, but I needed to think about the charge.

"Who messed with your head, anyway?" Diane asked.

"What makes you think anyone did?"

"I saw it last year. Took you weeks to let your guard down with me. You weren't that way the first summer. Back then, you were relaxed and open."

"You see too damn much," I said.

"Years of therapy. And I'm a writer. I notice things. Billy gave you such a hard time because he sensed your confusion. He planned his campaign accordingly. He just didn't reckon on how tough you were."

"I think stubborn's the word." She didn't know the half of it. She'd have enjoyed hearing about this morning's confrontation.

"Whatever. You avoided answering my question. It was Geoff, wasn't it."

So I was right. The word had spread. "Stow it, Diane." The sun was down, the sky inlaid with coral and turquoise. Bats silently swooped and darted above us, ridding the air of insects. "Who told you?"

"Buddy." Her voice had lost the harsh edge. "What happened?"

I paused, uncomfortable discussing the mess I'd made of my personal life. "Geoff used some of my work—without attribution—in his dissertation. He was on a deadline. . . . "

"Don't make excuses for him, Frankie."

"The department refused to accept his dissertation until he did more work."

"They let him off easy. What did *you* do?"

"I kicked him out in May, moved my stuff to Tucson, found a job. He went ballistic . . . threatened to come after me if I left."

"Did he do it?"

"He disappeared. I figured he'd show up here when he calmed down."

"Meanwhile, you escaped to Lon's line shack to lick your wounds in private. I'm sorry," she said, catching the look on my face. "But I tried to warn you—"

"When?"

45

"That first summer. I told you Geoff refused to pay for services rendered."

"I thought you were joking."

"Joking? It was no joke, Frankie. Geoff was an opportunist. When he couldn't use his charm instead of cash with me, he turned to you."

That hurt. I didn't answer, couldn't answer. All I could hear was Geoff's voice shouting obscenities as I loaded the Jeep, the scream of tires on asphalt. Then silence—the silence of an old movie. The silence of my dreams.

"He wasn't worth it, Frankie. None of them are. Adopt Lateran's motto: *Screw Them before They Screw You.* Maybe we could trade places next Saturday. The boys would love a change. Just remember to save the best one for last. I always do." She bent to toss her empty can into the ice chest, and the edge of her black shorts rode up, displaying a large circular bruise on her pale skin.

"Jesus H. Christ, Diane."

"Some men are hard to please."

I stared at her, not knowing how to respond. She was wrong. We weren't much alike, after all.

"Don't knock what you don't understand, Frankie," she said, running a hand lightly over the bruised hip. "It could happen to you."

"Over my dead body."

"You're the expert."

Expert on what? Dead bodies? Disturbed lovers? Miserable relationships? Suddenly I didn't want to know the answer. I disengaged.

She read the withdrawal in my eyes. "Hold on a minute," she said, her voice a monotone. "I'll get you the second installment." Turning, she sauntered stiffly toward the trailer.

So who was her rough lover? He had to be someone I'd met. She'd talked with Buddy since last night. Milo? No—she'd shut him down in public. Randy or Bill? Pete or Alf? One of the cowhands? One of the miners? I'd be looking at all of them with new eyes.

The manila envelope seemed heavy, as if a burden had been shifted into my arms.

"This is everything but the last couple of chapters." She waved a finger in the general direction of the green notebook. "I'm not really sure how it's going to end."

"I'll start it tonight." I turned abruptly, anxious to get away from the evidence of brutality, from a personality I couldn't fathom.

"He's in there," she called after me, so softly I could barely make out the words. "See if you can solve the puzzle."

When I didn't answer, Diane turned up the volume on the tape player and carried it into the mobile home. Gloria Gaynor's voice singing "I Will Survive" followed me as I trudged slowly back to the restaurant.

FIVE

I was midway through a country helping of cherry pie when Killeen joined me. I didn't hear him come in, just felt him loom next to the table and pull out a chair. The rest of the tables were occupied by that time, families mostly. The Boveys, whose Paradise Ranch covered a chunk of Nevada and Utah, sat at a table for seven. One chair was empty. I didn't know the family well, although I'd exchanged pleasantries with Ruth and the children when our paths crossed in town. It had been Lon's idea to loan me the line shack when he discovered that, without Geoff around to share expenses, my paltry budget had been stretched to its limit. He'd stopped by once a week to make sure I was coping, but had never crossed that invisible formal line between acceptable and unacceptable behavior. Just as well. Married men had nothing to give except momentary pleasure. If I'd wanted that, I'd have knocked on Bill's door.

Lon caught my look, smiled, and nodded hello. His glance drifted past me to take in Killeen, then continued to where Diane paused in the doorway. She laughed at something a young girl said, the sound carrying over the din of the Sunday evening crowd. Lon's blue eyes seemed to darken. The girl was Gabbie, his twelve-year-old daughter—old enough to sense the sexual undercurrents zinging through the room at Diane's entrance, young enough to need protection from the grittier side of Pair-a-Dice.

Lon snapped at his four small boys who were busily fashioning airplanes out of placemats. One sailed across the room to land nose-down in my beer. Lon picked up the offending youngster, tucked him

48

under one arm, and carried him outside. Ruth shrugged and offered an apologetic little smile, as if overwhelmed by the reality of dealing with four hyperactive children.

"Gosh, I'm sorry, Frankie. He didn't mean to ruin your drink." Gabbie rushed over to rescue the soggy aircraft.

"Pretty good shot, if you ask me."

"It was, wasn't it." She crumpled the paper into a ball, got her errant brother a new placemat, and slipped into the empty chair. As if by magic, the boys quieted, distracted by the book she pulled from her skirt pocket.

Lon, chastened child in tow, paused next to my elbow. Close up, I felt an adrenaline tug, the natural electrical attraction of the alpha-male. It was something I hadn't noticed before; I'd been too wrapped up in Geoff and the aftermath of our affair. My reaction, now, was the first sign that life was returning to an interior landscape devastated by a volcanic eruption.

"Run into any mud holes recently?" Lon asked. The week before, I'd buried the Jeep up to the axles on the road behind his line shack. He'd happened along while I was winching myself out of trouble. He'd found the situation very amusing.

"Nope. I've been careful. With any luck, it'll stay dry for another few days."

"Heading home soon?"

"End of the week."

"Drop by the ranch, and I'll give you some jerky for the trip. Old family recipe." He held out his hand to Killeen. "I don't think we've met. I'm Lon Bovey."

"Killeen." He stood to shake hands. The physical contrast was striking—short and square next to tall and lean. I watched them size each other up. Lon flexed his right hand to restore blood flow. I almost laughed. Point one to Killeen.

"Welcome to Pair-a-Dice, Killeen. You staying long?"

"Don't know yet."

"Well, if you need a job, come on out to the ranch. I can always use a strong hand." The double entendre put Killeen neatly in his place. Score tied at one apiece.

Lon moved away as a different waitress delivered heaping plates to his table. She'd started work while I was at Diane's. The girl looked fresh off the bus and seemed overwhelmed by the new faces and unfamiliar routine. She mixed up the Bovey boys' orders, which resulted in a tussle over plates. Lon patted her arm, told her not to worry.

49

"Just how much of the state does Bovey own?" Killeen asked after the waitress took his order.

"States," I corrected. "He's got property in Nevada, Utah and Idaho. In Europe, it would be considered a fair-sized country."

"A force to be reckoned with."

"I'd stay on his good side."

"What do the kids do for fun around here?" Killeen looked at the table full of Bovey children. I described the local attractions while he ate. Pair-a-Dice had no swimming pool, no fishing hole. "Mortal Kombat" was the sole arcade game in the general store, but nobody had much spending money. The school had a television set and a satellite dish, so the younger kids gathered there during summer vacation. Diane kept an eye on them. The older boys got summer jobs on the ranches or on road crews. They spent their nights drinking beer, shooting rabbits, and watching the stars from the beds of their pickups. Most of them were married and had two kids by the time they were eighteen.

"So they grow up fast—not necessarily a bad thing."

"'Scuse me," said a voice by my side. "You're sitting on John Wayne."

I shot up, knocking over my tea. Righting the glass, I searched for signs of life on the seat of my chair. Nothing. I looked at the boy.

"I'm sorry," I said. "But I don't see anyone."

"I know," he said. "Mommy doesn't see them either."

"Them? There are more?"

"Bruce Wayne's there," he said, pointing to the chair on my right. "And Mike Wayne's over there." Killeen had chosen the only unoccupied chair at the table, between Batman and Rooster Cogburn.

"Well, I guess I'll have to get another chair then. Will your friends mind sharing a table with us?"

"Oh no," he said, an earnest expression in his hazel eyes. "They like comp'ny. They just don't like people squushing them."

"I can understand that. I don't like people squushing me either. What's your name?"

"Tommy." He was suddenly shy, no doubt remembering that he shouldn't talk to strangers. I crouched down to his level and held out my hand. He shook it gravely.

"My name's Frankie. And this is Killeen. Do you live here?"

"Uh-huh. My mommy's over there." He pointed to the waitress who came in from the kitchen with two plates of food. She stopped as she saw us. "Her name's Sylvie."

"Is Tommy bothering you?" Sylvie asked, in a worried tone. She wore a simple indigo dress with a white dishtowel tied around her waist as an apron, navy-blue deck shoes on her feet. Her body was fine-boned, slim. She was probably twenty-three, but could pass for sixteen.

"Not at all. We're just getting acquainted." I stood, borrowed a chair from another table, and set it beside Killeen. "Imaginary friends," I said in answer to his look. He didn't seem to mind.

Sylvie mopped up the tea before bringing me a fresh glass. Tommy, satisfied that his friends were in good company, trotted across the room in his mother's wake.

"Interesting place, Pair-a-Dice," Killeen said. "Grand theft auto, judo at dawn, rattlesnakes at lunchtime, and imaginary friends. What next?" He watched Tommy stand patiently beside his mother. "Isabel and Randy brought them back from Elko this morning. He's a beautiful child, isn't he?"

"Yes," I said. Tommy had light-brown, curly hair in need of a cut, centimeter-long lashes around hazel eyes, and high, slanting cheekbones with a dimple on the left side. White, even, baby teeth showed bright against smooth skin tanned the same golden brown color as my own. About four years old, I guessed.

"My father was in the Army, stationed in Germany. My mother was German. Blonde, like her," Killeen said, referring to Sylvie.

She was calcite, I thought, yellow calcite: soft, translucent, reflecting bright light from three perfect cleavage planes. A blue rubber band pulled wispy blonde hair back from an oval face. Her cheekbones were delicate, and her small, freckled nose turned up at the end. The blue eyes were too big for her face, like a six-year-old's on the first day of school.

"My mother's family disowned her when she married dad," Killeen continued.

"That must have been tough on her—on all of you."

"You get on with your life. You have no choice."

But some wounds never heal, I thought, as Sylvie brought Killeen's pie à la mode.

"Tommy can sit here with his friends if he wants," I offered, suddenly needing the uncomplicated conversation a child offers. "We won't mind."

"Are you sure? He spent the afternoon with Isabel over at the motel, but there's no one to watch him now."

"Then he's probably pretty tired." I turned to Tommy. "Would John Wayne mind if you sat on his lap for awhile?"

Tommy held a silent conversation with the occupant of the chair. "Okay," he said, and climbed onto the chair. I hoped Bruce and Mike weren't jealous types.

"How do you like your new town?" I asked him.

"It's okay. Nicer than the last one. I was alone a lot. Now I get to sleep in a trailer," he said proudly, "with a bathroom!"

"You sleep with a bathroom? Isn't your bed kind of crowded?"

"No, silly," he giggled. Only children under ten appreciate my wit. "The bathroom isn't in my bed. It's in the trailer!"

"Well," I said, "I'm glad we got that straight. Where do all your friends sleep?"

"On the floor. They guard the door. The lock's broke."

"Broken," Sylvie corrected, collecting our plates.

"Has he eaten?" I asked.

"Yes. He's fine, thanks."

At that moment, Tommy hopped down off John Wayne's lap to chase a grasshopper into the corner. Apparently he didn't need my companionship as much as I needed his. Sylvie followed him with her eyes while she spoke to us. "Can I get you anything else?"

"Just my check, please." I pushed back my chair. "Sorry, Killeen, but I've got to run. I'll see you tomorrow."

"You heard anything more about the murders?" Killeen asked.

I stopped dead, then slowly took the check from Sylvie. Thoughts of Geoff, fieldwork, the message in my room, and my conversation with Diane had combined to push the murders out of my mind. That was stupid. I handed Sylvie the money, dropped a tip on the table.

"No, have you?"

"They've identified the bodies, but won't release the names until next of kin have been notified. No arrests yet."

I leaned against the back of a chair. "What about those tire tracks you found?"

"Wondered how long it would take you to remember them." He grinned. "Followed 'em clear across the range into the next valley west of here. About halfway along I realized I was back-tracking the guy—he left the highway north of Wells, cut across the mountains, and came the back way into Pair-a-Dice. I lost his tracks at the highway."

"Why do you think it was a man?"

"He made one stop along the way, a run-down cabin—"

"Ezekiel Thomasson's place." I said it carefully, was rewarded with the faintest of reactions. He paused, as if digesting the information.

"Guess so. Left footprints all over the place. Sandals, I think—the all-terrain kind. Bigger'n mine. Maybe nine-and-a-half, ten."

"I hate to disillusion you, but that's roughly the size I wear."

"I know. You left a track on my kitchen floor. Find what you were looking for?"

"I think I found what you wanted me to find."

"Mebbe. Time'll tell."

Tommy came back, hands cupped, to show us his treasure. When he opened them a crack, the grasshopper jumped down and crawled under the screen door. Freedom. Tommy climbed on Mike Wayne's lap—I wondered who the hell Mike Wayne was.

"Have you told Buddy?" I asked.

"Nope. Figure he'll show up for dinner sometime soon. So I'll keep Tommy company for awhile." He smiled down at his companion. "He can tell me all about his friends."

"When you see Buddy, will you ask him if he's found out anything about that tooth I gave him last night?"

"Sure thing."

"And Killeen?"

"Yeah?"

"Somebody left something in my room . . . "

"Is that right?" His expression matched the innocence of Tommy's.

"Know anything about it?"

"Room was locked?"

"Yes."

"Then it must have been somebody with a key."

The fish wasn't taking the bait. "Thank you, Sherlock. See you tomorrow."

I looked back from the doorway at the oddly touching scene: the bear of a man and the small, vulnerable boy, heads together, sharing confidences.

I'd planned to go straight back to the room and transfer data from the paper field map to the Mylar office copy. I switched direction in mid-stride, not ready to face my small drab room and my memories of Geoff.

On the street that ran behind the school, I passed Walker, dressed in his moth-eaten Pendleton shirt and a Stetson that had once been white. Now it matched the yellow-brown dust of Pair-a-Dice.

"Evening, Walker," I said.

No reaction. His eyes remained focused on the ground as he cut through the schoolyard to the lean-to he called home. Hurrying, hurrying, like the White Rabbit in Wonderland. The warped wooden door creaked as it slapped shut behind him. I wondered what his castle looked like.

I didn't know Walker's real name. No one did. Freda said he'd appeared in Pair-a-Dice twenty years ago with a sack full of aluminum cans. He'd stayed, a tumbleweed come to rest. Alf and Pete fed him, Freda hired him to stock the bar, and Diane let him stay in the lean-to in return for sweeping out the school at night. During the day, he walked, picked up cans, stared alternately at the mountains, the sky, the dirt. I'd sighted him five, sometimes ten miles out of town. He never spoke, never looked at me directly. But tonight I felt as if his eyes followed me when I turned the corner.

The new neon sign lit up the parking lot of Freda's Black-Light Bar. Toe-tapping music—"Chattahoochee"—poured through the open double doors. This jukebox held more contemporary fare. The place smelled of sawdust and varnish from the yellow-pine bar that stretched across one side of the room. Freda nodded from the other end of the bar as she handed Randy a Coke.

Freda Schultz had been raised in Pair-a-Dice. She'd left after high school, moving to Reno to work in the big casinos. Four years ago, at 45, she'd taken a bullet in the back during an attempted robbery. She was paralyzed from the waist down, the bullet still lodged by her spine. She'd come back to Pair-a-Dice with the insurance money, built a log bar the size of a barn. It sported four pool tables, a wall of poker slot machines, and the largest dance floor in a 40-square-mile radius. Three or four times a year, she imported a band, and people would flock from as far away as Winnemucca and Salt Lake City.

After skirting a bunch of line-dancers, I straddled a stool at one end of the bar.

"Careful, Frankie," Freda said. "Billy touched up the finish after he put in the boxes."

Apparently Bill had talents I didn't know about. A dim fluorescent glow emanated from the top of the bar. Three two-foot-square insets covered in heavy museum glass contained mineral samples, labeled and arranged in neat rows. The varnish around the edges was slightly tacky, but not enough to stick to Diane's manuscript. The box under my elbows contained arsenopyrite, chalcopyrite, galena, quartz, and sphalerite. The crystal faces and cleavage planes sparkled.

Freda's electric wheelchair glided smoothly on a platform behind the bar, keeping her eyes level with mine. Without asking, she put a Guinness in front of me.

"Heretic," I said, after taking a long swallow. "You'll be lucky if the locals don't burn you at the stake."

"I'll take my chances. Group of thumpers due in tomorrow. A British-Canadian team. Secretary called ahead to make sure I'd have plenty of liquid refreshment on hand. They were less worried about food."

Every year or two, geophysical crews evaluated the valley and mountain passes for potential deposits of oil and gas. Some groups set off explosive charges, some dropped heavy metal plates that thumped the ground with enough energy to send vibrations into the subsurface. Instruments monitored the data generated as the seismic waves were reflected back to the surface. Looked like I was going to have company at the motel. Loud company.

"Guinness is food. How long'll they be here?"

"Ten days or so. I'm bringing in a band from Salt Lake on Tuesday. Should be lively."

That was an understatement. Pair-a-Dice was turning into a happening place. Maybe I'd camp out in the mountains on Tuesday night.

"Who's handling security?"

"Hired that big guy you been hanging out with."

Word traveled with the wind in Pair-a-Dice. "Killeen?"

"Uh-huh. Figured he could handle just about anything those thumper jocks dish out. Excuse me a minute, hon." Freda rolled along the bar, started mixing a drink for a kid that looked fourteen. I wandered along the bar looking at the new additions.

"Watch this." Freda's eyes twinkled in her gnomish face as she switched off the light in the middle box. She made me wait. I suspected she enjoyed the kick that comes with anticipation. A black light flared, throwing purple shadows on her face.

"Oh . . . " The crystals glowed green, red, purple—the magic of a fortune-teller's booth at a summer fair. Bill had gathered all the fluorescent minerals together in one box. The mineral names were printed in beautiful bold script, almost calligraphy, on small oblongs of paper.

"Billy said they were just collecting dust in the storage shed," Randy said from behind me. "Might as well collect dust here where people can enjoy 'em."

"Didn't even charge for the labor," Freda said.

You can't put a price on a labor of love. I realized I didn't know Bill any more than I'd known Geoff. It was as if I took everyone at face value and saw nothing beneath the surface—a clueless scientist. "I didn't know he was interested in minerals."

"He wanted to be a mining engineer," Randy said. "He was at Mackay when Ma died. He had to quit to take care of me."

People crowded around me. I stepped away from the bar and the ranks closed, blocking the magic.

"Billy said, if you showed up tonight, I was to give you a game of pool."

"Does that mean you're going to throw the game?"

"Nope. Fair and square." Randy handed me a cue. "'Course, you don't stand a chance."

"Them's fightin' words." I left a tip next to the empty Guinness bottle, followed Randy to a table. He'd already racked the balls.

I broke. I even managed to sink one before Randy ran the table. He talked while he played, filling me in on the hunt for the killer. The police from Salt Lake City to Reno were scouring the countryside along Interstate 80. They hadn't caught him yet, but at least there were no new victims.

"Try again?" Randy asked, racking the balls.

"No thanks. My ego couldn't stand it." I stuck my cue in the rack on the wall. "Besides, I think you're wanted on the dance floor."

While he'd concentrated on the table, I'd watched three young things worshipfully follow his every move. Their eyes rarely moved above his tush encased in skin-hugging Levis.

"They're not going anywhere." His tone was matter-of-fact. Where else was there to go in Pair-a-Dice?

"Well I am. Got work to do." I imagined Randy's covey sighing with relief at my words. "Tell Bill thanks for remembering." I was at the door when I realized I'd forgotten Diane's manuscript. The bar was bare.

"Freda? Have you seen the manila envelope I left on the bar?"

"Kept it for you. Just a minute." She rolled back to the point where I'd been sitting, pulled the envelope from under the bar, heard my sigh of relief. "What's in it?"

I didn't think Diane's manuscript was a secret. Not then. "A novel Diane's working on. She asked me to read it."

"Any good?"

"Yes. Very."

"Tell her I'll buy a copy when she's finished. Hell, tell her I'll market it for her if she wants. Publicity wouldn't hurt this place, either."

I tucked the manuscript under my arm. "I'll tell her." When I walked to the door, Randy was involved in an intricate two-step with one of the girls. He winked at me as he swung her around.

I jogged back to the motel along streets that were silent and bare. There was a light on in the bedroom of the Tucker place. I imagined Killeen lying there, staring at the framed label, planning the next step of his mission—whatever that might be. I wondered if our paths kept crossing because he felt like a stranger in Pair-a-Dice or because I provided convenient cover, distracting people from looking at him too closely. Or was I somehow a part of his plans?

Diane's mobile home was dark, and her Harley was gone. A light went on in the kitchen of the old Airstream trailer next door as I passed. The windows were cranked wide open. Tommy's high-pitched voice carried clearly in the dry air. "Don't cry, Mommy."

"I'm just happy, honey. Hop into your jammies now, and I'll read you a—" Running water drowned out the words. "Sure, we'll search for Goldbug."

"Bruce Wayne says look in the banana car."

"He's awfully smart."

"Like me." The words were garbled, as if he had a mouthful of toothpaste.

"Just like you. I'm so very lucky to have you, Tommy."

"We love you, too, Mommy."

I hurried by, feeling like an interloper. I wondered if Sylvie and Tommy would end up as characters in Diane's novel. I hated the thought. I wasn't sure why—maybe because they'd lose their innocence. And innocence was in short supply in Pair-a-Dice.

Two hours later, after bringing my office map up to date and drawing a geologic cross-section, I settled down in bed with the manuscript.

EASYTOWN—Chapter 6

I hitchhiked into Easytown on an early Fall day, when the clouds hung low above the valley floor and nestled like cotton batting around the peaks. A few snowflakes touched my cheek, while from the canyons came the echoes of gunfire: hunting season had begun. Had I known that in one desolate canyon the quarry was human . . . but I didn't know. Not then. And so I stayed, reveling in anonymity,

quietly writing my story . . . eventually looking the other
way.

I didn't dream that night because I didn't sleep. Reading Diane's
novel was like spying through rusty keyholes and half-drawn curtains
on the secret lives of the Pair-a-Dice residents. How much of it was
true? I had no way of knowing. I tried to stop reading, but my fingers
refused to gather the heavy paper and stuff it back into its envelope. I
put down the last page, realizing I needed to know the ending—
because Lon Bovey seemed to be heading for a fall.

Diane didn't call him Lon, of course. Nadia's lover's name was Von
Boyle. But I'm as good at anagrams as the next person is.

Near dawn, I realized my mistake. Grabbing paper and pen, I
dashed off a note to Freda asking her to keep quiet about the manuscript. It was a sop to my conscience. I'd closed Freda's barn doors,
but the horses, I was sure, were long gone.

Six

On my way to breakfast I handed the note to Isabel, who was changing the linen in Room 1 at roughly the speed of sound. She looked at me accusingly from eyes the color of deep glacial ice. "Needs a stamp," she said, tucking the envelope into her pocket.

Isabel was a stickler for details. I attributed that to her Army training. Her husband, a Gulf War veteran, had died overseas a few years ago, just after they'd bought the motel and store. Pair-a-Dice was a hundred miles from where they'd been raised, not too close, not too far from their boisterous families. They'd planned to raise a brood of blue-eyed, black-haired Basque-speaking kids. Denied children to boss around, Isabel attempted to organize everyone else's lives.

"But it's not as if you need to go out of your way," I said. "You have to open the store anyway. You can just stick it in her box."

"Regulations are regulations, Frankie." She'd been around the Army too long.

I asked her to add it to my bill. Returning to Room 6, I grabbed my wallet before carefully locking the door. I don't know why, since Killeen had no trouble getting in the day before—probably while I was checking out his place. I guess I harbored the illusion that a locked door would discourage all but the most determined intruder.

When Pete opened up at five-thirty, I was sitting on the top step. By the time I'd claimed my usual stool the coffee was poured. Fern silently watched me add milk to the heavy brew and gulp the contents.

"Rough night, honey?" She refilled my cup, slid a roll in front of me, and broke a couple of eggs on the grill.

"How'd you guess?" A rhetorical question. I'd made the mistake of checking my appearance in the mirror this morning—the raccoon look was not attractive.

"I didn't sleep much either," she said. "Never realized how uncomfortable it was sleeping with a gun under the pillow."

"They'll catch him," Pete said. "Only a matter of time. You going to Emmajean's memorial service, Frankie?"

I wasn't sure I belonged at a memorial service for someone I barely knew, so I hedged. "If I get in early enough."

"It'll be over at the schoolhouse tomorrow evening—around seven. Milo's gonna officiate."

Milo was a justice of the peace, not a preacher. How he'd managed to win an election was a mystery, but at least he'd keep things short and sweet.

"I'll try to make it." I tucked into the bacon and eggs, avoiding more questions.

———

I took a different road into the mountains, one that cut through much farther north. When I pulled off the road into a dry streambed screened by the bend in a low ridge, I was tempted to brush out my tire tracks, but pushed aside my fears. I refused to become paranoid.

About fifty yards upstream, I struck an abandoned campsite. A storm, probably Saturday's, had scattered the ashes, leaving sinuous black trails like skinny kingsnakes. A charred label from a can of pineapple clung to the leaves of a sagebrush. One or two days of high-desert sun will fade almost any paper, yet these colors were bright. I picked up a pine branch from a haphazard woodpile. Poking around the center of the fire pit, I dug up a blackened bean can and a melted plastic water bottle.

In the open area, tracks had been washed away. But at the edge of the site, under a lone piñon, I discovered footprints made by running shoes about my size. Nearby, half-buried by pine needles and dust, was a cotton work glove. Not a cowhand's glove—the blue and white stripes looked new, fresh off the shelf. Without knowing why, I tucked the glove into a vest pocket, touching something smooth and hard. The projectile point. I could have sworn I'd left it up on the mountainside, exactly where I'd found it yesterday. I must have left my wits behind instead. . . .

After two days without finding a trace of the limestone marker bed, I decided to switch to problem number two, proving whether the contact between the Permian and Triassic beds was a low-angle fault. On the geologic map, the contact resembled the outline of an egg with a bird's beak poking out the side. The line was roughly eighteen miles in circumference, but only in the northern half were Permian beds missing. I started smack in the middle of that nine-mile arc.

I traversed the slopes as heat built up, magnified in narrow canyons where air did not move. A storm front was moving in, humidity rising. Beneath the field vest, my work shirt clung damply. Even my braid felt heavy, so I twisted it up under my hat, exposing my neck to dive-bombing flies. I pulled a red cotton scarf from my pocket, soaked it in water, and tied it around my neck. Even more flies arrived to suck the moisture. Sometimes, you just can't win.

I zigzagged around the base of Red Mountain, moving generally north. The ravines here ran roughly east-west. I already knew that beds farther above and below the contact showed an angular discordance. That was expected. In most parts of the world the two periods, which represent the end of the Paleozoic Era and the beginning of the Mesozoic Era, are separated by a time of nondeposition and erosion: an unconformity. But if a fault separated the two units, there would be evidence of shearing and folding. The forces that had torn the rocks would cut out parts of the units.

When blocks of the earth's crust are compressed, they break at low angles and ride up over each other creating thrust faults. That's how the Himalayas were formed (are forming still), and the Alps. Large parts of the northern Basin-and-Range and Rocky Mountain provinces underwent compression during the Mesozoic Era, usually, but not always, emplacing older rocks above younger rocks. Geoff had found evidence of this in his field area farther south. My hypothesis was that I was seeing the unusual, a thrust fault that cut nearly parallel to the dip of the beds, pushing younger rocks over older, cutting out section.

Slowly, a pattern began to emerge, evidence I'd missed earlier. In one outcrop, masked by overhanging trees, Triassic beds rolled over and the section was repeated—signs of compression. Further down-section, where the soft, yellowish Triassic siltstone slumped down over hard gray Permian limestone, I used my rock hammer to cut micro-trenches, hoping to expose the contact. The soil development was too deep. I'd need a bulldozer to find anything.

At the bottom of the next ridge, just before the mountain slope curved sharply to the west, I found a small outcrop of striated, fractured limestone. Calcite crystals, calcium carbonate deposited when water percolated through the fractures, shone dull-white. The undulating crystal surfaces mirrored the grooves carved into the surrounding rocks as the slabs slid past each other, a miniature version of what I envisioned had happened to the section as a whole. I was close.

Big hairy deal, my younger brother Jamie said when I described what I was doing in Nevada—it wasn't brain surgery, after all. But farther west at Carlin, Eureka, and Battle Mountain, gold-bearing waters had percolated through the fractured and crushed rock of fault zones, leaving behind microscopic residues of gold. And oil companies spend millions tapping oil and gas deposits in folded sedimentary rocks associated with thrust faults. So a lot more than reputation was riding on my interpretation of the data. I had to be careful.

I drained a can of grapefruit juice as I studied old black-and-white aerial photographs. I'd scoured the nearby slopes, knew they had nothing more to tell me. The photos confirmed this. But about a half-mile away was an area where I'd mapped the contact as exposed, instead of covered. I remembered finding that outcrop the first season, at the end of a day when light was fading. I hadn't had time to go back. I might have missed something. I started walking.

At 11:30, I stumbled across the ancient trail I'd found the day before. Since it pointed in the direction I was headed, I followed the trail west around the flank of the mountain until the trail intersected the road I'd taken that morning. At this juncture, the road followed an old riverbed. Unsure whether the trail continued due west or crossed the river bed, I sat in a patch of shade above the road and munched an apple, letting my mind and eyes search the sparsely wooded slopes. Sending up a cloud of dust, Killeen's truck passed below me heading east, back toward town. I didn't move. He couldn't have seen me.

I wondered where he'd been. West of here, the dirt road connected up with the highway that ran from Wells north to Twin Falls, Idaho. There were faster ways to get to Wells—or to Idaho. Maybe he wanted to gamble in Jackpot or explore some of the old mines and prospects. It wasn't any of my business. He didn't owe me an explanation. But I was curious as hell.

After Killeen's dust settled, I started west to where a widening of the canyon, an old water-cut bench or terrace, perched above the road. The day slowed to a crawl. Even the birds lay still, hidden behind their screens of deep-green needles. I jumped when a locust sprang from the dust at my feet, clicking like a rattler. The sun glared straight down on the road, hemmed in by black-and-gray cliffs of Permian rock that sucked heat from the atmosphere, pumping it back at me in waves. Any normal person would be holed up in the shade. I questioned my intelligence.

The hair rose on the back of my neck. A faint yelping drifted on the air, a chorus reminiscent of a trip to the local animal shelter. I realized I'd been hearing the sound continuously since I started up the road, the pitiful, helpless call for attention getting louder as I neared the bench. I quickened my pace.

The road doglegged north following the cherty limestone cliffs. As I rounded the bend, the old river course opened up into a small valley. I was back in Triassic siltstone, easily eroded. Fifteen feet above the roadbed was a wide flat bench carved by the river long ago. I climbed up to the level area consisting of roughly four acres on the north side of the road, another two on the south side, all dotted with trees and sparse clumps of grasses. I'd parked here the day I'd mapped the contact, two years ago.

The yelping stilled. It had come from my right, where sagebrush grew up against the cliff of Permian chert. I trod softly through the brush and trees, the only sound the rubbing of branches against denim. Two cows, startled from their siesta under a pine, trotted off in the direction of the road. When I reached the cliff face, a small coyote pup poked its nose out of a shallow undercut and whined. Apparently something had happened to mama. Three more noses sneaked forward. They couldn't have been more than a few weeks old.

I poured water from my canteen into my palm and they crowded around, pushing and shoving for position. Most of the water landed in the dust. I took off my hat. My braid flopped down and touched the dirt where I sat. While I lined the straw crown with plastic wrap from my sandwich, one of the pups grabbed the braid and started pulling. Another wrestled for control. This wouldn't work. I stuffed the braid back up under my hat, dug a shallow hole with my rock hammer, and lined the hole with plastic. When I poured water in, the pups lapped as if they hadn't been fed in a week, although it could only have been a day or two. I refilled the impromptu dish and looked for signs of mother.

Three buzzards circled in lazy formation low in the pale sky. On the ground, one set of tracks had been made since the last rain. They headed in a semi-circle around the edge of the valley. I'd followed them halfway when I heard the whimpering of an animal in pain.

The coyote was under a piñon pine, both rear legs caught in a trap. Her wild thrashing had left drops of blood on the pine needles, but she hadn't been able to twist enough to chew herself free. Dusty and unkempt, she lay now, exhausted, dehydrated, panting from the heat, staring up at me with pained gray eyes the color of my own. She must have been trapped for a day, maybe two.

I cursed the trapper. If the coyote had been able to speak, I'm sure she'd have echoed my expletives. I tied the red scarf around her muzzle. She didn't even try to snap, just whined softly. Then I looked at her legs. They were caught at the narrowest part of the tibia, above the ankle. She winced as I felt along the bones, but they didn't seem to be broken, only lacerated. What had saved them was a stick, a hair thicker than the bones, which also was caught between the bands. Using another stick, I pried open the trap enough to gently free her feet. She didn't move.

I placed pieces of my ham sandwich near her nose and gingerly removed the scarf. She took one swipe with her tongue, tasting the sandwich. Another swipe. While she decided whether she liked mayo on rye, I dug a second water hole, lining it with the wrapper from my potato chips. She wolfed down the rest of my sandwich, potato chips, and cookies, before drinking the water. I refilled the hole while she licked her legs.

She tried to stand. I crouched, five feet away, willing her success. The hind legs collapsed. She tried again, stood shakily for a moment, lost her balance. I wondered if I'd have to carry all fifty pounds of her to the pups. The third time, she trembled in front of me and took a tentative step. I held my breath as I brushed tears and sweat from my cheek. She sniffed the air, catching my scent, then turned slowly and limped off in the direction of the den. She looked back only once. There was silence when she reached the pups. Lunchtime.

After burying the trap under a pile of rocks, I filled in the makeshift bowl and used a pine branch to brush away our tracks. I sifted dust over the site, then returned the way I'd come, sweeping as I went.

I didn't want to eat the remains of my lunch near her former prison. Where soft Triassic siltstone met resistant Permian chert, a spur jutted out from the hillside and threw a finger-like patch of shade over the bench floor. When I reached it, I stopped short, staring in disbelief. I'd walked right by my evidence while tracking the coyote.

I hauled the camera out of my pack. Erosion of the valley wall had stripped bare the contact, and I could see the surface layers in vertical cross-section. The cut was no more than 20 feet high, but that was enough. The Permian limestone and chert dipped to the west here at about 40 degrees. But the beds were no longer flat layers: they'd been dragged along the contact, curving upward like a hand cupped for water. The Triassic rocks curved down against the fault plane in the opposite direction. The adjoining beds looked like the hands of a soprano, fingers hooked, singing a Wagnerian solo—a classic thrust fault. Not an unconformity. Not a simple depositional contact between two rock units. I quickly sketched the scene in my notebook, humming tunelessly. One problem solved, one to go.

After snapping a half-dozen frames, I put away my camera and clambered up the rocks to take compass measurements. Nearby, seeming to emanate from the black rocks, came the musical plink-plink of dripping water. I jumped down, stared, searching for the source of the sound.

The cliff was nearly bare, a dipping face of polished black chert. Tiny translucent white specks dotted the rock, sponge spicules from a long-ago sea. Here and there, in a cleft or fracture, wind-borne seeds had taken root: beavertail cactus with their magenta blossoms, creamy white bitterroot, one perfect Sego lily. That was all. No openings that I could see. But the elusive sound persisted.

To my right, a double-trunked, gnarled old juniper grew flush against the rock. I felt a breath of air against my pants. Pushing aside the branches, I stooped to peer inside a cave.

Picking up a handful of pebbles, I tossed them, one at a time, into the cave. When I didn't get a rattle or snarl in response, I stepped between the twin boles of the juniper. Water that had carved the old stream bed and bench had swirled up inside, dissolving the limestone that was interbedded with the chert, leaving behind a cave roughly fifteen feet deep. The floor was covered with sand mixed with guano dust. I could stand, barely, but my hat brushed the hummocky limestone ceiling. Soft light filtered through a large hole high up at the back of the cave, where water had eroded along a bedding plane. The back wall was a lower layer of chert that glistened when an errant beam of light glanced off its surface. At its base, a shallow limestone basin caught the dripping water. The basin edge showed grooves where it had been ground by harder rock into an oval shape. The floor of the cave was dry; the excess water must seep out through fractures in the basin. I tasted the water; it was soft and sweet.

I explored carefully, not wanting to disturb the site. On a waist-high shelf to the right of the basin, a fragment of woven basket still held a small chunk of yellow ochre, another of earthy red hematite, a transparent quartz crystal, a carved bone disk. I gently lifted the disk, the cross-section of a leg bone with a large central hole. Around the edge were small grooves, like minute marks on a watch. On one side of the disk, the tick marks went all around both the inner and outer circumferences. On the other, the ticks went half-way around the two edges. The marks were grouped in sets of 26 to 30, each group set off by tiny dots. Not a lunar cycle. A woman's record of the passage of months? Movement of the planets? I had an archaeologist friend in Tucson who might know.

Next to the basket lay a shriveled-up leather pouch. It looked so fragile I was afraid to touch it. On the floor, near the basin, small chunks of thin-bedded limestone lay in a haphazard pile. I picked one up. Even in the faint light, I could see that the limestone came from some other place, far away. The rocks contained black, branching invertebrate fossils, graptolites, millions of years older than the oldest rocks in this range. People, long ago, had left offerings in this magical place. The surface had been scratched with parallel lines—some wavy, some jagged—and rows of dots. Yellow ochre and white power had been rubbed into the marks. I dropped dilute hydrochloric acid on a white dot—the limestone groundmass around it fizzed, the powder didn't. Not calcite, then. Maybe gypsum.

After carefully replacing the rock, I sat beside the basin to eat. Air flowing down the makeshift chimney carried the worst of the musty smell out through the opening. The dim light and the musical dripping sound were soothing. I wanted to stay forever . . .

As I brushed the crumbs from my jeans, a truck motor slowed and stopped nearby. I couldn't tell whether it had come from the east or the west. A door slammed. Peering from the cave opening, I saw a man in a tan Stetson, rifle in hand, stride to the tree where the trap had lain. He paused, swept off his hat, and scratched his head. Grabbing the binoculars from my pack, I focused on the perplexed figure. Milo. I stifled a laugh. Jamming the hat back down, he walked slowly around the tree, then glanced up. He lifted the rifle to his shoulder, scanned the hillsides with the telescopic sight, and pointed for an interminable second at the juniper screening the cave.

The scene wasn't funny anymore. Although I knew I was invisible, I felt hunted.

Milo shifted the gun, continuing his 360-degree inspection of the valley walls. My knees started to tremble, and the shaking spread through my body until I lost control of the binoculars—they landed with a soft thud in the dirt at my feet. Milo swung around again until the rifle pointed at the rocks above the cave. The sound must have traveled up through the opening in the ceiling. He had taken two steps toward me when an antelope jackrabbit erupted from the brush near the cave mouth. He fired one shot. It passed through the hare, pierced the juniper branches, and clipped my binoculars before dying somewhere in the shadows behind me.

Belatedly, I threw myself behind the protective limestone wall; the pulsing in my wrists and temples thrummed against cold rock. Outside, cows lowed as they stampeded across the valley. I hoped they reduced Milo to pulp.

No such luck. When a smattering of courage returned, I allowed one tentative eye to probe the sunlit valley. The hare lay still, black eye glassy as a new marble, blood soaking the sandy soil. Rifle over one shoulder, whistling "Don't Fence Me In," Milo strolled back to his truck. He hoisted another trap from the bed, positioned it under a piñon not far from where the first had been. It took him a few minutes. I stayed put until the truck noise faded away.

Before leaving the cave, I found the spent bullet, sticky with blood. As I placed it alongside the leather pouch, I heard a scrabbling sound. Pebbles trickled through the opening at the rear of the cave. Then footsteps above me, hurrying away.

Not Milo. And this was about the limit of Walker's territory. Killeen, perhaps, doubling back? Or was someone following me, watching as I trudged up and down the hillsides? Had he seen me release the coyote, find the cave? Uneasy, I rinsed blood from my fingers with water dipped from the basin, then peeked outside. The hare's carcass was gone. Only blood remained.

To go, or not to go? Easy decision for someone with no weapon. I'd wait until both the stranger and Milo were well away . . . but I hoped my Jeep didn't disappear like the hare.

For the next half-hour, I worked on my map, shifting with the puddle of light as the sun crossed its zenith. This area was once railroad land, a checkerboard of Government and private ownership. Over the years, the Bovey family had bought anything that came on the market, so that now their holdings sprawled across hundreds of square miles. The ranch house was centrally located, just this side of the Utah line. Lon acted as if he owned the whole territory—in reality, he leased

Government grazing rights on a large percentage, including this valley. Apart from any moral consideration, I doubted that his foreman had the legal right to trap animals here. Or to shoot at scientists.

Of course Milo could be acting on his own initiative. Scary thought. On a professional level, I got along well enough with Milo. He'd stopped by the line shack from time to time, checking to see how I was doing. But he treated cows more charitably than he treated his wife. Cows were worth money.

A half-hour later, field notes completed, anger abated, heart rate back to sixty beats per minute, I said farewell to the cave and its ancient contents. When I slipped out, the coyote pups were quiet, probably sleeping off their meal; they'd normally be active at night, anyhow. Hugging the perimeter to protect myself from prying eyes, I crossed halfway around the valley. I scanned the nearby slopes with my dented binoculars. Nothing moved. Nothing was out of place. The cave would be my secret—except, perhaps, for whoever had removed that hare.

I activated the trap by tossing a rock at it, brushed out my footprints, left no sign I'd been anywhere near the place.

Take that, Milo.

SEVEN

I checked the Permo/Triassic contact as far as I could in both directions before circling back to the Jeep. None of the exposures were as good as what I'd found in the valley, but I proved the map was accurate.

The Jeep was intact where I'd left it. No tracks; no visitors. It was too late in the day to search for the marker bed. Besides, it would be at least a thousand feet above me. Problem number one would have to wait until tomorrow. Right now, I yearned for company, for the dubious safety of Pair-a-Dice.

The town seemed deserted. Randy's wall hadn't grown much, and his tools lay scattered in the dirt. A car with a Canadian license plate was parked in front of Room 1, but the place was as quiet as a church on the day after Christmas.

I showered quickly and changed into canvas shorts, a sleeveless white blouse, and sandals. My feet said thank you. When I picked up the field bag I used as purse, I noticed something wrong: the side flap was latched. This morning, I'd been in a hurry. I'd grabbed a mechanical pencil without bothering to lock the flap in place. The air seemed too cold, all of a sudden. I turned off the air conditioner, welcoming the silence while I checked the rest of the room.

Someone had made a careful search of my papers and maps, rifled through my books and aerial photographs, even unwrapped and re-wrapped rock samples that were stashed in boxes on the floor. I'd left a location map on the bed . . . leather beanbags still anchored the corners, but the spread was unwrinkled, smooth. I remembered perching on the edge to lace my boots. The impression was gone . . .

Isabel came with fresh towels every other day, changed the sheets every fourth day. The rest of the time I made my own bed. I wasn't obsessively neat. Whoever searched my room had left it neater than he'd (she'd?) found it. They'd know I'd been working near the valley where the traps were set, near the dirt road Killeen used. Had they followed me? Had they removed the hare? Had they found Diane's manuscript?

I glanced at the warped headboard, fastened to the wall with rusty screws. This morning, at the last minute, I'd stuck the manuscript in a dark brown folder, slipped it between the headboard and the wall. I'd hooked the elastic band around a big splinter near the edge of the back. I reached in now, tugged—the folder slid smoothly from its hiding place. If this was what the intruder was after, he'd left empty-handed.

So who was my intruder? Killeen had been on some mission to the west of the mountains today, but he'd gotten back with time to spare. Anyone in town might have talked to Freda, including Lon and Ruth Bovey; they might now know that the manuscript existed. Milo might suspect I had something to do with freeing the coyote, might be checking me out. Isabel always knew what was going on around town, but I'd trusted her with my things for three years. Bill or Randy? They weren't shy—they'd probably have left a note. Buddy? No reason I could think of, unless he thought I was involved with the murders. Absurd. The murderer? God, I hoped not. That would mean he was someone from town.

I gave up. The list was too long and I was too hungry. I'd given most of my lunch to the coyote. I replaced the folder in its hiding place, wondering if Isabel had changed the locks after she'd bought the place . . . wondering if my room key would indeed open all the other doors . . .

The Pair-a-Dice Store was closed for the day. I'd missed picking up my mail by five minutes. High-pitched voices came from the laundromat on the far side of the building. Next to the Bovey wide-cab truck, five heads—four dark-auburn, one platinum—bent over something in the dust. Noting the sticks clutched in the boys' hands, I wandered over to take a look.

"The living room's bigger than that," complained the oldest boy, Peter. (The only reason I remembered his name was that Ruth and

Lon had followed the list of Apostles I'd learned in school: Peter, Andrew, James, John.) "We have to move the walls out."

"More thtickth," sighed John, who was missing two front teeth. "Longer thtickth."

The other boys followed him toward the cottonwoods at the rear of the store, leaving Gabbie to dismantle the miniature log cabin.

"Hi, Frankie—" Gabbie stopped, confused. Looked up at me with eyes the color of that green glass button. "Is it okay if I call you that?"

"Sure. I like it better than Ms. MacFarlane."

Ruth stepped out of the laundromat, her brown eyes concealed by huge dark glasses. She was one of the few women I knew who could stand eye-to-eye with me. Today, in Tony Lama boots, she was even taller. "Oh, it's you, Frankie."

"Don't tell me your machine broke down."

"On wash day, too." She shook her head. The cloud of auburn hair glinted in the sunlight. Sunglasses slipped down her freckled nose revealing a multicolored bruise below her left eyebrow. She shoved them back in place with a quick, jerky movement. "They won't be able to send anyone out until Thursday."

"You okay?" I couldn't keep myself from staring at her eye even though I couldn't see through the dark lenses.

She shrugged, watching her daughter. "I just have to be more careful around the horses. Isn't that right, Gabbie? Blackie kicks."

"Yes, Momma."

And the moon is a Twinkie, I thought, as the boys arrived from their scavenger hunt. But how could I help someone who didn't want my help? "Well . . . stop by if you need to talk," I said.

Ruth nodded, shoulders slumping, before retreating to the mountain of wet clothes that sat in a basket just inside the door. Gabbie remained silent, waving one delicate hand when I said good-bye. I wondered how much she knew.

The Pair-a-Dice Bar was empty, for once. Sylvie heard the screen door slam and poked her head out from the kitchen. She had on the same navy blue dress as the day before. Tommy peeked around from behind her.

"Want the special?" she called softly. Her voice had a slight accent or musical overtone that I couldn't place.

The place reeked of fried liver and onions. "No thanks. Where is everybody?"

She stepped out wiping her hands on a towel. The topaz-blue eyes were friendly. "Over at the Black-Light. Eddie said someone was arrested this morning. I don't know who. Opal and Alf are getting the details from Deputy Montana."

"Eddie who?"

She gave me a strange look. "Eddie Killeen—the man you ate dinner with last night."

"Oh. That Eddie," I said, as if I knew fifty men with that name. At least now I knew what the "E" stood for.

"What would you like to eat?"

"Can you do a hot turkey sandwich, dinner salad with tomato, and iced tea?" God, what I would have given for Mexican or Szechwan fare, spicy enough to clear out my sinuses. I was sick of bland food.

"I can handle that." The gold hair retreated. Over the hum of the ceiling fans I could hear her singing—sounded like "Amazing Grace." She had a pure, effortless soprano. I wondered if hymns had ever before been sung in the Pair-a-Dice Bar.

Tommy carried my iced tea carefully to the table, then slid into the booth across from me. He had a milk mustache and clutched some dingy, shapeless stuffed animal—a shark or a dolphin, I thought. I automatically handed him a napkin from the black metal holder on the table. I have five nephews, and one on the way.

"Am I sitting on anybody's lap this evening?"

"Nope. They're all in the kitchen with Mommy. They like her singing."

"So do I. Do you like to sing?"

"Yes. But Mommy's better. She knows lots of songs."

"Tell me about your animal, " I said, pointing to the decrepit thing.

"Daddy sent it to me. When I was a baby. Least, that's what Mommy says. It's a dolphin. That's a mam'l, not a fish."

"Yes, I know."

"Lotsa people don't."

He stroked the dolphin's head as Sylvie brought my plate. The salad looked like a real salad with lots of tomato and carrot and red cabbage mixed in with the lettuce.

"Italian okay?" she asked, handing me a cruet.

"Wonderful."

She retreated to the kitchen taking it for granted that I welcomed Tommy's company.

"What's a mam'l?" he asked, watching me swallow a bite of sandwich.

"Mammals are animals that have hair, that give birth to live young instead of laying eggs, and that feed their babies milk." Maybe if I snowed him with facts, he'd change the subject. He thought for a minute while I ploughed through my dinner.

"I'm a mam'l," he concluded. "You're a mam'l."

"Yes," I said around a mouthful of salad.

"Why did Daddy send me a dolphin? Why not a teddy bear?"

"I don't know, Tommy. Have you asked your mom?"

He shrugged slightly. "She told me a story about a boy who was drowning, and a dolphin came along and saved him. So I guess it's supposed to keep me safe."

Sounded reasonable to me. I finished my dinner in silence, while Tommy stared off into space. Sylvie switched to Gershwin. The acoustics in the kitchen were wonderful. Her voice echoed off the metal surfaces and hung like crystal raindrops in the humid air.

"How do mam'ls make milk?"

Uh-oh. The record was stuck in a groove. Time for obfuscation. "Mammals have special glands, called mammary glands . . . they're like great big sweat glands. Are you following?" He nodded intently. "But these mammary glands make milk instead of sweat." This was getting complicated. "And the babies drink the milk until they're old enough to eat solid food."

"Do I have mam'ry glans?"

"Well, no, Tommy, not really. Only females have them. Like your mother."

"And you?"

"Yes."

"Where are they?"

Help. I much preferred teaching college kids who were intimately familiar with mammary glands. "They're breasts, Tommy." I pointed to one of mine, sneaking a look around the room to make sure no one had come in while I was talking.

"Oh, those," he said. "Yeah, Mommy's got those." Pulling out the neck of his red-striped tee shirt, he peered down at his chest.

I stood up before he could ask the next question. I'd forgotten how curious a four-year-old could be. "I've got to go now, Tommy. Thanks for keeping me company. Would you get your mom for me, please?"

"Okay. 'Bye, Frankie." He ran off to the kitchen.

I paid Sylvie. "Have you seen Isabel today?"

"Not since noon when I stopped by the store."

"I loved your singing."

She stopped transferring my dishes into a gray plastic tub. Her eyes opened wide, startled, as if no one had ever complimented her. "Why thank you."

"Your voice has a faint accent . . . "

"I lived in Jamaica for three years. My father was a minister there. I helped him teach school." She noticed my surprised look. "In Jamaica, you only have to go to school till you're fourteen. So at fourteen I started teaching the little ones."

"Why did you leave Jamaica? Wasn't it paradise?" For a moment, I thought she wasn't going to answer. She wiped the table with a damp towel, sweeping the crumbs into her left hand.

"It was. But there was a hurricane . . . Dad died. I had to go live with my mother's sister in Connecticut."

"I'm sorry."

"Don't be. It was a long time ago." But she wiped the table for a third time as if erasing memories.

It was barely 6:30 when I stepped outside. Several hours of daylight left. The Boveys' truck was gone from the laundromat. I trotted over to Freda's place, humming "Summertime" an octave lower than Sylvie sang it. "I Got Plenty O' Nuttin'" would have been more appropriate.

The dirt strip in front of the Black-Light Bar looked like a swap meet on Saturday morning. But inside the building no one played pool, no one danced; the jukebox brooded silently in the corner. Freda fiddled with the TV, trying to pull in a station, but the cloud cover interfered. Everyone else clustered around Buddy.

Killeen stood up and gave me his stool. Freda rolled her wheelchair over and handed me a Guinness.

"On the house," she said, as I reached into my pocket. "Buddy told me about Geoff. I always thought he was an odd one."

"How so?"

"I don't know exactly . . . He acted like he was better than us, smarter. He asked questions, but wouldn't pay no attention to the answers."

It was true, I realized. I was just too involved to notice. "Did you get my note?"

"Isabel dropped it by after the store closed. I only told Gabbie about the book when she stopped in to get some lemonade for the boys. She's read every book in the school library at least twice. Wants to be a writer. She won't tell nobody."

Only her mother or father, who might already have searched my room for the damn thing. For my own protection, I had to return that manuscript tonight. "I hope not," I said to Freda's retreating back.

Freda didn't hear me. Backing up, she refilled a couple of glasses before picking up a half-dozen empty bottles. The glass clanked into the bin under the bar. "Walker," she called loudly enough to carry over the buzz of voices. "Bin needs emptyin'."

Walker stumped out from the storeroom behind the bar, hoisted the plastic tub without breaking stride or removing one hand from his pocket, and turned away. At the storeroom door he paused, found my eyes in the mirror, held them with a pale, unnerving stare. I looked away first.

The buzz of conversation got louder when Buddy stood up. His eyes had deep circles, and the skin was taut across his prominent cheekbones. He stretched his arms high to loosen his muscles; one hand dropped to massage the back of his neck.

"What happened, Buddy?"

"Sorry, Frankie. Killeen can fill you in. I'm late already."

"Will you be back? I need to talk to you."

"Emergency?"

"Not yet."

"Then how about if I stop by the motel on my next break . . . around 10:30?"

"Great," I said. Did I have a choice?

Half the crowd left with him, still murmuring questions. The rest drifted over to the pool tables and the jukebox. Randy wasn't around, I noticed. No thrills for the teenage girls. Killeen took the stool next to me. "Well?" I said.

"Deputy was murdered this morning—over on 93," Killeen said.

Oh, God. Poor Buddy. No wonder he didn't have time for my little worries.

"A friend of his?" Stupid question. Out here, where they had to drive hundreds of miles a day on their routes, the deputies knew each other pretty well. I took a swig of Guinness, felt exhausted all of a sudden.

Killeen's expression was grim as he told the story. A deputy was headed south, about halfway between Jackpot and Wells, when he stopped to help a stranded motorist. The deputy radioed in, but didn't sound suspicious. The vehicle, hood up, was off the northbound lane. A figure was bending over the engine. Deputy Hogue made a U-turn and pulled up behind him. Couldn't read the dusty license plate. He told the radio operator that he was going to check on it and radio back. He never did. A trucker found Hogue lying in front of his car ten minutes after the deputy's last transmission. He'd died from a shotgun blast to the head.

There weren't any suspects. The sheriff assumed the murderer was in Idaho by now, but the trucker didn't remember passing anyone who drove suspiciously. Didn't remember passing anyone at all. His mind was in neutral.

I nodded, knowing how it is on these roads. You focus on the horizon, you concentrate on staying awake.

"Then the killer's vehicle was operable," I said. Had he waited for someone to kill?

Killeen read my look. "Seems so. He was able to drive it away. Now they got the police in three states on the alert."

And there were a hell of a lot of dusty license plates and shotguns in this country. It seemed hopeless. But I didn't say it.

"They'll get him," Freda said, slapping another Guinness on the counter.

I hadn't heard her arrive. I was thinking about Killeen, driving through the mountain range from the west this afternoon. I wondered if his plates were dusty.

"You told her the other news yet?" Freda asked Killeen.

"I thought someone would have told you already. They arrested Bill this morning . . . for the murder of that girl in Wells."

EIGHT

"Bill Anderson?" My gut said no. Pranks, yes. Getting drunk and hurting someone in a fight, yes. But not premeditated murder. My thoughts must have been easy to read on my face.

"Why not?" Killeen said. "How well do you know Anderson?"

"Well enough."

"Anyone's capable of killing, Frankie."

"I don't even kill spiders."

Slowly, with one blunt finger, he wiped the condensation off the outside of his glass. "Some day you might not have a choice . . . that spider might be too big to carry outside."

"I've met tarantulas and wolf spiders. I just use a bigger cup." The words sounded naïve, but I didn't try to take them back. I felt that if I opened the door a crack, he'd tell me about the people he'd killed, a soldier's stories of where and when and why. I didn't want to see his pain or his scars, didn't want to know him that intimately. So I brought the conversation back to safer ground. "What happened with Bill?"

"The police found out he was in Wells Saturday night. He got thrown out of Nita's place for yelling at one of the girls, so he went to see Emmajean at the service station. They had words about her boy. The other attendant heard him threaten to cut off child support."

I hadn't known he was paying child support. "But did anyone see him with Emmajean later?"

"I don't know."

"It sounds pretty circumstantial. Does Randy know?"

"Haven't seen him."

Randy didn't need this, on top of everything else. Bill meant everything to him. I'd drop by the shack to see how he was doing—it was the least I could do. But I wanted to find Isabel first. "Isabel around?"

"Left just before you got here. She's sweet on Montana, you know."

"What?"

"Yeah. They're keeping company."

"You don't say." He'd found out more about Isabel in three days than I had in three years. I wondered if Killeen had ferreted out the details of her husband's death. Isabel hadn't volunteered any information, and I'd been afraid to broach the subject.

"You want company over to Anderson's place?" Killeen watched my reaction in the mirror behind the bar. How had he guessed where I was going?

"That depends." I took a deep breath. I might as well challenge him in the middle of a room full of people. "Did you search my room today?"

He didn't seem surprised. I wondered if anything surprised him.

"If I'd searched it, you wouldn't know I'd been there."

It wasn't exactly a denial, but I believed him. I don't know why. Maybe because I wanted to. I needed to trust someone. "What were you doing on the western side of the range today?"

"Had some business in Elko. Took the scenic way home." He wore one of those take-it-or-leave-expressions I found so irritating. But at least he hadn't answered with a question. "You can ask Montana about it," he said, grinning.

"He just left . . . as you well know."

"I visited the library."

"Checking back issues of the newspaper?" It was my turn to ask questions.

"Among other things."

"Did they have anything to do with a boy named Johnny?"

He checked to see that there was no one standing close. Freda was at the other end of the bar. "It had . . . has . . . everything to do with a boy named Johnny."

"Why are you suddenly answering my questions?"

"Because trust is a two-way street."

I drained the last of my Guinness and set the bottle gently on the bar. Freda switched on the black-light, and the minerals glowed with a cool beauty.

"Want to take Isabel along for protection?" he asked. "If she'll go, that is."

"She may have searched my room. That's why I'm looking for her—to ask if she knows anything, saw anybody."

"Montana trusts her."

"But do I trust Buddy? Trouble is, I don't know why anybody would do it." I wasn't going to mention the manuscript.

"But somebody did."

"That's the bottom line," I agreed. "Come on, Killeen. Let's go. But if you touch one hair on my head—" Trust only went so far.

"Don't get your pigtail in a snit, woman. I'll keep my distance." He reinforced his point by telling Freda where we were going before he followed me to the door. "My truck or yours?"

A moot point, since I'd walked. His Texas license plate was dusty, but readable from a distance. Reassuring. Of course, he could have washed it off. . . .

Isabel wasn't at the motel. Killeen just looked at me. Waited. I nodded, and we headed over to Randy's shack.

Bill and Randy lived in a shack on the back edge of town. They hadn't heard of landscaping; the closest trees were a block away. The building was an architectural nightmare of tar paper, shingle siding, brick, and cement. No plan. No clear form. But it kept out the rain, they claimed, and it had a terrific view of the mountains.

A lumpy old couch in a putrid shade of green occupied the sagging front porch. Randy sprawled, boots up on one arm, head on the other. He faced west, where the sun glowed behind Red Mountain. He didn't even turn his head as we pulled up, just kept staring at the mountains from under the brim of his hat.

A pack rat scurried from behind a cushion as Killeen and I reached the steps. Killeen leaned against a post. The front window had a bullet hole in the middle surrounded by a spider web of fractures. The bullet had come from inside the house. The front door looked like a reject from somebody's closet. The old yellow paint had weathered to ivory— what was left of it anyway, a few strips here and there. Someone had tried to kick a hole in the door, but it was solid. And dented.

Randy's green-checked shirt was sweat-damp and unsnapped to the waist, exposing an almost hairless, muscular chest. I said his name softly as I sat on the top step. "What happened?"

"Billy's in jail."

"I know. But why? I thought he was in the clinic having tests."

"He was. They released him this morning. Gave him medicine for an ulcer, and a special diet. He was arrested in the grocery store. Don't know if they'll let him be on that diet in jail." He sounded lost, a little defensive, like a child separated from its mother on a crowded beach.

"They had to have some reason for suspecting him. . . . "

"Of course they did. They've always got a reason to get Billy. He *hands* them reasons—makes it easy. Listen to what my stupid, jackass brother did this time." Randy swung his feet around, thumped them on the boards. "On second thought, let's go in. I need somethin' to drink." He held open the front door for me and flicked on the light. Killeen moved silently behind us.

I'd never been inside. The place was spotless, swept. No piles of clothes or papers on the floor, no dirty dishes in the sink. The long wall of the kitchen/living room was floor-to-ceiling books, science mostly—biology, metallurgy, chemistry, geology. But there were rows of classics and old *National Geographics*. A brown virgin-vinyl couch sat against the opposite wall. Above it hung faded color photographs in cheap wooden frames. One showed a woman with dark- blonde hair sitting on the brown couch. Beside her, cradling a baby in his arms, was a young Bill. Both were smiling. There was a baptismal shot with Bill, baby Randy, and a priest. He was the only adult male in any of the photographs.

"That's Father Vincent," said Randy. "He took most of the pictures. Thought Billy would make a good priest. Billy had other ideas, of course."

In a later photo, a teenage Bill held up the carcass of a mountain lion. The rocky hillside under his boots was covered with snow; a rifle leaned against a tree. Forming a circle around the other photos were school pictures showing Bill's and Randy's maturing faces. But there were empty slots, as if their mother had planned for a future she never saw.

"How old were you when she died?" I asked.

Randy followed my look. "Ten." His voice was a rough whisper. "She was a teacher," he said. "Taught us as much as she could before the cancer took her. . . . We think it was from the nuclear testing at Dugway, but we couldn't prove it." He ran a hand over the spines of the books. "Billy always said the only talents he had were with mining and women. But when Ma died, there wasn't any money. He had to come home and take care of me." He turned his back on the library, wandered like a sleepwalker toward the refrigerator, and stood in front of it as if he couldn't remember what he was doing there.

I took out a beat-up copy of *Gray's Anatomy*, flipped through, saw the yellow highlighting. "What do you want to be?"

"You won't laugh? No, of course you won't." He looked at the floor, then over at me. "A vet," he said.

"You read all these?"

"Yep. I get 'em from the used bookstore in Elko. Or wherever. Billy brings me some." His voice trailed off. A three-legged cat hopped neatly from the top of the refrigerator down to the drain board as Randy handed me a soft drink. He didn't seem to notice Killeen standing just inside the door. Killeen, big as he was, had a way of blending in with the furniture.

"Tell me about Bill," I said.

Randy stared at his Mountain Dew for a moment before popping the tab and gulping down the contents. He twisted the empty can between his hands until it snapped in two with a metallic crackle. He tossed the halves into the trash bag under the sink. "There isn't much to tell," he said.

Deputies had canvassed the whole town of Wells (which wasn't saying much). In one of the bars they'd learned that Bill had been in town Saturday night. He'd been mad when I didn't show up for a confrontation at Freda's bar. Angry with Buddy, too. So he'd driven to Wells, to Nita's place, which offered sex in addition to gambling and booze. He'd left Wells about eleven, after gassing up at Emmajean's station. He must have been her last customer; she'd left work at eleven.

Bill said he drove straight home. But he didn't remember whether he passed Buddy on the road. Didn't remember much of anything very clearly—except the girl at Nita's place had long black hair. Like mine, I thought. Her name was Rose. She said Bill yelled at her and started throwing things. Rose launched a few ashtrays herself. Nita chucked him out of the place.

Randy had been down at headquarters for half the day giving statements and talking to his brother. So far, there wasn't any physical evidence linking Bill to Emmajean's murder. But he didn't have a good alibi for the Wendover murder either, and the police were still checking on Salt Lake City.

"Did they ask if you had an alibi, Randy?"

"Yeah. I told 'em I took a turn with Diane about 10:30." He looked at the floor, shifted his weight from one foot to the other.

"I'm sure she provided half the countryside with alibis."

"Good thing, too. Wish Billy weren't so particular. But he and Diane don't get along too well. Not sure why, exactly. Maybe he just doesn't like blondes."

Emmajean was a blonde. "Do Bill a favor, Randy. Don't say that to the sheriff."

His eyes glistened, reflecting the ceiling light. "We gotta get out of Pair-a-Dice, Frankie—Billy and me. This wasn't what Ma wanted for us. Will you help me?"

Did I want to interject myself in their lives? Most emphatically not. But I have a tough time saying no to beseeching blue eyes. "Please, Frankie?"

"I'll talk to him before I go." I handed him my empty can, watched him twist it in two as he had the first one.

"Thanks," he said gruffly. He reached for the cat, stroked the tawny fur with long smooth movements. Its yellow eyes turned to slits; a rumble issued from deep in its throat.

"Don't mention it. You still working for Pete?"

"Yeah. Missed most of today. But Billy told me to get back to work tomorrow or he'd tear a strip off me. Didn't want me to visit him in jail again."

I touched his hand. "See you in the morning, then."

"Bright and early." He didn't look like he'd get much sleep that night.

I turned to go. "They'll find whoever did it, Randy."

"For Billy's sake, I sure as hell hope they make it quick."

It was eight when Killeen dropped me back at the motel. We'd been silent on the drive from the Anderson house. "He could've done it, Frankie. Could've snapped."

"I know." I stepped down from the truck, stuck my head in the window. "Thanks, Killeen. For coming with me."

"You take care of yourself."

I stood in the courtyard, confused by the day's events, until the crickets were the only night sound. Then I shook myself and walked to the office. Isabel answered my knock and invited me into the rear apartment for iced tea. My bladder was going to work overtime tonight.

The apartment looked like Isabel: small, unfussy, organized; earth tones, simple furniture, blinds at the windows. I sipped iced tea; learned nothing of import—at least, I didn't think so at the time. . . . The owner of the Canadian car parked in front of Room 1 had checked in around lunchtime. Said he was on his way to a conference. Isabel hadn't seen anyone in or near my room, but she'd spent the afternoon at the store. No one else had a key to my room. However, all the locks could be opened with a master key; she hadn't re-keyed the locks when she'd bought the place two years ago. Maybe someone had made a copy of the master.

"Two years ago? But you were running the motel the first summer I was here."

"Ted, my husband, was in the Middle East at the time—military intelligence. I'd already finished my hitch with the Army, and since I couldn't be with him, I came back to Nevada. Kept me busy. When he was killed, I decided to buy the place. It had been for sale for years. We'd been saving for a house. For later," she added, "when he got out."

It was a small world, I thought. Killeen was military intelligence, too. Curiouser and curiouser. I stood up.

"How did Ted die?" I asked, rinsing out my glass and setting it on the drainboard. I didn't really expect an answer.

"I never learned the details of his last mission . . . and in the end it didn't matter. He was dead. Life goes on."

Life goes on . . . life after Ted, life after Geoff. For Bill and Randy, it was life after Mother and Emmajean; for Freda, life after legs.

"I'll keep an eye on the place while you're out in the field," Isabel said.

"Wednesday or Thursday should be my last day. Just a couple more areas I want to check out. Can I ask you something personal?" As if I hadn't already invaded her privacy.

"You can ask."

"Are you and Buddy a couple?"

"I guess you'd call it that. We're keeping it quiet for the moment. I'm not ready to get married again. He isn't either. His first marriage was a disaster. And when my family finds out I'm seeing a divorced man, they'll disown me."

"Did you see Buddy last Saturday night?"

"Sure. Saturday nights, he takes a long break—parks around back and doesn't leave until after ten." I didn't ask what went on for two hours. "That's the other reason we have to keep quiet about our relationship. The dispatcher knows, but she turns a blind eye as long as Buddy puts in enough overtime to compensate. He keeps his radio on, though there've been a few times I've wished he hadn't. But nothing much happens during the early evening along his route. . . . The drunks take to the roads later on."

Back in my room, I locked the door and stuck a chair under the handle. Two hours to go until Buddy showed up. It was so humid and still, I had to turn on the air conditioner. I hated the fact that it covered the night sounds. After another shower, I settled down to skim

Diane's opus for a second time, looking for details I'd missed the night before.

On the surface, it wasn't a depressing book. The stiletto humor dug as deeply into the fabric of small-town society as the first chapters had into mores and customs around the globe. But now I sensed a brooding undercurrent of despair.

Did I understand Diane any better than I had before? Not really. The tattoo, for instance: why Our Lady of Sorrows? Why not Our Lady of Fatima, or Guadalupe? In the book, the lurid rendition of Mary, her heart pierced with seven swords, signified Nadia's own traumas, her conscious identification with the Mother of Christ. Like Mary, Nadia was at the mercy of powerful men—her father, brother, priest—while still a young, relatively innocent girl. She insisted there were other similarities between their lives: becoming pregnant out of wedlock via a holy being (which stretched the allegory, as far as I was concerned—since when was a priest a god?); delivering her child far from home; losing the child; and fleeing her own country to live among foreigners for a time. To Nadia, Mary represented the most powerful positive force on earth. Where men destroyed, women sacrificed, shouldered despair, endured, offered solace and hope, rebuilt. The three people who stayed on Calvary until the end demonstrated the immense strength of women. A valid point, but I still had trouble placing Nadia, or Diane, at the same level in the sororal hierarchy as Mary.

In Easytown, Nadia felt needed—as a teacher, as a whore, as the lover of a complex, powerful man confined by the strictures of his family, his role in society. The reader knew the relationship was doomed. So did Nadia. But the relationship had nothing to do with love, at least on her part, and everything to do with power. Whereas Nadia controlled the frequency and the times of their secret meetings, her lover controlled the tenor. Victim and victimizer, abused and abuser: sometimes it was tough to tell one from the other.

Diane was at her most perceptive when she dissected Pair-a-Dice, revealing relationships and political factions I hadn't suspected. I'd never wondered how a town of one hundred and fifty subsistence-level citizens and a few wealthy ranchers could support three bars and two restaurants. The answer lay in the town's proximity to Utah, where the church/state boundary was blurry, and where liquor, gambling, and whores were scarce. Pair-a-Dice, in its less-than-splendid isolation just across the border, offered anonymity to those who observed church strictures publicly, yet had other, socially unacceptable needs or cravings.

The novel read like an exposé, becoming more factual and less humorous as the story progressed, almost as if another narrative voice were intruding, one very familiar with Lon Bovey, alias Von Boyle. In the manuscript, the Boyles had been acquiring land by intimidation for the past century and a half. They held legal title, but always bought low after threatening the smaller landowners, sabotaging their water supplies, or appropriating their herds piecemeal—a euphemism for rustling. The family simply moved the unbranded cattle onto Boyle land just before roundup. Sometimes it was necessary to kill the branded cow if she clung to her calf. Those carcasses were conveniently buried. Nadia speculated about what else was buried on Boyle land. And who.

After skimming those chapters a second time, after seeing Ruth Bovey's face this afternoon, I wondered, too. I no longer was surprised by Diane's intimation that Lon had raped and brutalized two teenagers years before. One had run away, the other had borne him a child. Neither had pressed charges. Wealth, whether here or abroad, buys a truckload of silence.

The last chapters were missing, so I didn't know how the book ended. But neither did Diane. Maybe she was waiting for events to play themselves out in Pair-a-Dice; maybe she feared the ending. I knew I did.

Pete had told me that Lon Bovey was going to run for Congress in the next election. It didn't matter whether the "novel" contained thinly disguised truth or fabrication—if it were published, then Lon's reputation, family, and political future would crash.

So how did this affect me? My room had been searched today, and it wasn't because someone found limestone fascinating. I suspected Lon knew the manuscript existed, even if he didn't know the contents. Had Gabbie passed the word along? Had Lon found out from Diane or Freda? Or was I jumping to conclusions?

The manuscript wasn't for show-and-tell. I decided to return it immediately, before Buddy arrived. It was only ten o'clock. That gave me half an hour.

It was a Tennessee Williams kind of night—humid, sultry, with an undercurrent of expectancy. The skin on my arms prickled. I half-expected to sniff magnolias and the musky scent of passion on the faint breeze. I smelled nothing but sage and dust mixed with my own sweat. The air bathed me like an August night in Tucson, thick with monsoon moisture. Tropical storms normally didn't get this far north, but I could almost smell the rain forests of Mexico. Stars peered through breaks in the cloud cover, but they seemed farther away than usual, as if a sheer veil had been dropped over the earth by a mischievous goddess. In the east, across the valley, mountains stood outlined against the growing light of the waning moon. Even the night birds were silent.

I drove up Easy Street to Diane's mobile home, not wanting to face the shadows that suddenly seemed threatening. In less than a minute, I pulled in beside her Harley. The light beside the front door was on and a faint glow came through the small bathroom window. Good, she was home. It was pitch black under the cottonwoods as I cut the motor and lights, so I stayed put until my night vision returned. I half-expected Diane to come to the door and check out her visitor, but she didn't, and the lights in the front of the house stayed off. Maybe she wasn't here after all. I opened the door and put one foot on the ground. Something brushed my bare leg before slinking under the Jeep. God, I hoped it was a cat or raccoon, not a rat the size of a dachshund. There was a rubbing sound as it squeezed through a gap in the aluminum skirting. I took two deep breaths before getting out and closing the Jeep door.

From the house came a muffled thud followed by scrabbling sounds. I ran up the steps to the screen door.

"Diane?" I called softly, urgently. No answer.

Someone moved quickly in the back part of the house, stumbled, grunted in pain. The sound carried easily in the heavy air.

I jerked open the door. "Diane?" I called more loudly.

As I stepped inside, a tall shadow moved in the hallway, caught momentarily in the tiny shaft of light that escaped around the almost-closed bathroom door. The rear door slammed open against the aluminum wall. The figure leaped out, landed easily on the ground, took off running.

As the footsteps receded, I dropped the manuscript on the living room carpet and crept cautiously toward the bedroom. Something rope-like caught in the open toe of my sandal. I tripped and fell on a warm solid object.

NINE

I untangled myself from the body with frantic, jerky movements and groped for the light switch on the wall. A truck started up in the distance. Close by, a motorcycle engine sputtered, caught, then roared away. It sounded like Diane's Hog.

Diane lay between the doorway and the double bed. I couldn't tell whether she was unconscious or dead. I'd tripped on the thin braid that ran like a rat's tail from the base of the shingled mass of hair. Next to her forearm, a pair of stainless steel barber's scissors caught my reflection, warped my lean body into a squatting gargoyle's form. In the soft overhead light, Diane's face showed mottled purple; bruises were darkening on her neck.

I dropped to my knees beside her shoulder, tilted back her head, and checked for breathing. Nothing. I lifted her neck, pinched her nostrils, and blew in four quick breaths. I was too scared to be gentle. I'd never had to do this on a real person. But it worked—her chest rose as the lungs inflated. I shuddered as my fingers touched the bruises, worried that I'd do more damage to the fragile skin. The jugular pulse was faint and irregular, but reassuringly present.

She still wasn't breathing on her own. I inhaled deeply, exhaled into her mouth, then paused to check her skin tone. I couldn't remember how long to wait between breaths, so I settled on four seconds, not sure I could count any higher. I didn't yell for help, afraid of wasting precious air.

After a couple of minutes, an eternity in that cramped space, her eyelids flickered open, then closed again. She was breathing on her own, shallowly, but effectively enough to bring some color back to her face. Or remove it. She now was the hue of butcher paper. I could distinguish the fine blue veins in her forehead. Her pulse was light, but regular. I left her head tilted back while I ran to the phone. A faint rustling sound, like pages of a book turning in the wind, came from the front room of the mobile home. The sheriff's office answered my distress call. I watched Diane and the hallway anxiously as the dispatcher took my information. No more noise. Maybe it had been the breeze. I prayed it had been the breeze. I felt exposed with the doors open and the light on. That truck motor could have been anyone. Even now, the attacker might be lurking outside or in the shadowy front room, watching, waiting for me to move. I picked up a statue from the bedside table—a carved figure of a tall African woman. It felt heavy, and I wondered if I were going into shock.

The dispatcher said it would be at least a half-hour before the helicopter got to me; the ground force would take more like an hour. I told her to call Buddy, who should be closer than that. She ordered me to keep everyone else outside until help arrived. It sounded simple, but I wasn't about to spend the time alone. Now that Diane was breathing again and the authorities were notified, I was starting to shake—for the second time that day.

My memory balked, unable to recall Isabel's number. Diane's phone book wasn't on the nightstand, and I didn't want to disturb the room by looking for it. So, keeping one eye on the front room, I crossed to the rear doorway and yelled for Killeen. The windows of the Tucker place were dark. Sylvie appeared thirty seconds later from the other side of the trailer. I wanted to hug her.

Diane's back door had no steps, just a sharp drop-off to the dust below. Sylvie stopped short, looking from the statue to Diane's prostrate form.

"Somebody tried to kill her—not *me.*" I set the statue down by the door.

"Who?" Sylvie's voice was a whisper.

"I don't know. I called the sheriff, but I don't want to wait alone. Can you get Pete?" I would have thought I'd yelled loudly enough to be heard three blocks away, but no lights shone in Pete's windows. He must sleep like the dead.

"I can't leave Tommy that long," Sylvie protested. "And I can't bring him here." She had a point.

"Have you had any emergency training?" I asked.

"A little. Cuts and things. Nothing like this."

Damn. "All right. Come on in." I helped her climb up beside me. "Watch her face for any change . . . Keep her head tilted back, and make sure she keeps breathing."

"What if she stops?"

"Scream." I felt for Diane's pulse. Still there. I closed my eyes for a moment and pictured my address book open to the "P" page—for Pair-a-Dice Motel. I only needed the last four digits for a local call. I felt my heartbeat quiet, my limbs relax.

Isabel answered on the third ring. She didn't waste time on questions I could answer later, bless her organized brain. She said she'd round up the troops and be over in a minute. I looked at Sylvie.

"I can take it—" I started to say, when a small head appeared at the doorway.

"Mommy?" He stood on the ground, eyes at floor level. They were focused on Diane. "She dead?"

Taking his small hand, Sylvie hoisted him into the room. He wore a sleeveless Superman pajama top tucked into blue underwear. The dolphin was under one arm.

"No honey. Just sleeping." The veins throbbed in her temple as she struggled to maintain a calm tone. I hoped she wouldn't faint.

In a flash, Tommy slipped between us. I'd forgotten how fast little ones could move. Kneeling beside Diane, he gently pressed his lips to hers.

"Why won't she wake up? Sleeping Beauty woke up." He looked at me accusingly as Sylvie picked him up. The red cape billowed out, settled over her arms.

"I don't know, Tommy." The life-and-death scene was turning into a farce. "Maybe her prince had more practice," I muttered.

Tommy didn't hear me. He stared over Sylvie's shoulder into the darkness outside. "You can't come in, Daddy. No room."

Another imaginary friend had been added to Tommy's circle. Sylvie's mouth tightened, and a kind of set patience replaced the tender smile. "Come on, honey, I'd better take you home."

I touched her arm. "It might be safer if you two stay up front until the others get here. He may still be out there." Sylvie turned paler still. "Besides, I could use the moral support. But please try not to touch anything."

Determined to protect whatever shreds of evidence remained, I used the tail of my shirt to cover my hand as I closed and locked the back door. I did the same with the screen door after I led them into the front room. When I turned on the floor lamp, there was no sign that anyone but me had been there in the last five minutes. No one hid in the corners or behind the furniture. Diane's desktop was strewn with papers, and the drawers were open. It had looked much the same the last time I'd seen it. The rest of the room was tidy, the curtains drawn. The place smelled like stale cigarette smoke. Even the walls and shades were stained.

Sylvie and Tommy perched on the edge of the dingy brown couch. She wore a pale pink tee shirt with faded blue-denim shorts. It was the first time I'd seen her in anything but the navy dress. A pink ribbon held her hair off her face—she looked like Alice in Wonderland. Tommy snuggled on her lap, pressing his face against her chest. His thumb crept up and found his mouth as Sylvie rocked back and forth, absently smoothing his hair and crooning a lullaby. Staring off into the night beyond the screen door, she looked frightened, lost. Tommy's eyelids drooped.

I left them alone and sat next to Diane, holding a hand that felt smooth and cold as a mountain stream. She wore no make-up. Her neck was splotched with small broken blood vessels and the smudgy bruises that turned darker as I watched. They tapered toward the back of her neck as if she'd faced her attacker. I wondered if she'd recognized him or if he'd been a stranger. . . .

Isabel was as good as her word. She arrived two minutes later with Pete and a surprisingly sober Alf. They left their truck lights on. I found the brightness reassuring. No one would jump out of the shadows. As I opened the door wide, two more trucks drove up—Killeen and Lon Bovey. Milo Gates arrived on foot.

"You know anything about first aid?" I asked Isabel from the doorway.

"I was a medic in the Army."

"All right. You can come in." I stood aside. The rest crowded after her before I could stop them. So much for protecting the crime scene. "No, damn it!" I said, pushing at them ineffectually. "The rest of you have to stay outside. Sheriff's orders."

"What happened?" Lon asked, shoving his way to the front.

I sighed, conceding defeat. "Somebody strangled Diane." Milo tried to brush past me to look at Diane. He froze. So did everyone else.

"You heard her," said Isabel from the hallway. "Outside."

When I turned around, she was pointing a handgun at the group. It could have been a pellet gun for all I knew, but the men quietly, carefully, backed out the door. The damage was done, however. They'd touched walls, the door, the kitchen table, and God knows what else.

Killeen was the last to leave. "Want me to take them home?" he asked, nodding at Sylvie and Tommy.

"No. They're safer here for the moment."

Killeen looked at me sharply. Shrugging, he joined the others in the yard.

"Don't worry, Frankie. We'll protect the perimeter," said Pete, as I shut the door on his full-moon face.

I crossed to Isabel who hunkered down, eyes on her watch, two fingers on Diane's wrist. "How long ago did you find her?" Isabel asked, when she finished.

"Fifteen minutes . . . twenty. I don't know. The paramedics should be here soon. The dispatcher said thirty minutes. How does she look to you?"

"Lucky. If you'd arrived a few seconds later, she'd be dead."

"Why isn't she coming round?"

"I don't know. Her pulse and breathing are stable, but she might have hit her head. I don't want to move her to find out. What happened?"

"I stopped by to give her something—oh, hell!" I ran for the front room. Sylvie hadn't moved. The manuscript wasn't on the floor where I'd dropped it. It wasn't on the desk next to the old IBM Selectric or on the table. I rifled through the papers on Diane's desk, but didn't find her green steno notebook, either. Had she had the presence of mind to hide it after I'd seen her earlier? With Sylvie sitting there, I didn't want to look in the drawers. Silently cursing my stupidity, I trudged back to Isabel.

"Gone?" she asked, studying my tight face.

I nodded, then slumped against the wall watching the steady rise and fall of Diane's chest.

"Want to tell me about it?"

Isabel already knew that someone had been in my room today. Now, in a soft voice, I told her about Diane's book, about hearing someone inside the mobile home when I stopped by to return the manuscript, and the noise in the front room when I called the sheriff. Isabel wanted to know what the book was about, but I wouldn't tell her. Diane might have been hurt because of it. I didn't want Isabel in danger, too. Besides, it was up to Diane, not me, to tell whomever she wanted. If she recovered.

"But you'll tell Buddy?"

"I suppose so. The manuscript may have nothing to do with this, but maybe the police can keep an eye on Diane until we find out for sure."

"And who'll keep an eye on you? You caught a glimpse of the person who attacked Diane. You read the manuscript."

"But I couldn't identify him. Or her. And I haven't read all of the manuscript." Hearing the whisper of denim brushing denim on the other side of the thin aluminum wall, I dropped my voice to a whisper, realizing belatedly that the windows were wide open. "Diane didn't give me the last two chapters. I'm not even sure they're written yet."

"Doesn't matter. You better watch your ass—"

The noise of a helicopter approaching cut off the rest of the warning. We joined Sylvie and Tommy in the living room and were shunted outside by the paramedics. Pete, Alf, and the others clustered around the trucks. Half the town had arrived, some in nightclothes. Families stood in small groups, speaking in hushed voices.

Lon Bovey broke away from Milo and Pete to corner me by the front door.

"Is she alive?" he asked in a tense tone. His voice carried easily, even over the distant whir of the helicopter blades. The murmurs from the crowd stilled while they waited for my response.

"Barely." The look on his face could have been relief, consternation, or anxiety.

"Conscious?" he asked.

"No."

"So you don't know who did it?" He shifted as he spoke so that his hat threw his face into full shadow.

"I didn't say that." I heard the sharp intake of his breath. I knew I was provoking him, but I was angry—about Diane, the manuscript, Ruth, the coyote. I wanted answers.

"Well do you know, or don't you?"

"I'll tell Buddy what I know when he gets here." I started to turn away. He grabbed my arm. The long spatulate fingers pressed deeply into the muscles of my left forearm. "Let go."

"When you answer my question." His voice was low, a soft, sibilant whisper.

I would have kicked him or stomped on his boot, but I was wearing sandals. It definitely would have hurt me more than it hurt him. Besides, I hate public brawls. Instead, I jerked my arm towards my body, twisted it down and around until he was forced to loosen his grip. My right elbow accidentally—well, sort of accidentally—caught him under

92

the jaw as he stepped forward. From a distance, it must have looked like he stumbled into me. I pushed him away.

"Don't touch me again, Lon. Ever."

His pale eyes glittered in the headlights; something dark oozed from his lower lip.

"Trouble?" asked Killeen from behind me. Milo walked over and stood next to Lon. Milo smelled like he'd inhaled a pitcher of beer and spilled at least one glass on his clothes.

"No trouble," I said. "Lon was just concerned about Diane."

"I'll talk with you later." Lon spun angrily toward the crowd. Milo threw me a look that said "I'll be back," before trailing after him.

"You certainly have a talent for rubbin' some people the wrong way, Frankie." Killeen's voice came over my left shoulder.

"Just overbearing men."

"Ever notice that the level of violence seems to escalate when you're around?"

I checked the marks on my forearm, wondering if the bruises would be the same size as those on Diane's neck. "No offense, Killeen, but things didn't start happening in Pair-a-Dice until you showed up."

"No offense taken." His tone was mild. "Same could be said for Sylvie and Tommy. And didn't you move into town the day Emmajean was killed?"

"Touché."

"You gonna leave now?"

"Why should you care whether I leave or not?"

"Just curious."

I'd heard that refrain before. "I'm not leaving until I'm finished."

"Why do you do it? Why do you work where people steal your Jeep, break into your room, strong-arm you?"

"There are risks in every profession, Killeen. Look at Freda. She was shot during a casino robbery. Isabel's husband was killed in the Middle East. You were in 'Nam, and yet you stayed in the Army. Why?"

"I loved my job. It was worth the risk."

"I feel the same about geology." I brushed back a few wispy strands of hair that had come loose when I helped Diane. I felt exhausted now that the adrenaline rush had worn off. "Maybe if I were just starting my fieldwork, I might quit, knowing I could finish next year or the year after. But I don't have that luxury. So I'll find a way to minimize the risks, to finish as quickly as possible, and then get the hell out. Besides, I've always felt safe back in the mountains—most people are too lazy to leave the comfort of their cars."

93

"Except me."

"Except you." And Bill, and Milo, and whoever took that hare back by the cave.

"And if someone wants to take a potshot at you?"

"They'll have to find me first."

"Don't say I didn't warn you, Frankie."

"Isabel beat you to it."

"You realize the vultures will follow the story. They ought to be here by breakfast."

Just what I needed—our killer could move about undetected amid the media chaos. "Then the sooner I head for the hills, the better," I said.

"Your funeral." Killeen went to stand by Sylvie who sat patiently on the tailgate of his truck, Tommy still tucked on her lap. Her fine-boned face was pale in the glaring lights; inky-gray shadows emphasized her eyes.

It was two hours before I could go home. I stayed out of the way for the first half-hour while Buddy and three other officers secured the area with yellow tape. After Diane was airlifted to the hospital, deputies methodically scoured the inside and outside of the mobile home for clues. As far as I could tell, they weren't finding anything important.

"Can I take Sylvie home?" Killeen asked Buddy.

"Don't see why not. I can talk with her later. Even if the guy's still around, she should be safe enough. There are lotsa folks within earshot."

"I'll watch out for her," Killeen said firmly. I shifted slightly, looked over at Buddy.

"You got a problem with that?" Killeen stepped closer, his body blocking my view of Sylvie. The passive face changed—the bones seemed to stretch against the skin, the muscles tighten. His eyes were deep black pools in the glare of the searchlights. He didn't raise his hand or his voice, but he intimidated me with his bulk, his energy. I was getting tired of men trying to intimidate me.

"Because she's white and you're not? Get real, Killeen. My problem is that one woman has been hurt tonight and I feel protective of Sylvie and Tommy. I still don't know why you're here in Pair-a-Dice, except that it has nothing to do with prospecting."

He relaxed slightly. "I didn't hurt Diane, Frankie. I was at my house, reading."

"And you have a dozen witnesses."

94

"At least," he agreed, matching my sarcasm. "You're gonna climb down off that fence sometime. Trust is a two-way street.

Bull's-eye. I wanted to let go, to trust my instinctive judgn people. It was like an ache that had been building since last summer, since Geoff had started to turn on me. I thought I knew him so well. I opened my mouth, but the words lodged in my throat.

"Actually," interrupted a soft voice. "It comes down to whether *I* trust him." Stepping in front of Killeen, Sylvie transferred the sleeping boy to his arms. Tommy's eyes opened, but he seemed content enough. She started for the trailer next door. Killeen caught up with her before she'd taken two steps. He didn't even send me one of those "I told you so" looks. I wondered if I'd have been as gracious in victory.

"Killeen!" Buddy called after him.

Killeen stopped, turned halfway around. Tommy looked small against his chest. "What?"

"I still need your statement. See me later."

"You know where to find me."

TEN

"Well, that's settled," Buddy said. He held up his notebook. "Ready to talk now?"

"Guess so. Buddy?"

"Yeah?" He looked up after entering name, date, and time in the notebook.

"Did Diane's injuries look like Emmajean's?"

"I didn't get a real good look at her. Why? You think this one might be different?"

"Yes." I dictated my version of the evening's events, including a summary of the missing manuscript and my run-in with Lon. It took a while. At intervals, Buddy whistled softly between his front teeth.

"But you can't identify the attacker?"

"A tall, agile person. Male, I think, at least my height. Not Pete—he moves like the Pillsbury Doughboy. Alf only comes up to my shoulder, and that's in his cowboy boots. All the women around here are shorter than I am."

"Except Ruth Bovey," Buddy said.

"Hadn't thought of her."

Ruth had always struck me as a follow-the-Good-Book-to-the-letter type, who wouldn't say shit if she had a mouthful. But she was in great physical shape. I'd watched her at roundup a couple of years ago; she could ride and rope with the best of them. If I were right about Diane's relationship with Lon, then Ruth might want her out of the way. Whether she'd actively remove her husband's mistress was another matter.

"Add her to the list," I said.

Buddy glanced up from his notes and over at the crowd. Lon was ordering people to go home and get some sleep. Buddy strolled over.

"Actually," he said mildly to Lon, "I'd like some of them to stick around until I have their statements." He called off names from his notebook. "Anybody else see or hear anything?" Nobody volunteered. "Okay, the rest of you go on home. You got anything more to say, Frankie?"

"In private." Buddy followed me to my Jeep. I told him what I'd seen that morning: the campfire, footprints the same size as those Killeen had seen at Thomasson's cabin, Milo and the coyote, the disappearing jackrabbit, Ruth's black eye. Buddy dutifully jotted down the hodgepodge of unrelated observations.

"Anything else?" He uncrimped his fingers from the pen, flapped his hand to get the circulation going.

"Bill still in jail?"

"Until we finish checking his alibi. If we determine the I-80 killer attacked Diane, then Anderson's off the hook."

"Did you check out Killeen?"

"Military intelligence, like he said. Got out six weeks ago. No blotches on his record—wheelbarrow full of commendations, in fact."

"Do you know why he's really here?"

"I know what he told me . . . in confidence. You'll have to make up your own mind if you want to trust him. Me, now—I don't trust anybody. Including you."

"Except Isabel."

He gave me a weary smile. "Word gets out."

"I'll keep your secret."

"Thanks."

I leaned against my Jeep and listened shamelessly to the interrogations. Lon had been taking a crib over to Milo's because Junior Gates had outgrown his bassinet. I saw the flash of surprise cross Milo's face at this piece of information, but he didn't contradict his boss. Lon's youngest had graduated to a real bed last winter, so Lon had offered to loan the crib to Milo. There it sat in the back of the truck: as Lon hoisted the headboard, a caster spun and flashed in the glare of the lights.

"You were delivering a crib at ten o'clock at night?" Buddy asked skeptically.

"Had paperwork to catch up on . . . finished a little after nine. Figured I'd run the crib by and surprise Milo and Nancy."

"Where was Ruth when you left?"

Ruth was already asleep. Since she got up at 4:30 every morning, she went to bed when the boys did. Lon was just pulling into Milo's driveway when he saw the two trucks racing for Diane's. He'd followed.

"Thought maybe I could help," Lon said, flashing the too-bright smile.

Buddy, not bothering to comment, turned to Milo. He'd been walking home from Freda's when he saw the trucks. Buddy would have to check with Freda to see what time he'd left—his watch was broken. He'd detoured to check out the ruckus.

Isabel, Pete, Alf, and the rest had nothing much to offer.

"Too many suspects, not enough time," I said, when Buddy finished. As a half-hearted attempt at humor, it failed miserably.

"Damn it, Frankie!" Buddy glared at me. "Do you have to make a joke out of everything?" He yanked off his cap, rifled the sparse hair on the crown of his head, jammed the cap back down.

"I'm sorry," I said, gently touching his arm. "It's my way of coping."

"Yeah. Okay." He tucked the notebook and pen in his breast pocket. "Just seems there's one crisis after another. First Emmajean, then Bert Hogue this afternoon. Now Diane. And I haven't had much sleep. . . . Doesn't look like I'll get any tonight, either."

"Buddy, until you find out who attacked Diane, and why, she's still in danger—"

"I'll make sure she's guarded, Frankie. And we'll get a statement as soon as she's conscious. That would be her best protection."

If she regains consciousness, I thought. But I left the more positive statement hanging in the air between us as Killeen appeared at my elbow. I wished he'd make more noise when he moved.

"Montana," he said, "there's something I want you to hear. You, too, Frankie."

Sylvie was sitting in the breakfast nook of the old Airstream trailer she rented from Alf. Tommy was asleep on one of the twin beds. The table sat four. I slid between the stove and table into the space next to Sylvie. I'm slender, but it still was a tricky maneuver. Buddy sat across from us. Killeen perched on a rickety camp stool in front of the stove. It was useless trying to fit his bulk into the narrow space next to Buddy.

The navy dress hung over a hanger, drops plinking from the hem into the stainless-steel kitchen sink. Nobody else seemed to notice the sound or the occasional creaking of the plastic cushions under our shifting weight. Sylvie studied her tightly clasped hands, which looked blue-white under the overhead fluorescent light. Buddy laid his pen and notebook, clean page up, on the brown Formica table.

"Well?" he said.

Sylvie looked up at Killeen, who nodded reassuringly. Like Alice, she began at the beginning, went all the way to the end, and stopped— efficient chronological order. As she spoke, the faint musical tone in her voice became more pronounced. I didn't understand the import of her words until she'd almost finished. Jesus H. Christ.

Sylvie's father was a fundamentalist missionary who'd worked in Jamaica. Sylvie was two when her mother took her back to Boston; the divorce had been final a year later. When Sylvie was 14, her mother died. With no other relatives willing to take her in, Sylvie rejoined her father on the island. The Reverend Birch was a scholar, and Sylvie was an only child, surrounded by books. As a missionary's daughter she was isolated, not allowed to date, expected to be a role model for the students at his school. The only young male she saw frequently was Raef Kingsley, a Jamaican who worked at the mission. She fell in love with him. Proximity had a lot to do with it. She was lonely, and Raef seemed to care about her. Maybe he did. He went out of his way to brighten her days with his easy laughter. But he never really got to know her. Nor she him. Their relationship might have passed, a girl's first infatuation, if a hurricane hadn't demolished the mission and killed Reverend Birch when Sylvie was 17.

After the hurricane, Sylvie moved in with an aunt in Connecticut, her only relative, and took a job as a waitress. Raef followed her to the States. Still lonely and confused, she married him on her 18th birthday. Tommy was born nine months later.

Raef had his green card, but had trouble finding work. He eventually joined a group of his countrymen who were in the import-export business. He was arrested for drug trafficking. Sylvie wrote to him in prison and visited him regularly. But as time passed, he became angry and accused her of infidelity. When he threatened her life and threatened to take Tommy away from her when he got out, she started divorce proceedings and made plans to disappear. But he was released six months early. When she got word he was on his way, she took off with Tommy, heading for California. She only had enough money to get to Laramie. From there, she worked her way across country as a waitress, never staying in one place very long: Rock Springs, Salt Lake City . . . Pair-a-Dice.

"I-80," I murmured. She nodded, looking miserable.

She thought she spotted Raef in Salt Lake City one day, so she grabbed Tommy and hopped on the next bus. When she got off at Elko, Isabel heard her asking for work at a restaurant. She offered to drive her to Pair-a-Dice, where Alf needed help. Sylvie jumped at the chance. She felt safer off the Interstate, until she heard about the murders in Wendover and Wells. The killer seemed to be narrowing his territory, focusing his search.

"He's out there . . . following me. I know he is," she whispered. "I didn't mean to involve anyone else. I just wanted to get away."

"Why didn't you call the police?" Buddy asked.

"Because I wasn't positive I'd seen him. I haven't had time to read the papers, so I didn't find out about the Utah murders until Saturday night. Even when that girl in Wells was killed, I didn't link it to Raef. He wants *me*. He wants Tommy. Why would he kill someone else?"

"We're not sure he killed anybody."

"Maybe not—but he's here."

"In *Pair-a-Dice?*" I asked. "You *saw* him?""

"No." The blue eyes were tortured. "But this was tucked beside Tommy's pillow when I got back from Diane's." She handed Buddy a mud-brown teddy bear. Instead of a bow around the neck, it wore a necklace of braided fabric, knotted at three-centimeter intervals. "Tommy said his daddy left the bear—as a present." She turned to me. "Remember when Tommy called to him at Diane's, Frankie?"

"I thought he was talking to an imaginary friend."

"So did I . . . until I found this." She pulled something from her pocket and slipped it over her fine-boned hand. It was a friendship bracelet braided from brightly colored ribbon and string. The knots were more closely spaced than on the bear's necklace. "Raef gave this to me when I left Jamaica. His mother taught him how to make them. He said they used to sell them to the tourists . . . until she . . . until she committed suicide."

"How old was he?"

She hesitated, searching her memory. Knuckles showed white on the clasped hands resting on the table. "Eight or nine. He was in an orphanage after that. He hated it. The woman in charge terrified him."

Buddy's hands stilled for a moment before he slowly closed the notebook. He picked up the bear. "Can I borrow this?"

"Do you have to? Tommy wouldn't understand if it were missing in the morning." When Buddy hesitated, she jerked the knotted ribbon from around the bear's neck, and pushed it across the table. "But take this—please." I want it as far away from me as possible, her look said.

That necklace scared the hell out of me, too. If Raef slipped in and out of people's bedrooms, had he been in mine this afternoon? Was he there now?

"I checked around outside," said Killeen. "Not a trace of him."

"I'm not surprised." Buddy carefully tucked the necklace in a plastic bag. "Do you have a picture of Raef, Sylvie?"

Sylvie picked up a faded red backpack, rifled through a wallet until she found a passport photo. She stared at it for a moment as if memorizing the details of Raef's handsome face. With trembling fingers, she passed it to Buddy. "Just this."

Buddy put the photo in a second plastic bag. "Get some sleep now. Killeen will keep an eye on you and Tommy." I saw the look that passed between the two men. I interpreted it to mean, "If anything happens to them, Killeen, I'm holding you responsible." But all Buddy said was, "I'll stop by tomorrow."

I stood up. Killeen moved back to let me out. Buddy followed me into the humid night. Deputies still bustled around Diane's home. Buddy shone his flashlight into the back seat of the Jeep before opening the door for me.

"Should always lock your car," he said.

"If I'd stopped to lock my car, Diane would be dead."

"Yeah. Well, if you call the station at ten tomorrow, I'll let you know how Diane's doing. The hospital won't release that information."

I looked around. The only person close enough to overhear our conversation was Milo. I lowered my voice. "Buddy, have they identified the Utah bodies?"

"Canadian women from Toronto, missing since they left a convention in South Bend last week."

"There was a car with Canadian plates in Room 1 . . . yesterday, I think. Isabel said the driver was on his way to a conference."

"Then she'll have the license number." Buddy jotted another note in his book.

"But what are the odds of a Jamaican immigrant killing Canadians in the middle of Nevada?" The only things I associated with Jamaica were bobsled teams, Colin Powell, coral sand, and reggae.

"About the same as one shooting up Americans on a Long Island commuter train, I expect."

"That was a long time ago."

"Frankie, if Raef Kingsley wasn't stable to begin with, transplanting him to the States, putting him in prison, and having his wife file for divorce wouldn't help."

"Were the women strangled with bare hands?"

"Nope. With something knobby, like—" He looked at the necklace in the plastic bag. "Like this cord. . . . And their bites were spider bites, gotten while they were tied up some place."

I felt the hairs on my arms stand up, and the night felt strangely cool. I was not overly fond of poisonous spiders. "What about Emmajean?"

"Strangled with gloved hands," Buddy said. "Don't worry, Frankie, we'll find the son-of-a-bitch."

"Diane was choked with bare hands. Or maybe someone wearing surgical gloves. The marks are pretty distinct."

"You sure?"

"I got a close look at those bruises."

"And Kingsley was around at the time. Maybe he'd already left the bear at the trailer."

"No. Sylvie and Tommy were there until I called for help."

"I can't picture someone carrying a teddy bear and trying to strangle someone at the same time," Buddy said. "It's ludicrous."

"Could there be two killers?"

"Or three. And God only knows how Bert Hogue's murder fits in."

"What about Bill?"

"If you're right, and there's more than one murderer, Anderson's not off the hook."

"Randy asked me to talk to him. . . . Any chance of that happening?" I half-hoped he'd say no. I didn't want to be any more involved with the Andersons than I already was.

"Tell you tomorrow morning." He took a step towards the mobile home still bathed in artificial light. Now that most of the crowd had gone, I realized something was missing.

"One last thing, Buddy."

"What." His face looked so drawn and tired, I hated to toss another complication in his lap.

"When I got here tonight, Diane's Harley was parked by the step. Did you guys move it?"

"You're not joking, are you." His sigh was just loud enough for me to hear. I shook my head. "I'll check around and see if somebody took it for safekeeping." We both knew that hadn't happened.

"The key should be hanging inside by the front door—under the sign."

"Sign?"

"The one that says: 'TAKE YOUR FUCKIN' PILL.'"

He gave me a half-smile. "I'll look. Meantime, go home and barricade the door."

For once, I did as I was told. I followed Isabel back to the motel and parked next to her truck.

"Darn," I said, locking the doors. "I should have told Buddy to have a priest on call—in case Diane needs last rites." Lugubrious thought.

"Do Mormons have last rites?" Isabel paused at her apartment door.

"How would I know? She's Catholic."

"Born and raised in Provo?" She sounded skeptical. "I suppose there could be a few Catholics in Provo. She told Ruth the other day that she might go back soon, to watch the aspens turn color in the Wasatch."

"What about her teaching job?"

"I don't know. Maybe she just wants to go back for a visit."

"Tell me something. Does Diane ever work out of Freda's bar, or Pete's? I've never seen her either place."

"Pete's Mormon—jack-Mormon, anyway. Figures a little drinking and gambling are okay, but whoring's another story. He's two-faced about it, though—owns the Pair-a-Dice Bar. Alf just runs it for him."

So that's why Fern and Opal could trade places without causing a ripple.

"Alf used to own a cathouse over by Reno," Isabel continued. "Feds took it in lieu of back taxes."

Which confirmed what I'd learned from Diane's book. "What about Freda?"

"Freda's Catholic, more or less. When Diane flaunted that tattoo, Freda asked her not to come back. Thinks it's blasphemous."

"What do you think?"

"I saw a lot worse in the Army."

"Thanks again for getting to Diane's so quickly. And for bringing the gun. Tell me—would you have used it on your friends?"

"My guns aren't for show. They know that. I came within an inch of hitting a bozo who tried to steal gas from me last year."

"Did he cry foul?"

"He tried. The judge threw it out." She unlocked her door. "Don't forget Emmajean's memorial service tomorrow evening."

"Will you shoot me if I don't make it?"

"You never know." She shut the door softly. I hoped she was kidding.

The clock next to my bed said 12:02 when I let myself into my room. My mind buzzed with contradictory "facts" about Diane, but I was too sluggish to sort them out. Even with the background white noise of the air conditioner, I had trouble falling asleep. So I pulled out the aerial photos. As I'd told Killeen, the faster I worked, the sooner I could get the hell out of Pair-a-Dice.

Back to problem number one, the elusive marker bed.

I'd already scoured the more accessible north, east, and south faces of Red Mountain. The west face was steep, erosion having followed a nearly vertical young north-trending fault. Along much of the face, blocks of limestone had slumped down, covering the contact between the older and younger Triassic units. Where not obscured (a rare situation), the contact occurred at the break in slope between the softer underlying yellowish siltstone and the resistant maroon-weathering limestone. Unfortunately, the first good exposures of the upper unit were well above the contact, as they were in sections I'd measured elsewhere on the mountain. The lower three meters of the upper unit were covered by dirt, grass, and scree. When I went back this time, I'd take a shovel.

The photos helped narrow down my choices. Of the three areas that looked most promising, two could be reached only from the top of Red Mountain. The third required a hike up a talus chute. I remembered the place, a shadowy spot under an unstable overhang. I'd moved through there at the speed of light when I mapped the contact. Gave me the willies to contemplate returning.

If I checked one locality each day, I could leave by dinnertime Thursday . . . as long as the weather cooperated.

Eleven

Three news trucks pulled into the courtyard at eight. I'd eaten early and was hiding in my room, using the time to tape up rock boxes and do one last load of wash. I wanted to be ready to clear out at a moment's notice.

I used Isabel's office phone to call Buddy at ten. Diane was conscious, but unable to speak—her larynx was bruised. They were going to keep her in for observation for another forty-eight hours. He'd been allowed to question her, but she'd had to write the answers.

Unfortunately, she hadn't been much help. She said someone had come in while she was in the shower. She heard him in the front room while she was dressing. She called out, then went to check. The room was dark. She never saw him, never heard his voice.

"She's sure it was a man?"

Buddy chuckled, the first laugh I'd heard from him in days. "Said she knows a man's hands when she feels 'em."

I bet. I crossed Ruth Bovey off my list of suspects. "Did you tell Diane the manuscript was missing?"

"Nope. Doc shooed me out. I'll tell her tonight."

"You guys find the last couple of chapters? Or a notebook?"

"Uh-uh." He sounded as if he had a mouth full of doughnut. I heard him sip something, probably coffee. "Drew a blank there. But I got permission for Billy to talk to you. Hold on a minute. It'll be recorded."

105

"Okay."

It was five minutes before Bill's voice came on the line. No preliminaries.

"How's Randy?"

"Upset, scared, sick of worrying about you. He wants to leave Pair-a-Dice. He asked me to convince you it's a dead end."

"Tell him we'll leave soon as I get out. Wherever he wants to go, we'll go."

"I'll tell him." Mission accomplished. There was a pause while I tried to think of something to say. "I loved the mineral displays, Bill."

"Yeah. They turned out pretty nice." He cleared his throat. "I didn't do it, Frankie."

"Randy knows that." I didn't commit myself one way or the other. "Did they give you a decent lawyer?"

"Fresh out of school, but smart. She'll do. . . . Great body," he added, trying to provoke a reaction. Some things never changed. When I didn't respond, he said, "Buddy told me about Diane."

"It might help your case."

"Maybe, maybe not."

"Don't you have alibis for the other murders?"

"Only Randy—for the law that's not enough. The murders were at night. And I was pickin' up a winch in Salt Lake last Wednesday. Got home late." Voices growled in the background. "Time's up, Frankie. I have a date with Father Vincent."

"You *are* getting desperate."

"They're not allowed to tape confessions. Watch Randy for me, will you?"

"But—" I was talking to a dial tone.

I could imagine their conversation: "Bless me Father, for I have sinned. It's been a *gazillion* years since my last confession. These are my sins. . . ." I hoped Father Vincent had a couple of hours to spare.

"How long you going to stand there, Frankie?" Isabel stood at my elbow.

I hung up the phone, expelling a long breath. "What a mess."

"Think he did it?"

"Opportunity, but no motive that I can see."

"He was paying child support to Emmajean's boy. Heard tell she wanted to up the ante. He was pretty sore last Saturday night."

"But even if he killed Emmajean, he'd still be paying. Did he want custody?"

"No."

106

"And what about the other victims? Any connections?"

"Not that I know of. Never thought he held a grudge against women —except Diane, of course. They rubbed each other the wrong way."

At least he was clear of that one. I realized, with a start, Diane's manuscript had skipped over the Andersons. It had confirmed Isabel's affair with Buddy and her abortive run for justice of the peace, explored Alf's and Opal's problems with the IRS, revealed Pete's association with the sale of those desert parcels. Diane hinted that Freda's confinement to a wheelchair was a ruse to bilk the insurance company and that Milo's wife had had an abortion two years earlier. But aside from suggesting that Bill and Randy were bastard descendants of Bloody Bill Anderson, she'd omitted them from the plot. I wondered why.

"What is it, Frankie?" Isabel was staring at my face.

"Just the manuscript."

"I'm in it?"

"Your name's Belisa."

She laughed, a deep laugh for a small woman. "I hate it."

"Tell me something, Belisa?"

"If I can."

"Did Lon really buy that election for Milo?"

"He's justice of the peace. And a lot of people who couldn't afford it had prime beef on their tables last winter."

So that part was true. "But Lon sold you this place. . . . Seems strange."

"He needed seed money to start his run for Congress."

Another piece matched. I tried to make my voice nonchalant. "Have you ever seen Freda out of that wheelchair?"

"Only when she was stuck in bed with the flu last winter." She gave me a strange look. "Freda can't walk, Frankie. I've seen the bullet hole—cut right between her ribs. No exit wound. Bullet's still there, in her spine."

"I needed to ask." I shrugged to ease the tension in my shoulders. "It's late—I'd better get going. See you tonight, Isabel."

"The school. Seven-thirty."

I hadn't planned to attend. But it might be interesting to find out who showed up . . . and who didn't. Besides, I'd rather not be shot, thank you very much. "I'll be there," I said.

The thumpers arrived as I stowed my gear in the Jeep. The motel bulged at the seams—reporters on one side of me, geophysicists on the other. If I hadn't felt compelled to attend the memorial service, I'd have checked out and camped in the hills. I still thought it would be safer than town.

The manhunt had been in full swing since dawn. Despite what Bill had said on the phone, the law was treating the attack on Diane as another incidence of the I-80 killer. The prevailing theory, according to Pete, was that the killer had shot Bert Hogue on his way to Idaho. Panicking, the man turned east into the mountains, crossing over to Pair-a-Dice. The state police had set up roadblocks on the highway in case he was still in the area. Helicopters crisscrossed the range looking for suspicious vehicles, while officers went door to door in Pair-a-Dice. *Nada.* I hoped they'd let me into the mountains.

Gunshots sounded in the vicinity of the schoolhouse a block away. My heart skipped a beat as people erupted from their motel rooms, jumped into trucks, and raced to see the showdown. Half of me wanted to follow, to get a look at the killer, the other half wanted to fetch my sack lunch and get on with my day. Five minutes later, when I got to Pete's place, the furor was over. I caught the rehash.

"Had him up against that shed, spread-eagled." Pete lifted his arms like a referee signaling a field goal. "Kept askin' him his name. Wouldn't say nothin'. They was puttin' the cuffs on him when Freda wheeled up in that chair. Ordered the stupid sons-a-bitches—her words—to let him go. Ain't never seen her so angry, 'cept that time she laid into Milo for killin' them lion cubs."

"Who?" I asked when Pete paused for breath.

"Milo."

"They arrested Milo?"

"Course not." Fern shook her head as she wiped the same spot on the counter for the fifth time. "They were after Walker. Only he don't talk."

I'd forgotten all about Walker, who tended to blend in with the local scenery. The police had let him go, Pete told us, after they found out he'd been working for Freda at the bar last night.

Fern plunked a large white paper bag on the counter and took my money. "You don't eat enough."

"Just watch me waddle to the service tonight," I said, hefting the bag.

I was stuffing the bag into my daypack when Killeen spoke behind me. I straightened up so fast I bumped my head on the door frame of the Jeep.

"Would you repeat that?" I said, rubbing my crown.

"About last night . . . I'm sorry."

"What for?"

"The crack about trusting people."

"You've nothing to apologize for. You were right."

"Not completely. You seem to trust Buddy, Isabel, Randy, Pete—people you've known for a while. You're careful with strangers, that's all."

"That's not all. Look, Killeen. I used to be able to trust my instincts, my reactions to people. I lost that when my fiancé turned on me. He became someone I didn't know. Now I don't know if he's alive or dead. How do you think I feel? If Geoff could pull a Dr. Jekyll, anyone could. Losing my instinct is like being in the middle of the ocean and dropping the compass overboard."

The silence stretched long. I closed the passenger door, walked around to the driver's side, looked over the top at Killeen.

"I'm sorry. I don't usually go on like that."

"Quit apologizing." He scratched his left eyebrow, then smoothed it with his forefinger. "I don't suppose Geoff could have followed you out here. . . . "

"And murdered a bunch of women, leaving their bodies along the Interstate? There's a big difference between stealing someone's ideas and murder, Killeen."

"You'd be surprised." He followed me around the car. "Where you goin' today?"

He was giving me another chance to get off the fence. I hesitated for a fraction of a second, no more. Hauling my mapboard out of the car, I flipped it open, pointed to a two-square mile area. "Back side of Red Mountain."

"See, that wasn't so hard."

"Easy for you to say."

"Want a field assistant? I work cheap."

Hell, yes, I wanted to yell. "Sylvie and Tommy need you," I said.

"They'll be fine. Alf has a shotgun under the bar; Opal's got a pistol in the kitchen. Ruth brought over a load of toys and books for Tommy. Gabbie's gonna baby-sit."

"You'll need a canteen and a pack."

"We can stop by my place on the way."

"Okay. Hop in. I'll be back in a minute."

It took two minutes for Fern to pack another lunch. "Somebody goin' with you?"

"Killeen."

She shook her tiny bird-like head. "Ugly as a horny toad." She slipped another apple and three huge chocolate-chip cookies into the bag. "But smart, real smart."

"What makes you say that?"

"Well, even after Freda gave Walker an alibi, the police still didn't want to let him go. Killeen asked 'em, kinda soft-like, if they'd looked at Walker's right hand, the one he always keeps in his pocket. It's missin' three fingers—couldn't have made those marks on Diane's neck, he says. So they let Walker go."

I handed Killeen the bag as I slid into the car, saw his eyes widen when he checked the contents. "You might work cheap, but you can't work hungry," I said. "Fern likes you."

"Fern likes any man with an appetite."

It was almost lunchtime before we parked at the bottom of the west face of Red Mountain. Of course, almost anytime was lunchtime as far as Killeen was concerned.

"This isn't going to be a picnic," I said, staring at the barren hillside. Seven hundred feet above us, surrounded by a cascade of talus, was an outcrop of limestone. We'd have to climb up the unstable talus, hoping that we didn't start a rockslide, until we reached the resistant ledge. The mountainside steepened above the ledge, ending in limestone cliffs that bulged out over the slopes. Except for that one day, two years ago, when I'd dotted in the contact, I'd avoided this area.

"You were going up there alone?" Killeen asked, eyeing the threatening cliffs.

"I didn't have much choice."

On the map, I showed him how I'd pieced together the Triassic stratigraphic section by correlating exposures at various points on the mountain. "I'm still looking for fossils that'll confirm the age of the youngest rocks in the section."

"Anyone know where you were going today?" He still stared at the mountaintop.

"No. I left the area marked on the map in my room. But even if Isabel checks it, she knows not to tell anyone else unless there's an emergency. Why?"

"Thought I saw something move up there."

"Nobody from town could have gotten here ahead of us. If it's the killer, he won't take on two of us."

He didn't look convinced, but he kept his thoughts to himself. "So . . . what am I looking for?"

I drew a *Meekoceras*. "Picture this in 3-D."

Killeen turned my notebook this way and that. "Tommy could do better."

"Have you ever seen a chambered nautilus, that coiled shell that shows up in beach shops? They saw it in half and mount it on velvet." I sketched the interior chambers.

"'Build thee more stately mansions, O my soul'?" He flung out his arms to accompany the sonorous rendition of Oliver Wendell Holmes.

"Yeah. I bought one for my grandmother once."

"Well, the nautilus is the closest living relative of the ammonite we're looking for. Two hundred million years ago, something affected the *Meekoceras* habitat, killing millions of animals. The seafloor that covered this part of the world was thick with their shells. Paleontologists call it a thanatocoenosis, a fancy word for a death assemblage."

A police helicopter swept down the narrow, V-shaped valley. Killeen met my eyes squarely. "Looks like history is repeating itself."

I didn't want to think about it. After taking a photograph of the hillside with Killeen as scale, I watched him remove a holster from his daypack. He checked the gun before strapping it on; we both shouldered into our packs. Handing him the shovel, I swung the pickax over my shoulder.

"Tilt at your windmill, Quixote," he said, behind me. "Sancho Panza's bringing up the rear."

His cheerful whistling echoed off the rocks. I hoped "The Impossible Dream" wouldn't bring the hillside crashing down on our heads.

Two-thirds of the way to the outcrop, I spotted a piece of maroon-colored limestone float filled with ammonites, some the size of my thumbnail, one as broad as my hand. I sank down on my haunches, staring, marveling at the internal symmetry of the fossil exquisitely preserved in recrystallized calcite. I didn't speak right away—I was trying to catch my breath from the climb. I took off my pack, pulled a sample bag from the pocket.

"Hell of a lunch spot," Killeen said, sitting down beside me.

"This," I said, dropping the rock into his hand, "is what we're looking for."

He turned the rock over, studying it from all angles. "Doesn't look a bit like your drawing."

I grinned. "The real thing is always better." I wrote the locality information on the sack, marked both it and the rock with my field number, stuffed the rock into the bag.

"Want me to carry it for you?"

"Not on your life. Float's not much help, but it may be the only evidence I find. Where I go, it goes."

"Does this mean we don't get to eat yet?"

"You got it. Never could climb on a full stomach."

Killeen muttered something about drill instructors, but he blazed a zigzag path up the mountain, eyes sweeping the ground at each careful step, searching for more fossils. I followed more slowly, willing the fossils to push away the overburden and spring from their hiding places. They weren't listening.

I was concentrating so hard on the ground, I almost walked past the outcrop. Killeen munched an apple next to the limestone ledge that jutted out five feet from the slope. He'd taken off his gun, stashed it with the shovel and his pack under the ledge.

"I'm on strike until I finish lunch. It's in my contract: page three, paragraph sixteen, item five," he said.

"What if I exercise my line-item veto?"

He lifted a boot-clad foot until it was level with my stomach. "It's a long way to the bottom of this hill."

Seven hundred feet, to be exact. I climbed the last three feet, shed my gear, collapsed next to him.

On this west-facing slope, shade would have been non-existent even if the sun had been out. The cloud cover acted like thick insulation, holding the moisture close to the earth so that I seemed to be breathing through damp gauze.

Killeen studied the peaceful scene in front of us: nothing in the distance but hills and valleys, no sounds but the drone of helicopters. "If there are oil and gas deposits here, whoever owns the land could be sittin' pretty in the future."

"It's a gamble. Costs a ton of money to sink a well and bring it into production." I took a bite of roast beef on whole wheat. God, it tasted good.

He took off his camouflage-patterned, short-brimmed hat, wiped his forehead with a sleeve. The reddish hair glowed in the gray light. "Life's a gamble."

"And I wouldn't want it any other way. Ready to play detective?"

Killeen wiped his hands on his fatigues. "Think I'm up to it."

I crouched under the ledge. "The fossils should be either just above or below this limestone bed. We need to find them in place."

"I'll take the low road," he said. "Just watch out for my head when you toss those rocks down the hill."

He pulled on blue-and-white cotton work gloves and started checking and shifting float at an amazing speed. I climbed up about ten feet and did the same, more slowly, bare-handed. When I reached a level where the loose rocks were held in place by dirt, I attacked with the pickax. Killeen alternated between the shovel and my rock hammer.

"'Breakin' up big rocks on a chain gang.'" His voice was rich, deep, mellow.

"'Breakin' rocks and servin' my time, oh yeah,'" I joined in. We exchanged grins. Anyone watching would have thought we were crazy.

Thirty minutes later, my shirt was soaking wet. Killeen called to me as I guzzled water from the canteen. "Found something." Excitement tinged his voice. He was hooked.

I slid down to where he sat, about five feet below the ledge. He'd uncovered a limestone bed about one foot thick. Disk-shaped white cross-sections showed clearly against the iron-tinged matrix.

"Damn, that's nice." I held out my hand. "You did it."

"What now?"

"You take a break while I photograph it, describe it, and bag it."

I managed the first two before the noise of an approaching helicopter forced me to look up. It was coming up the valley at eye-level, heading straight for where I sat. I waved, figuring it was the police coming to check on us. By the time I realized the markings were wrong, the helicopter was hovering sixty feet away, wash from the rotors blowing dust into my eyes. The pilot maneuvered the craft until it faced the hillside, like a bull about to charge. As I opened my mouth to yell, the mountaintop exploded with a deafening roar. I scrambled upward for the safety of the ledge, slipped, fell. The air thundered. The rocks on the hillside shivered, and gave way.

Twelve

I was flat on my back, Killeen's body covering mine so that I couldn't see, could barely breathe. The earth beneath us trembled, the roar of falling rocks went on and on. I felt him grunt once, and then go still. Eventually, the noise abated, and the rockslide slowed to a trickle. The helicopter was gone.

When I pushed at Killeen, it was like trying to shift a dead horse. I wriggled my torso to the right until my chest was free enough to draw a deep breath. Breathing, I decided, was a wonderful adaptation.

I was still holding my field notebook. I set it to one side, using a rock to weigh it down. With my free hand, I touched Killeen's neck: his pulse and breathing were slow and regular, but his eyes stayed closed. The skin behind his left ear was bleeding, swelling. I tapped him lightly on one dusty cheek.

"Killeen! Wake up!" I tried to keep the panic out of my voice. Our legs were buried under a layer of angular rocks. Even if I could free us, I had no idea how I was going to lug a two-hundred-and-forty-pound man all the way to the Jeep. I shoved with both arms, moving him just enough to dislodge some of the rocks. I could see his legs, now. Using my torso as a lever, I heaved again, this time managing to turn him over. But he slid ten feet down the hill before I dragged him to a stop. Around us, the rocks moved like a viscous river.

My canteen had disappeared, but my pack was still tucked under the ledge beside Killeen's. I climbed back up, rifled through his pack until I found bottled water. As I squeezed some onto his face, another section of the hillside came loose and thundered past. I dug my boot heels into the slope, grabbed Killeen under the armpits, and hung on for dear life. Our section of the slope moved another twenty feet. When I looked down, Killeen's eyes stared blankly into mine.

"Can you see?" I asked, checking his pupils. They weren't dilated.

"Who am I?"

"The geologist somebody's trying to kill?"

"Yes, sir. Welcome back."

"How long was I out?"

"About ten minutes. Rock must have hit you behind your ear."

"I know where it hit," he said, sitting up and touching the knot with gentle fingers. He stared at the devastation below us, winced as he twisted his head to look up at the ledge that had saved our lives. Blood oozed from the bottom of the swelling.

I dug out the first-aid kit to clean and dress the inch-long cut. "Headache?"

"Oh, yeah." He downed four painkillers. "I'm gonna live," he said, "but the fossil bed's covered again."

"I know. It doesn't matter."

"Like hell."

"Well, I'm not going to risk trying to dig it out again." I stood up, my knees shaking so violently I could almost hear them chatter. I sank down, took a couple of deep breaths. "I'll find another exposure, on a safer slope. You hurt anything besides your head?"

He felt his legs, wiggled his feet. "Bruises, no broken bones. So what else did we lose?"

"Nothing much—my canteen, the pick and shovel, my rock hammer. I'd put the camera away before the helicopter arrived. Your stuff's okay, except your hat."

"Could have been worse," he said, shouldering into his pack. "A whole lot worse. Let's get off this damn mountain."

"I'm . . . glad you were here, Killeen." For the second time in thirty minutes, I offered my hand. "Thanks."

Shrugging, he took it. "It's nothing." His eyes sought, and found, the white Jeep, barely visible through the screen of dust-choked air. It sat, untouched, on the opposite side of a sea of rock, where the road forked, one branch dropping into the valley below us, the other circling to the top of the mountain. "Thought about how we're gonna get over there?"

"Very carefully," I said.

"I'll drink to that."

"It's on me."

"If we live that long," was his cheery reply.

I'd always found that the best way to descend an unstable slope was to run like hell, never pausing long enough to get trapped by shifting talus. I went first, cutting downslope at an oblique angle, figuring that my lighter weight would be less likely to dislodge the rocks. I stopped only once, reaching back to grab Killeen's hand when a section of the slope gave way. I didn't complain about the wrench to my shoulder caused by the jerk of his weight. At least I was still alive to feel pain. And so was he. I didn't want a death on my conscience.

We didn't speak until we reached the Jeep where, as if by mutual accord, we turned to face the mountain. It looked raw, newly created. The only spot that would still match my photos was that isolated ledge of rock that had saved our lives. I took a photograph, an "after" to match my "before"—weight loss on a monumental scale.

"Dynamite?" I asked.

"Something like that. Remote control, maybe. Who in Pair-a-Dice knows how to use explosives?"

"The Andersons worked for a mining company in Arizona last winter. Bill's in the clear, but Randy's a possibility . . . except that he doesn't fly a helicopter."

"Who around here owns a Bell Jet Ranger?"

"What's a Belgian Ranger?" It sounded like a breed of dog.

He sighed. "That chopper."

"Oh. Lon Bovey uses a helicopter—I don't know what kind—to monitor the cattle and commute into Salt Lake. There's an airstrip behind the ranch house. You can see it on aerial photographs."

"Who pilots?"

"Lon or Ruth. And I think Milo took lessons." I couldn't remember where I'd learned all that; my mind collected and stored seemingly useless information. "Did you get a good look at the pilot?"

"Nope. Helmet, dark glasses, gloves. Could have been anybody."

"He must believe we're dead, or he'd have come back by now."

"That's somethin' in our favor. Course, he could have booby-trapped the Jeep just in case he missed us the first time."

We turned simultaneously toward the Cherokee. "I wouldn't know a bomb if I sat on one," I said.

"Don't worry." There was grim satisfaction on his face. "I would."

While he went over the Cherokee inch by inch, I waited in the shade of a juniper. When Killeen finally pulled himself out from under the truck, he looked like he'd just escaped from a refugee camp in a third-world country. He also looked disappointed.

"All clear." He slapped his pants, raising a cloud of dust.

"Killeen?" I handed him a can of grapefruit juice with a picture of a duck on the front.

He didn't answer until he had drained the can. "Hmm?"

"Can we prove someone triggered that rockslide?"

"Not without shifting a hundred tons of rock. And I'm not volunteering."

"So he'll get away with it."

"Looks like it."

"Damn."

"Cheer up, Frankie, he'll probably try again. Must want you real bad."

"Maybe he was after you? Or a two-for-one special?"

"Doubt it. I didn't catch a glimpse of Diane's attacker."

"Or read her manuscript, either," I murmured, stooping to tie my boot.

"Manuscript?"

I stood up. "The one in which she reveals all the dirty little secrets of our friends in Pair-a-Dice. She asked me to read it."

"And Bovey's in it?"

"Generations of Boveys are in it, along with everyone else in town. But I'm *assuming* those are the reasons that hillside came down."

"What else could it be?" Killeen's pores exuded innocence.

I played my trump card. "You tell me. . . . And don't give me that line about looking for a place to settle down."

At least a minute elapsed before he answered. "I'm looking for a grave. An old, old grave, that doesn't even have a marker."

Somehow I knew, had known since I read Easy Thomasson's hand-writing on the back of the spinach label. "You've been following me, hoping I'd lead you to that camp I found."

"That's right."

"That wasn't what you told Buddy, was it?"

"I gave Buddy a reason he'd understand. It bought me time."

Time to search for an unmarked grave. "Johnny's parents were murdered?" He nodded, staring off at the scarred hillside. "For God's sake, Killeen. What if your snooping worried someone in Pair-a-Dice?"

"It's possible."

"I wish you'd told me."

"I didn't know you, did I?"

"Hop in," I said. "We've a stop to make on the way home." Hell, what was another hour or two when we should, by rights, be dead?

117

Killeen and I didn't talk for the first part of the drive. The adrenaline had worn off, leaving me limp. Killeen withdrew into some world inside his head. But when we came to Easy Thomasson's cabin, I paused for a few minutes to tell Killeen what I knew of the cantankerous old drunk who had left such an imprint on the area. Some of the story I'd learned from Pete, some from Diane's manuscript.

Ezekiel Thomasson was dumped off the train one night while it was taking on water. He'd made the mistake of winning too much in a craps game. He had a pair of dice in his pocket, a gun, and the clothes on his back. He homesteaded a place up this canyon, living on game and piñon nuts, and set about building a herd of wild horses. He was forty when he started, Pete said, and tougher than year-old licorice. He got older and tougher in that one-room log cabin—alone.

The Boveys attempted to buy him out, burn him out, wear him down. They failed, but not before a few had died. Later, when the government decided it was illegal to gather mustangs, some brave civil servants tried to close down his ranch. They reconsidered after Easy shot up their vehicles. It was less trouble to wait for him to die.

Easy died twenty-five years ago. Pete's father found him a month later. He'd missed his monthly trip to Pair-a-Dice for whiskey and Skoal.

While I talked, Killeen and I stared at the cabin. The roof had fallen in but the railroad-tie walls were intact. Easy's indomitable spirit still haunted the place.

"And those yellow roses he planted out front bloom every summer," I said, shifting into first and wheeling back onto the road.

"You're a romantic, Frankie MacFarlane."

"It's our secret. Want to share yours?"

"When we get to that camp."

I left the Jeep parked just off the road. We had to hike around a low hill to reach the site. The air was quiet now that the helicopters had crossed the valley to explore the eastern range. Every once in a while, I could see flashes of light, reflections off their Plexiglas bubbles as the sun fell beneath the cloud layers. But the sound didn't carry this far.

The closer we came to the clearing, the more tension emanated from Killeen's big body. His face was expressionless, but his shoulders were taut as we stopped at the edge of the hollow among the trees. No footprints but mine broke the clayey crust. For that, I was thankful. I had worried that other strangers might have trampled the camp, removed its worn treasures. But it was as I'd left it, serene, still.

"I found her tooth, with the button, among the roots of that piñon." I pointed, wanting Killeen to meet his ghosts before I entered the site again. "Her shoe was in two pieces . . . there, and over there."

Killeen's eyes tracked my shifting finger. He took one hesitant step forward, paused as if a thought had grabbed him by the shoulders, turned back. "You coming?"

"No. This is personal. Tell me the story after you explore. This might not be what you're looking for." I sank down, hugged long dusty pant legs with long dusty arms, rested my chin on my knees. I couldn't remember ever feeling this weary.

"It's the place. But it'll wait a few more minutes." He hunkered down next to me and told the story simply, without embellishment.

In November, 1906, John and Bessie, Killeen's great-grandparents, had headed north after the fallout from the Brownsville Massacre. They stopped with relatives in Killeen, Texas, where they adopted the name of the town in place of their own. But the disgrace of the dishonorable discharge followed them. John Killeen couldn't find work. They moved on with their young son, Johnny, heading north and west, traveling alone. They were following one of the overland trails to California, when they passed through Pair-a-Dice. There, a white man had commented on Bessie's beauty. He was Henry Bovey, Lon's grandfather. Uneasy, John had driven up into the hills and unhitched before taking the mules back to town for supplies. On the return journey, someone had killed him and stolen the mules.

Johnny Killeen, age five, was out collecting firewood when his mother was attacked. He heard the commotion and sneaked back. While Henry Bovey raped and killed Bessie, a younger man held the horses, out of sight, at the edge of the clearing: Lon's father, Jake Bovey. He was fifteen.

Just before dawn, Jake came back for the boy who'd sat all night by his mother's body, waiting for his father to return. Jake told him they had to leave quickly, his father wasn't coming back. They headed for Easy Thomasson's cabin, the only safe place Jake could think of, leaving Bessie there on the ground. On the way, they passed John, shot in the back. The boy stayed with Easy for a week, never talking, hiding in the root cellar when Henry Bovey came looking for him. But it was from Easy that Johnny learned the Bovey names. He never forgot. Finally, Jake returned with enough money for Johnny's train ticket back to Texas. The five-year-old traveled alone, his father's Army discharge papers pinned to his coat—the only address Jake could find back at the camp.

"What with a bunch of wars in between, nobody was able to get here till now. I promised Grandpa I'd find her, bury whatever was left. Put up a marker."

"He's still alive?"

"Died six months ago."

"I'm sorry. What about the Boveys?"

"Well, Henry and Jake are dead. Wouldn't be right to punish the living. They had nothing to do with it. Wish I could have thanked Jake and Easy, though—without them, I wouldn't be here." He stood up, dusted off his rear. "I'm going to look around."

"Want help?"

"You're as much a part of this as I am."

I moved around the perimeter of the clearing. I sensed, rather than saw, Killeen fall in behind me. A small dry wash curved among the trees, little more than five feet deep. Pieces of gray-weathered wood littered the near bank; in the channel, a rusty wood-burning stove leaned drunkenly. We wandered down the wash, spying pieces of purple glass, parts of a wheel, a skillet with a hole in the bottom, the ribbed metal plate from a washboard. But no more human remains. We circled back toward the clearing.

"I'll need to spend more time here . . . rake the hollow and the wash," Killeen said. "Too late to start today." He touched my shoulder as I started toward the Jeep. "Thank you for bringing me here."

"My pleasure." And I meant it.

Thirteen

I would have sold my soul that evening to be back in Tucson wallowing in my parents' spa. I settled for a shower, standing under the stream until the water turned cold. I looked at the bed. The lumpy mattress pulled at me as surely as the Sirens beckoned Ulysses. But I was strong. I dragged my bruised, aching body out the door and over to the Pair-a-Dice Bar to stoke the furnace with the Tuesday-night special.

It seemed like years since I'd last eaten there. The restaurant overflowed with people who'd come for the memorial service—or Freda's band. Alf had set up folding tables on the bar side; Sylvie jogged between them, taking orders. Not an empty seat in sight. The cigarette smoke was so thick, I started to cough. A small brown arm holding a teddy bear waved from a booth at the rear where Tommy sat between Ruth and Gabbie. The Bovey boys were seated across the table. Ruth, busy wiping Andrew's face with a damp napkin, didn't see me as I threaded my way between the tables.

"Hi, Frankie," said Tommy.

"Hi, yourself."

Ruth's head jerked up. She couldn't have looked more surprised if I'd sprouted wings and a halo. The heavy foundation and eye shadow she'd used to conceal the bruises showed dark-beige as the blood drained from her face. Gabbie's eyes darted from Ruth to me, unsure of what was going on.

"You're . . . " Words failed Ruth. She tried again. "You're looking well tonight, Frankie."

I couldn't say the same for her. But what had she started to say? That I was alive? In one piece?

"Thanks. Apart from some bumps and bruises, I feel great."

"Bruises?" Her tone barely carried above the noise in the restaurant.

"Killeen and I tangled with a few hundred tons of rock."

She stiffened, fixed her eyes on my forearm which sported a large bruise. "And is he . . . all right?"

I let her suffer for a moment. She worried a paper napkin, folding it into tiny pleats. Gabbie reached behind Tommy to touch her mother's shoulder. I wondered how long she'd tried to be the buffer between her mother and the world.

"Seemed to be," I said.

Ruth slumped a little, whether from relief or disappointment, I didn't know. "You look hungry," she said. "I think we can squeeze in one more."

The children obligingly shifted closer together. James took the opportunity to squirm under the table and up onto his mother's lap.

"Will I squish anybody?" I asked Tommy.

"No. They're outside with Daddy."

I'd forgotten about Raef, the specter who moved through the night like a shadow. Where did he stay during the day? He couldn't be "outside"—the manhunt would have uncovered him by now. He must have crossed into Idaho or gone back to Utah. We were safe for a while.

I looked at Gabbie as I sat down next to Peter. "Everything go okay today?"

"The kids had a ball. Opal gave them free ice cream and the run of the restaurant."

As if hearing her name, Opal arrived with a glass of iced tea and a plate heaped with fried chicken, mashed potatoes and gravy, mixed vegetables, and a dinner roll.

"All we have left," she said, plunking them down in front of me. Sweat beaded her broad forehead; the pile of red hair leaned like tule reeds in a windstorm. She slid a ticket under the edge of the plate before stacking the children's dishes. "Dessert, Ruth?"

The chorus drowned out Ruth's answer. A minute later Opal was back with seven bowls of red Jell-O. The jiggling cubes wore little white caps of whipped cream, straight from a can, no doubt. The kids loved it. Ruth pushed hers around, but didn't eat. Her mind seemed far away.

"Why don't you take the boys outside, Gabbie," Ruth said. "But make sure they don't get too dirty. I'll join you in a minute."

I watched them leave. Gabbie turned at the doorway for one last look at her mother.

"How long have you and Lon been married?" I asked.

"Seven years." A lifetime, her tone implied. "Warren, my first husband, died when Gabbie was two. Head-on collision."

"I'm sorry."

"So am I."

"How'd you meet Lon?"

"He was a friend of Warren's. Lon's wife, Ann, had died the year before. She'd had polio, and was an invalid for years. Lon and I . . . just sort of drifted together. I was looking for someone to lean on, I guess. Gabbie needed a father, and he wanted children. It seemed to fit, somehow."

"Gabbie's growing into a beautiful woman," I said, hoping she wouldn't react, fearing she would.

The graceful fingers trembled as she gathered the auburn hair to drape across one shoulder, exposing bruises at the edge of her collarbone. Her lips pressed into a tight, straight line. "I know," she whispered. "Sometimes, I wish she were ugly."

I had my answer. But I tried for one more. "Ruth, did Lon hurt Diane?"

Her face closed up. "You don't understand. I can't—won't—speak against my husband."

I tossed money on the table, slid out of the booth. My whole body ached when I straightened up. "Thanks for sharing your table, Ruth. See you at the service."

She caught up with me at the door. "Frankie?"

"Yes?"

"Isabel said you'd talked to Buddy today."

I nodded, wondering what was coming next. Judging from Ruth's face, it was important.

"Diane's going to be all right, isn't she?"

"As far as I know."

"Thank God," she said, scrubbing tears from the corners of her eyes. She even managed a smile. "The children have been so worried about her."

And you, I thought, have been worried sick that your husband killed her, killed me, Killeen, and how many others? Why in the world are you protecting him? You're right, Ruth. I don't understand. But I couldn't bring myself to say the words.

123

"Why don't you have them make her a get-well card?" I said. "I'm sure she'd love that." And I turned on my heel and walked into the dusky glow of high-desert evening.

Behind me, Ruth collected the next generation of Bovey men.

———

Among the people straggling toward the memorial service were Dead-heads, bikers, wranglers rigged out in their dancing duds, and thumpers looking for free food. I followed the crowd, eavesdropping on their gossip. Objects were missing from Pair-a-Dice: clothes from a clothesline, rags from the gas station, a teenager's mountain bike, vegetables from Freda's garden. The search for the strangler had been called due to darkness, but not before the police had found a car with dusty Canadian plates ditched just across the Utah line. Like bloodhounds, the media had rushed off to track the story.

The two-story wooden schoolhouse, the most imposing building in town, sat in the middle of patchy grass. A sand-floored playground nestled in one corner of the yard, a cement basketball court in another. Huge old cottonwoods dotted the side yards—good climbing trees if you could shinny up the first eight or ten feet. At one time, the second floor of the building had served as the high school. Now, since the teenagers were bussed into Wells, the upper floor held the town library, an amalgam of outdated textbooks, paperback romances, thrillers, and westerns.

Emmajean's memorial service was to be outside, illumined by fifties-style Tiki torches that put off more smoke than light. The poles resembled two rows of staggering drunks. They probably looked straight to the guys that set them up, the unsteady wranglers who leaned affectionately on the shoulders of their wives and girlfriends. Off to the left, under a cottonwood, Isabel and Freda stood guard over a sawhorse-and-plank table laden with cakes, cookies, breads, and punch. Two torches smoked at either end. As I watched, one young man distracted the women while another poured something from a bottle into the punchbowl. I decided to steer clear of the refreshment table. God knows what they'd put in the brownies.

Randy loped over when I paused just inside the gate in the white picket fence. I hadn't seen him since I'd stopped by Pete's addition that morning to discuss my phone call to Bill.

"Boy, I'll be glad to get shut of this place," he said. He gestured at the building behind him. "I'll miss the school, though. My earliest memories are of Ma teaching here. Bill says she came here right out of college."

"What did your father do?" Distracted by the sight of Lon Bovey working the crowd, it took me a moment to notice the awkward silence.

"Don't know. Anderson was Ma's name."

"I'm sorry—"

"It's okay. You didn't know . . . *They* made it rough for her though."

"So why did she stay?"

"I've wondered that myself. She had no family left, and she could have taught anywhere. But she just couldn't tear herself away."

Whether the wistfulness of his tone or the words themselves made my stomach plummet, I wasn't sure. It reminded me of my conversation with Ruth a few minutes before. I looked from Randy to Lon and back again, registering the similar height, build, profile, the same confident carriage. . . . Add two bastards to the Bovey family tree.

A multitude of questions danced in my head. If Randy didn't know who his father was, did Bill? And whom did he hate? His mother? Lon? Did Bill avoid Diane because she was his father's lover? What would Randy do when he found out? Bill had clearly inherited his father's libido—had he also inherited his temper? Did he punish Emmajean because she pressed him for money?

"You know, Randy," I said, "you're right. The sooner you and Bill get away from Pair-a-Dice the better."

"Amen to that."

"Randy, did Lon stop by the motel this morning?"

"Might've. I saw Ruth just after you left. Isabel opened up the store early for the thumpers, and Ruth stopped by for the mail."

Lon spotted me then. The grin froze in place as he paused mid-handshake. Appearing nonchalant, unhurried, he covered the ten yards between us in record time. In typical Bovey fashion, he attacked instead of retreated. But then, I doubted he'd run from a fight in his life, especially with a woman. I struggled to keep my feelings from showing on my face. But knowledge is tough to hide.

"Would you find my wife and hurry her along, son?" he said to Randy. As if the world waited on Lon Bovey. And did I imagine the slight emphasis on the last word?

"We had dinner together," I said. "I left her in front of the restaurant, collecting the younger Boveys."

If Lon was concerned about what I might have learned from his wife, I couldn't see it in his face. My eyes left his long enough to take in

Randy's confused expression as he hopped over the fence. People in this town were used to doing what Lon wanted.

Drawing myself up to full height—six-one in my Birkenstocks—I could almost look Lon straight in the eye. Could have used the extra inch my Justin boots would have added.

"There have been Boveys in this territory for eons, Frankie. We don't take kindly to visitors interfering in our affairs."

Sounded like a campaign slogan. "Hardly *eons*, Lon. Merely a wink of geologic time. And speaking of geology, did you know that dynamite blasts produce characteristic peaks on seismographs? I'm sure the one this afternoon was recorded in Salt Lake. And any seismologist worth his salt would be able to tell a natural rockslide from a blast-induced slide." I was talking through my hat, but he wouldn't know that.

"If that seismologist was alerted to look for that specific peak."

"Done."

"You're lying."

I kept my mouth shut, letting him stew.

"And even if you aren't," he continued, "there's nothing to connect me to that hypothetical blast."

"Motive and opportunity, Lon. The manuscript and the helicopter." Milo sidled up. Just what I needed—a pincers' attack.

"Tell Ms. MacFarlane what I was doing this afternoon, Milo."

"You was herdin' cattle on the other side of the valley?"

"That's right. And did I take the helicopter out today?"

"No, sir. It sat on the pad all day."

Lon's look was triumphant. "That'll be all, Milo."

"I need to start the ceremony, Lon." Milo's voice held a hint of a whine.

"I'll be right there."

He watched Milo walk away. "Give it up, Frankie. You're outclassed."

I was angry, or I wouldn't have responded. "I wonder if the tabloids would be interested in Diane's manuscript?"

"Manuscript?" He smiled. "What manuscript?"

Okay, so he'd found and destroyed the bulk of the novel—I refused to cry uncle. "The last two chapters are riveting," I countered. It was a shot in the dark at a moving target.

"They might be, if they existed." His eyes pinioned mine, as if the force could draw truth from my soul.

The look didn't faze me. Seeing the effect of my first shot, I fired again, speaking so low Lon had to lean forward to hear me. "I wonder if anyone in Wells heard a helicopter the night Emmajean was killed."

"You wonder too damn much."

There was a crunch of gravel behind me. Lon's expression changed, became affable.

"Nice talking to you, Frankie. Maybe I'll see you later." He didn't wait for a reply. Parting the crowd, he made his way to the front row of chairs. The rest of the people took his cue and filed in behind him.

"Rilin' that man could get you killed." Killeen voice was pitched for my ears only.

"I'm afraid you're right."

"Did he do it?"

"The blast?"

"What else?"

I wasn't ready to share the "what else." "You bet. But Milo gave him an alibi we can't break. Unfortunately, I gave him two more reasons to come after me."

"Not too bright."

"I've had better ideas. But I wanted to draw him out in the open. Shall we take our seats?"

Emmajean's husband and son were in the front row. The boy, Bobby, looking more like Lon than Bill—pale eyes, cleft chin, black hair—but some features skip generations.

Ruth took the seat next to Lon. Their boys were playing hide-and-seek with Tommy among the cottonwoods in the side yard. Sylvie and Randy joined us in the back row. Randy smiled as "Ollie-ollie-oxen-free-free-free" echoed in the descending darkness. Milo droned on about someone I didn't know, and my thoughts drifted back to the mountains, now hidden from sight.

Without warning, Gabbie appeared behind us. "We can't find Tommy," she said her voice high-pitched and scared. "We've looked everywhere!"

For Sylvie it was one more blow. Eyes closed, she swayed and toppled forward. Killeen caught her before she hit the chair in front. Randy hooked two fingers in his mouth and whistled loud enough to be heard from one end of Pair-a-Dice to the other. Milo stopped mid-sentence. Two hundred heads swiveled to stare at the back row. Lon, brows drawn in an angry line, hoofed it to the back row. Ignoring Killeen, Randy and Sylvie, Lon confronted me as if I were the only adult present.

"What's the meaning of this, Frankie?" He used the same tone Sister Isabel Agnes had the time I'd run a stolen nun's habit up the school flagpole.

"Tommy's missing."

"Who's Tommy?"

I realized he probably had never met Sylvie's son, even though Gabbie had been baby-sitting the child all afternoon.

"Mrs. Kingsley's son," said Gabbie. She stared at the ground as she spoke, her words barely loud enough to hear. "He was playing with us over there." She pointed to the cottonwoods, where the rest of the children huddled in a silent group. "Andy was 'It.' Tommy didn't come when everybody was called in."

"Maybe he went home," Lon said.

"Tommy's five," I said. "He wouldn't leave Sylvie." Not knowing if they'd been formally introduced, I gestured to Sylvie, who sat with her head between her legs. The crowd had formed a tight circle around us. For Sylvie's sake, I didn't want to broadcast that the police had been searching all day for her husband. She had enough problems.

"His father was in town last night," I continued. "He threatened to kidnap Tommy. But Tommy doesn't know that—he'd go with him voluntarily."

Lon gave me a probing look, a short nod. "Then we'd better start searching."

Within minutes, Lon had organized two-person search teams. Sylvie described what Tommy had been wearing, the same red-and-white striped tee-shirt he'd worn the day I first saw him. It seemed like years ago.

"Lon?" It felt odd to have him on the same side.

"What?" He sounded impatient.

"Tommy's father might be armed." The last thing I wanted was people shooting at anything that moved, but the warning might avert an ambush.

I thought he was going to swear, but he reined it in. "Horse of a different color," he said.

The level of excitement rose when he announced there might be gunplay. The crowd dispersed like chaff on the wind. Killeen and Randy disappeared for five minutes, reappearing with holsters fastened to their belts. Shiny black handles reflected the torchlight. We tried to convince Sylvie to stay in the schoolyard with Freda and Isabel, but she was adamant about joining the search. I was teamed with Randy, Killeen with Sylvie, Lon with Milo.

"Out there in the dark," Killeen said in a low voice, "I could arrange for Bovey to have a quiet accident."

Was he serious? Killeen had as much reason to fear and despise Lon Bovey as I did—maybe more. A Bovey hadn't murdered my forefathers —at least, that I knew. But then, I knew next to nothing about my Apache ancestors.

A quiet murder . . . the blame would fall on the I-80 killer. I perched on the watershed, staring down each side of the divide into ravines deep as the Grand Canyon.

If someone had told me a week ago that I would consider aiding in murder, I would have deemed him or her certifiably insane. I was learning a lot about myself. I wasn't sure Lon Bovey deserved to live—he'd come too damn close to taking my life, Killeen's life. I believed he'd attacked Diane, perhaps killed Emmajean. Tonight's truce was only temporary. What about tomorrow? Would he be waiting for me on some lonely hillside?

Killeen waited, arms crossed over barrel chest. Adversity had produced a quiet, self-possessed man. Maybe that's what Lon needed, a little adversity.

"No," I said. "But let's bring him down with as much fanfare as possible."

"Wise choice."

Randy and I started our search at the school. While Randy took the ground floor, I climbed the old wooden stairs, worn in the center by the footsteps of generations of Pair-a-Dice children. Shadows loomed large on the upper landing, illumined only by a low-watt bulb in the ceiling. I hesitated halfway up the stairs, emotions swirling. I felt pulled in multiple directions: find Tommy; discover who attacked Diane; recover Diane's manuscript—the only evidence that would provide a motive for Lon's attempt to kill me. And I wanted to stay alive and healthy until I could leave Pair-a-Dice. To accomplish one or all of these, I was going to have to shelve my fatigue and emotions and allow the left side of my brain to take over completely. I'd had to do it before, in the aftermath of Geoff's deception and departure. Geoff . . . I hadn't thought of him all day. I'd been too busy surviving, coping. How did he fit into all that had happened lately? For a moment, it seemed he stood there in the shadows at the end of the landing. I squeezed my eyes shut, then looked again. Nothing. A trick of lighting.

Downstairs, Randy clumped through the classrooms, opened cupboards and closets, all the places a small boy might hide. Or be hidden.

Spurred on by the thought, I climbed the rest of the stairs. In front of me, the door to the library stood ajar. When I pushed, the door crashed back against the inside wall.

"You okay, Frankie?" Randy's voice echoed in the stairwell.

"Fine. I don't know my own strength."

His chuckle sounded relieved. "Scared the shit out of me."

"Me, too."

"Call if you need me."

"Ditto." My reply was lost in the sound of his retreating footsteps.

I flicked on the lights. The rectangular room had recessed casement windows bordering uneven hardwood floors that creaked when I moved across them. At the base of the first window niche, someone had piled pillows—a nest for reading, for dreaming. The window framed old cottonwoods muted against the rapidly darkening sky.

To the left of the door, guarding the entrance, stood the checkout desk, a replica of the water-stained bar in Alf's place. I tried to picture Alf checking the pile of returned books that were stacked haphazardly at the near end, but the image would not compute.

The library was stuffy with the heat of day gathered on the second floor. A central aisle extended all the way to the back of the room, ending at another window enclosure; ancient wooden stacks lined up on either side of the aisle. A familiar smell wafted from the shelves— dust mixed with old leather, fading ink and sour urine, as if a mouse had made itself at home.

I had to get moving, but my feet felt heavy, reluctant. I heard Randy stumping around downstairs, a crash like tumbling buckets. I peered over the counter before hesitantly moving down the center aisle.

The overhead fixtures threw wedges of shadow between the stacks. I'd have traded a kingdom for a flashlight. I wouldn't mind being outside in the twilight, but I hated closed-in areas where I had no room to turn, much less run. I should have stuck with Randy.

"Tommy?" I called. My voice couldn't have carried more than halfway down the room. The only answer was a breath of air rustling the page of a book somewhere in the shadows ahead. Someone must have left a window open.

I moved quickly down the center aisle, more confident that I was alone. I felt no presence, heard nothing but faraway shouts as I approached the window at the end of the room. It was opened exactly one quarter, so that the wooden cross-lattice was aligned with the upper edge of the lower casement. Under it, a nest of cushions surrounded a stash of books. The topmost book lay open, exposing pages of old typescript on onionskin. In the dim light I turned back to the title of the book: *The Genealogy of the Bovey Family*, by Nora Benton Bovey, 1938. An inscription, in precise handwriting, covered the bottom of the title page: *To Helen Anderson, in recognition of your interest in the Bovey Family history—June 12, 1970. Dorothy Bovey.*

Had Dorothy discovered that Lon had fathered a son by the Pair-a-Dice teacher? Who else knew?

I thumbed quickly through the thin pages until I found the family tree, taped inside the back cover. The handwriting there was different, a teacher's writing. Helen's work. Lon's grandmother, Nora Benton Bovey, died in 1970 at age ninety-five, two months after his father, Jake. Dorothy Bovey, Lon's mother, died ten years later. Lon had been married to Ann for twenty years. No children. But Bill's and Randy's names were included on a side branch. Was Helen trying to document their parentage so that her sons would inherit? Then why hadn't Helen told them about Lon? Why hadn't she kept the book at home?

Bill and Randy might not know the truth, but two other people did—whoever left the genealogy in the nook, and Diane. She had added the marriage of Lon and Ruth and the births of their boys. Gabbie was listed, too, as Grace Anna Bovey. But Diane had noted in the margin that Gabbie was the adopted daughter of Ruth and her first husband, Warren.

I turned back to the page that had caught my attention. The passage was from Nora Benton's diary, a bride's first impressions on arriving at the Bovey spread in 1891. I sank back on my heels, feeling blood drain from my head. My fingers felt leaden as I turned the page.

I arrived at Paradise Ranch on an early Spring day, when the clouds hung low above the valley floor and nestled like cotton batting around the peaks. A few snowflakes touched my cheek, while from the canyons came the echoes of gunfire. Had I known that in one desolate canyon Henry's quarry was human . . . but I did not know, not then. Soon it was too late to leave, and so I looked the other way . . . and prayed for a way out.

Fourteen

Diane had plagiarized whole paragraphs from the genealogy. She must have known she'd be caught. She'd never have chanced sending it to a publisher unless she was planning to rework the second draft. Even then, Lon could probably block publication. He must not know this copy of the genealogy existed.

Randy's boots sounded loud on the hardwood floor. I whirled, and the book slipped from my hand raising a cloud of dust from the cushion.

"Find anything?" he asked.

Should I tell him, or shouldn't I?

"Nothing. Just somebody's light reading."

I picked up another book from the stash in the niche, John McPhee's *Basin and Range*. The pages were dog-eared and dirty. It, too, had an inscription: "Merry Christmas, Walker, and Happy 1993! Diane." I set it carefully on top of the Bovey genealogy, hoping Randy wouldn't notice my shaky fingers.

"Me, neither. What next?" He started double-checking the shadowy aisles between the stacks. My brothers always did that, too, as if I were incapable of doing something by myself. Usually it irritated the hell out of me, but this time I was thankful Randy was occupied. It gave me time to pull myself together.

I slid Nora's book beneath one of the cushions and stood up to close the window. Glancing outside, I could see the refreshments table where Freda guarded the food. A few children played under the table. I saw a skinny arm snake up to grab a cookie. The Tiki torches were beginning to burn low. A rangy figure joined Freda. Together they turned and looked up at the library window. I thought I saw Walker's lips twitch. I jerked the window closed and backed out of sight of the watching pair.

Randy and I reached the door at the same time. "Let's check Diane's trailer," I said.

"There's yellow tape all over the place," he offered in the same tone he would use to describe a spilled beer.

"Which makes it a good place to hide." I flicked off the lights and closed the door behind us. "Tommy's been there before. It's familiar ground."

He pulled on his hat brim until the shadows hid his eyes. "After you, kemo sabe."

Tonto and I walked to Diane's, calling out at intervals, in case Tommy was within earshot. The search perimeter had widened, so that now the other voices came from far away, sporadically, on puffs of wind. We didn't talk, just searched the night with our eyes and ears, and occasionally with the flashlight Randy found in the janitor's closet.

The yellow caution tape was still in place; the front door was taped shut. We slipped around to the back door, the door Tommy'd climbed through last night. Randy moved easily, silently, as if he'd had a lot of practice in skulking. I flashed on the day he and Bill had stolen my Jeep. Bill was a good teacher.

Either the police had failed to tape this door, or the tape had been removed. There were no telltale pieces on the ground.

"See?" I whispered, pulling on the handle. "We won't be doing anything illegal."

"I'll let you explain it to the cops."

"Chicken."

He clucked softly as he followed me into the tomb-like darkness. I led the way into the living room by the dimming light of the flashlight. After closing the blinds, I turned on the table lamp next to the sofa. The room looked cleaner than I'd left it except for the powder on switchplates, doors, tables, cabinets and desk drawers. Water had pooled under a bowl and pan in the dish drainer. I smelled the faint aroma of vegetable soup.

Randy's eyes followed mine. "Somebody's been here," he whispered. "Today."

I couldn't control the shiver that started at my neck and slid all the way to my toes. I nodded, put a finger over my lips.

He pointed to the rear of the trailer, and I nodded again. Randy and the orange flashlight glow moved silently toward the bedroom. His other hand held a gun.

The living room was empty, which suited my plan. As soon as Randy was out of sight, I rifled through the desk for a photocopy of the Bovey manuscript. Zilch. Diane didn't have a computer, so there was no backup disk. And she hadn't made carbon copies of the typescript from the electric typewriter on her desk.

The walnut-laminate bookshelf under the window yielded titles on education, psychology, Western history, poetry, short stories, and *How to Write a Damn Good Novel.* A thick manila envelope was tucked between the volumes: *The Literary Merit of the Plays of Catherine the Great*—Diane's master's thesis. I wondered if she'd plagiarized that, too. She and Geoff would make a great pair.

I dropped to my knees, peered under the couch, the desk, the kitchen table, looking for the manuscript I dropped the night I rescued Diane. The police had vacuumed; I found nothing but a paper clip caught under the edge of a square sofa leg. The leg sat flush against a tan metal wall—a file cabinet, not the trailer wall.

I pulled my head out from under the sofa skirt. A folded bedspread, one of those ubiquitous beige-black-red Indian prints that were used in the sixties and seventies for everything from clothes to curtains, covered the file cabinet. Ashes had overflowed an ashtray; the ashtray and butts were missing, but the square mark was plain on the coarse cotton surface. I lifted the edge of the spread, almost afraid to look.

I could hear Randy in the bathroom, now. There wasn't much time. The police were thorough, the two drawer handles had been dusted for prints. The top drawer was light, empty except for the tape Diane had been listening to while she scribbled in the steno notebook. On a hunch, I pocketed it before gently pushing the drawer closed.

The bottom drawer squeaked when I opened it, the sound covered by the noise of Randy using the toilet. He hadn't bothered to close the door.

The bottom drawer held the mimeograph masters for Diane's exams. I let out the breath I'd been holding for God knows how long. I didn't blame Diane for not wanting to leave them in her school office, the whole town probably had keys to the schoolrooms. I shoved the drawer closed with my foot, shifting the whole cabinet back an inch. A yellow triangle stuck out from under the metal. I lifted the lower handle and pulled on the triangle—two manila envelopes slid out, their clasps entwined. As Randy checked the hall closet next to the bathroom, I stuffed the envelopes under my print blouse. Being long-waisted and small-breasted has some advantages, after all. I was buttoning my denim vest when Randy sauntered into the room. His gun was back in its holster.

"Cold?" he asked. Disbelief tinged his tone—the trailer was stifling.

"Nervous," I said.

Turning off the lamp, I joined him at the back door. As if to justify my lie, the handle turned by itself and the door swung outward. I jumped back, bumping Randy, who dropped the flashlight.

"Son of a—" Randy groped for the flashlight.

"Stay where you are!"

We froze like jackrabbits facing oncoming traffic. I didn't recognize the voice behind the blinding light, but it didn't matter. He held a gun.

"Buddy?" Randy said. His voice broke on the second syllable.

"Yeah. What the hell you doin' here?"

"Looking for Tommy," I said. "The back door was unlocked. Somebody's been here. They cooked a meal."

"Move over," he said. Pulling himself into the trailer, Buddy flicked on the overhead light. Using a long wooden cooking spoon, he fished two empty cans from the trash container under the sink and stood them on the counter: pineapple slices and vegetable soup.

"Remember that camp I found in the hills?" I asked Buddy. "Same brand of pineapple."

"Did you touch anything?" he asked.

I paused for a minute wondering how to minimize the damage. Randy was quiet as a mole. "I closed the blinds," I said.

"Show me."

I turned the rod on the blinds beside the front door. A person sitting at the kitchen table had a perfect view of Sylvie's trailer next door.

"Anything else?" Buddy pressed.

"We searched every place a small boy could be hidden." Not to mention a few where he couldn't. "And Randy used the bathroom."

Randy cleared his throat. Buddy sighed. "God save me from amateurs. Can you locate that camp on a map?"

"It's already done. Back at my room."

"Let's go. We're wasting time." He said nothing more about our trespassing.

"Have they found Tommy?" I asked.

"Not yet. Whoever has him moves like a ghost."

I wanted to tell Buddy about the rockslide, but didn't want to talk in front of Randy. So, as we circled back by the school, I watched their flashlight beams stab the shadows on both sides of the street, and listened to them talk about Bill. Buddy figured he'd be released by morning.

"Hot damn. You mean it?" Randy asked.

I could see Buddy's grin in the dark. "Looks like Frankie'll have to stick a chair under the doorknob again."

"Maybe jail's reformed him," I said. I started to laugh, and couldn't stop. I was clutching my stomach while tears overflowed. Buddy pointed his flashlight at my face.

"Holy shit," said Randy. "Turn it off, Buddy."

Blessed darkness surrounded us. No streetlights; just dense air and the call of Tommy's name, like a children's game on a summer night.

"Ollie-ollie-oxen-free-free-free," I shouted. The words were swallowed up by the cloudy Great Basin sky. "I'm okay. Really. I'm okay."

Randy put his arms around me—the teenager, older than his years, comforting a woman who'd lost all vestige of youth in the past four months. He and Buddy didn't know about this afternoon, didn't understand. I was shaking. The left side of my brain wasn't strong enough.

"Randy?" I whispered.

"Shhhh."

"I need to talk to Buddy. Alone."

Randy hugged me. He'd make a fine man, I thought. Helen would be proud of him. Lon should be proud of him. But Lon would never acknowledge his Anderson offspring. At that moment, I hated Lon for what he'd done. And for what he hadn't done.

"See ya back at the schoolyard, then," Randy said, as he let me go.

"Be careful," Buddy said.

"I got Lizzy. I'll be fine."

"Lizzy?"

"His gun," Buddy answered. "Now, what's got you shakin' like the temperature just dropped forty degrees?"

I sat in the dust of the road and told him about my day at the office. I told him everything—or *almost* everything. I wasn't about to give him the manila envelopes still cradled against my chest. At least not until I'd had a chance to read them. And I omitted my claim to possessing the last two chapters of Diane's book. It didn't seem important just now. I heard his jaw snap shut when I told him about the rockslide and my confrontation with Bovey in the schoolyard.

"Holy Hell, Frankie! Why didn't you call me?"

"Because I couldn't prove anything. Milo gave Lon alibis for last night and today."

"You're the most stubborn Goddamn woman I've ever met. Alibis can be broken, for Christ's sake! That's my department."

"Lon's too careful. Too power—" I faltered on the last word. "I was angry. I wanted to strike back."

"You were stupid."

"Impetuous, maybe."

"Stupid." He stood there, hands on hips, shaking his head. "Come on." He helped me up. "Let's stop at the school before we get that map from your room."

Most of the searchers had drifted back. The torches had burned out; truck headlights illuminated the yard. Isabel, Ruth, and Gabbie watched the children and dispensed refreshments. There wasn't much left.

"Find anything?" Ruth asked Lon. She must have rubbed her eyes. The make-up was smeared—dark circle below met bruises above her left eye. She looked like a panda.

"Not a trace," Lon said, raking fingers through his thick silver hair. He accepted a piece of zucchini bread, the last from the platter. "It's as if he'd sprouted wings."

I avoided the punchbowl and poured a cup of iced tea from an urn that must have been seventy years old. Buddy went from group to group, checking to make sure the entire area had been covered. Sylvie and Killeen stood off to one side.

"Can I get you anything?" I asked Sylvie.

She shook her head, half-leaning against Killeen. Her face was so pale, it almost glowed in the darkness. Haunted, scared. A parent's worst nightmare was coming true.

"I drove Freda over to the bar," Isabel said behind me. "She figured she had to get things moving over there before the natives got restless. Walker's still looking. Freda says he's got a sixth sense."

"We'll need it," I said. "The first five sure haven't helped."

There was a murmur of excited voices near the schoolyard gate. Two figures crossed the gravel paths, one tall and awkward, one small and lithe. The little one led.

"Tommy!" Sylvie's high-pitched cry silenced the milling crowd.

"Hi, Mommy." Tommy grinned as he dropped Walker's two-fingered hand and launched himself into her arms.

"Where have you been?"

"For a bike ride. With Daddy." He pulled a stuffed animal from under one arm and held it next to her nose. "He did give me the teddy bear, Mommy. I told you. And the necklace. Where is it? Daddy wants to know."

Buddy broke the awkward silence that followed. "What happened, son?"

"I went to the bathroom. Daddy was in the hall. He wouldn't hurt me, Mommy. He has a big-boy's bike. We rode by the railroad tracks."

Sylvie set him down, then sank to her knees. "What did you talk about, honey?"

"Things. My bear. I 'membered to say thank you, Mommy."

"That's good." She hugged him again, as if to reassure herself that he was real. "Can you remember any other things he talked about? It's important."

He wrinkled his forehead. Light dawned. "Oh. I almost forgot. Daddy says he's gonna find a way we can all be together, forever and ever. That's what he said: 'forever and ever.'" He looked at Sylvie accusingly. "Did you promise to stay with him, no matter what?"

"Yes, honey. I did." Her voice sounded hollow, like wind in a reed. Behind her, Killeen's face was shuttered.

"Well, that's okay then."

Ruth and Lon stood at the edge of the circle. There was bleak acceptance on her face. He frowned, despite the fact that the search had turned out well.

Buddy crouched next to Sylvie. "Tommy," he said. "Where did your daddy leave you?"

"At our trailer. He told me to count to a hundred and then Mommy would come. It was our little game. But I got stuck in the teensies. I had to start over lots of times. Then Walker came. I was hungry."

So he was next door with Raef when Randy and I searched Diane's trailer. Stupid me. Had Raef heard us rustling about? Had he laughed at our silly attempts to track down Tommy? Was it kidnapping for a father to take his son for a bike ride?

"Tommy," said Buddy. "Did your daddy have a car or a truck?"

"No. Just a bike."

"How about a gun?"

"Uh-uh."

Buddy squeezed his shoulder. "Thanks, son. You can get some food, now." Buddy loped to his car and grabbed the CB.

Killeen handed Tommy some bread and cake, carefully wrapped in a napkin. "I've been savin' this just for you."

"Thank you." At least, I think that's what Tommy said. His mouth was full of chocolate cake.

Tommy trotting by her side, Sylvie crossed to Walker and took his hand in both of hers. Standing on tiptoe, she whispered something only he could hear. The gaunt face jerked slightly, as he rested his good hand on Tommy's dark curls. His eyes met Milo's, then Lon's, with a fierce look, before striding off toward Freda's bar.

Milo flipped him off. Lon, for once, was silent.

Killeen followed Walker to the Black-Light Bar, leaving Randy to keep an eye on Sylvie and Tommy. Buddy drove me to the motel. My door was unlocked, all the lights were on. I was positive I'd locked my room when I left. Buddy pushed me out of the way before nudging open the door with the barrel of his gun.

The room had been searched. Not carefully this time. Someone had ripped through the place as if they'd been in a hurry. The dresser drawers were upturned, clothes from the closet torn off their hangers. A dusty bike track ran down the middle of the rug, crossing papers, maps, and underwear to the bathroom door. I followed Buddy into the bathroom. Someone had taken a shower, leaving short curly black hairs on the drain cover and a dirty wet towel on the ancient linoleum floor.

Buddy stared at my hair, long and straight as an arrow shaft. "Damn," he said.

One person? Two? Three? Had Lon and Milo bothered to search for Tommy? Or had they torn apart my room instead, looking for the elusive last chapters of Diane's novel, not bothering to lock the door when they left? If so, that particular bullet had struck home. Lack of success would explain the disgruntled look on Lon's face. But they didn't have a mountain bike. Neither had tightly curled black hair. Raef, I suspected, had both.

"Anything missing?" Buddy had his notebook out.

I picked through the rubble, trying to disturb the scene as little as possible. "Some grapefruit juice, stew . . . rope, duct tape." I double-checked the maps and papers. "Nothing else."

"You think Kingsley trashed the place?"

"No. I think Lon and Milo did, while we were searching for Tommy." I pointed to the tire track. "Raef came later."

Buddy pushed his hat back and scratched the bald dome. "You told me the manuscript disappeared when Diane was attacked. So what do you have that Bovey wants?"

"He thinks I have the last two chapters of Diane's novel."

He backed up and closed the door, then checked to make sure the window was shut. "You withheld evidence?"

"Not exactly."

"What 'exactly'?" He crossed his arms over his chest.

"Well, when I confronted Lon earlier, I . . . kind of . . . implied I had Diane's last chapters."

"Wonderful. Do me a favor, Frankie. Let me handle Bovey from now on."

"Ball's in your court." I had already resolved to head for the hills by first light. But I didn't tell Buddy. I was sure he'd tell me to stay put.

If he thought I gave in too easily, he didn't show it. "I'll talk to Diane in the morning," he said, putting away his notebook. "You'll have to stay with Isabel tonight. Can't have you messing up the place before the lab boys get here."

We locked the door behind us. His car was parked in front of the office. While he called in, I stepped into the office. Isabel was directing two grizzled thumpers to the Black-Light Bar. There'd be a hot time in Pair-a-Dice tonight.

I waited until we were alone to tell her about the room. I'd let Buddy fill her in on the other details. "I'm almost finished, Isabel. I have to check two areas, then I can go home. Tomorrow morning, before dawn, I'm heading back into the range. I'll camp overnight up on top of Red Mountain. No one will think to look for me there. But I want you to tell everyone that I've gone to Elko. No matter who trashed the room, I'll be safe if they think I'm a hundred miles away."

"You'd be safer in town."

"When someone has a key to my room? As safe as Diane?"

She had no answer.

"I'll have to trust my instinct," I said. "Take my chances."

She gave in. "You can sleep on the couch tonight. You got enough food for the trip?"

"Everything's freeze-dried or canned. No fresh stuff."

"Come on. I'll open the store for a minute. Got some apples and oranges in today . . . and a few decent tomatoes. Freda grows them."

I followed Isabel out the door. She already was ten paces beyond me, moving at her usual Warp II. She swatted Buddy on the ass as she went past. I resisted the impulse. I was in enough trouble as it was.

I caught up with Isabel at the back entrance to the store. Five feet above our heads, a yellow bug-light glared, creating a netherworld of long shadows.

"Are you still carrying your gun?" My whisper seemed loud as a shout in a tunnel.

Isabel patted the small of her back where something dark snuggled in her waistband. Reassuring. She unlocked the back entrance, leading me through the storeroom to the double-aisled grocery section. The post office counter was at the front on the right, open wooden cubbyholes climbed the wall behind. A bin on the floor collected mail pushed through a slot in the store wall. While I selected apples, oranges, tomatoes, trail mix, block-ice, and milk, she sorted mail.

"Couple of things for you," she said. I heard the thump as she canceled a stamp. "Might be important."

I settled the groceries by an ancient manual cash register before accepting a letter and a nine-by-twelve manila envelope. The manila envelope had my name and general delivery in block caps, heavy black ink, no return address. But it must have been local, because she'd had to cancel it. Through the heavy paper, I could feel the spiral wire of a notebook. My mind flashed a picture of Diane, lying on the ratty chaise, scribbling on green paper. Something was wrong with the picture, but I'd have to worry about that later. Something else bothered me: if these were the final chapters, untyped, what was in the manila envelopes tucked against my chest?

"The letter arrived earlier today. I forgot to bring it to you," Isabel said, avoiding my eyes.

Isabel, forgetful? Must have had something important on her mind. The letter was from my younger brother, Jamie. I had the odd feeling that it bore bad news. I couldn't take any more tonight. Opening a plastic grocery bag, I stuffed the mail inside. "Thanks, Isabel. How much do I owe you?" Tomatoes cost less in Point Barrow, I'd wager.

Isabel had her hand on the gun when we slipped quietly out the back. We stood there for a moment until our senses identified all the sights and sounds. The ground seemed to vibrate in time with the drumbeat and bass-guitar riffs emanating from Freda's, while the wind moaned around corners, pushing ineffectually at the cloud cover. Dry lightning sparked over the mountains. The air was damp enough to drink, but the rain held off. Seemed as if even the crickets felt too lazy to rub their legs together.

Isabel didn't offer to carry one of the bags the short distance to the motel. Buddy and his car were gone; a piece of yellow tape stretched across the doorway to my room. With the crime rate soaring in Pair-a-Dice, I probably should invest in the company that manufactured caution tape.

I disobeyed Buddy's order, ducked under the tape, and took what I needed from the room. But I stepped carefully around the litter on the floor. Isabel cursed the mess, but didn't question my right to enter. She even stood guard while I loaded the ice chest into the Jeep.

"Do me a favor?" I asked, when were back in her apartment. She handed me an armload of bedding, I handed her a topographic map with the areas circled where I planned to work for the next two days.

"Sounds like a last request."

Ha, ha. Maybe she had a point, but my sense of humor was deserting me. "Show this to Killeen or Buddy—no one else."

"Your secret's safe with me." She locked the map in the steel office safe. After checking her hair in the hall mirror, she headed for the door.

"Where are you going?" My voice seemed high and sharp, even to my ears.

She paused, the door half-open. "To the dance, of course. It's not like Pair-a-Dice is a mecca for bands. Want to come?" It was as if kidnapping, threats, and attempted murder had never happened. Bootscooting music thrummed on the air. I recognized the insistent tempo but not the song.

"God, no." My bruised body ached for rest. "Just be careful," I said.

As soon as she was gone, I pulled out the envelopes I'd lifted from Diane's trailer. The first held Diane's last will and testament. I scanned the single handwritten sheet. Her possessions were left to Ruth Bovey, to be held in trust for Gabbie. The second held seven pages from Nora Bovey's book. I stuck the sheets back in the envelopes and placed them on the kitchen table where Isabel would find them in the morning.

I hadn't wanted to open my mail in front of Isabel, so I'd left it in the Jeep with the groceries. But my subconscious finally figured out what had bothered me at the store. If that envelope Isabel had given me contained Diane's notebook, then someone else had mailed it this evening—Diane had been incommunicado in Elko since late last night. That meant at least one other person in Pair-a-Dice knew where the notebook was. . . .

I had to open that envelope tonight. I grabbed a butcher knife from the kitchen, keys from my daypack, and opened the door a crack. Except for the unceasing wind, the night was quiet as a rock lab at midnight. The band must be taking a break. I ran lightly to the Jeep, fumbling in my hurry to get the door unlocked. The edge of the plastic bag stuck out from under the ice chest where I'd stashed it. As my fingers closed on the bag, I heard gravel crunch.

"Forget something?" said a voice behind me.

I whirled, knife held at gut level. Not that it would do much good against the gun on Milo's hip.

"Just finishing my packing," I said, lowering the knife. "You can tell Lon I'm leaving in the morning."

"I'm not his errand boy."

"Could have fooled me."

"I want the manuscript." The gun slid into his hand. The barrel looked awfully big at close range.

"Lon destroyed it."

"Not all. You have the most important part. You have the ending."

"There is no ending."

"What do you mean?"

"I lied. Diane didn't have time to finish the book."

"I don't believe you. Lon thinks you have it."

"Lon's wrong."

"If you're lying now, you'll be sorry."

I hoped it was the bravado of a schoolyard bully. I hoped he knew more about cows than he did about women. I could almost hear the gears turning in his thick skull as he stood there thinking it over. He tossed the gun from one hand to the other, watching for a reaction. I held very still, praying the bullet would miss me. In the distance, the band started up again. Distracted, Milo turned his head

"Why's the manuscript so important to you?" I asked.

"Now why do you think, you silly bitch?"

Either the dance beckoned or Milo tired of the game, because he didn't stick around for an answer. Just as well. I didn't have one.

I heard his footsteps stop around the corner of the motel. In case he was watching, I left the envelope and letter where they were, tugging the ice chest to cover them completely. Thanks to Milo, I'd have to wait until morning to read my mail. Maybe Milo'd do us all a favor and shoot himself.

Taking a felt-tip pen and a couple of three-by-five cards from the pocket of my field vest, I made two crude signs: WARNING: RATTLESNAKE ON GUARD. I taped them to the front side-windows. Did Milo know me well enough to call the bluff? Just in case, I added a makeshift alarm.

Testing the doors to make sure they were locked, I retreated to Isabel's apartment. The air conditioner cooled my overheated skin, and covered the music. I might even be able to catch a few hours' sleep. But before turning off the light, I wrote a short note describing Milo's interest in the manuscript. After sealing the envelope, I wrote Buddy's name on the front and placed it on top of Diane's will. I hoped the note wouldn't be my last testament.

Midnight. I was just settling down for a short summer's nap, when Isabel let herself in. She carried her pistol in her left hand, keys in her right. Her smile was bright enough to light the sky.

"Caught Milo snooping around your Jeep. You scared the living bejeezus out of him."

Son of a gun. It had worked. "You saw my signs?"

"Yeah."

"I put some pea gravel in an empty can balanced so it would roll if anyone bumped the Jeep." I was so tired I was laughing and crying at the same time.

"Milo sure saw the light. He won't be back tonight."

But would someone else? On a scale of one to ten, the day hadn't even reached one. Tomorrow—today—*had* to be an improvement, I thought as I turned out the light.

I should have remembered MacFarlane's First Law of Anthrodynamics: It's only when your trolling motor quits in the middle of the lake during a summer thunderstorm, that you discover you forgot to bring the oars . . .

FIFTEEN

Before sunrise I was on the road. I hadn't even waited for Fern's cinnamon rolls.

I drove three quarters of the way through the range before turning north off the dirt road onto a track that led up the west side of Red Mountain. I felt the safest place to camp was up on top, and I wanted my truck hidden before most of the world was awake. I'd been on that Jeep track several times before when I mapped the Triassic beds, but there'd been a lot of erosion since last year. In one place the road was barely the width of my truck. Not a comfortable feeling.

I parked the truck in a natural bowl of maybe three acres. Cattle hadn't been up there for years, if ever, and a veneer of grass cloaked the bottom. In the center was a spring, an overgrown seep that trickled around before spreading out and sinking into the soil. Nearby, three standing rocks had collapsed against each other, making a small pyramid-shaped shelter. Dirt had piled up against the sides and blown in upon the floor of a space only large enough for me to crouch down. When I scratched around at the base of the rocks, I found slivers of dirt-encrusted brown chert, identical to the projectile point I'd found Sunday, when Killeen had awakened me from my nap. I brushed dirt from one curved flake, feeling oddly connected with the person who'd fashioned that point—as if time stood still in this place. It was comforting, somehow.

I ate my meager breakfast, an apple and a handful of raw almonds, while leaning against the shelter. Clouds stretched to the horizon, but I figured they'd just ease on by, as clouds so often do in the high desert, tantalizing those below. Dragging the plastic bag from under the ice chest, I read last night's mail. My brother's note enclosed a longer letter from my graduate advisor, Sarah Barstead. Jamie's message was scrawled on the back of a hospital questionnaire: "Hi, Kiddo— Sorry to be the bearer of bad tidings. Wish I could have brought the news myself, but I've been filling in for another resident (need the bucks to repair the MG—again!). Dr. Barstead tried to call you, but was told you're out in the hills. Mom and Dad are worried—you haven't called since July, and they expected you home by now. They know about Geoff. I think they feel pretty helpless, being stuck in London at the moment. *I* know you can take care of yourself, but I promised them that if I don't hear from you by Monday, I'll fly up to scope out the situation. . . . Wish things had turned out differently. Love, Jamie."

Sarah had written because she couldn't reach me by phone. She wished she could have delivered the news in person. Geoff was dead. The police had boxed up his office files and personal effects. She was sorry. . . .

She'd enclosed two short newspaper clippings. I smoothed the folded articles against my thigh, unwilling to accept the raw data—as if not reading them would negate the reality of death. My hands trembled. I squinted at the horizon, the ground, anywhere but at the flimsy newsprint. But I felt the words burn my palm, until I had to look. One short blurb described the discovery of a body not long after I had left for the field. The second, dated two months later, filled in the details. A boy chasing his dog had stumbled across Geoff's remains at the bottom of a campus arroyo. He'd been dead for months. It took weeks to make the positive identification—they'd had to order his dental charts from England. The cause of death was unresolved. The forensic pathologist suspected an accidental fall from the cliffs above, but hadn't ruled out murder or suicide. She was waiting for the results of additional toxicological tests that might, or might not, resolve the issue. Although the investigation remained open, the body had been shipped home to England for burial.

My chest had the empty, hollow feeling that comes after an intense argument, after hurt so deep that a piece of you is missing. I'd been waiting for him to show his face all summer, sure that he'd find his way to Pair-a-Dice to finish his dissertation. It had been the most important thing in the world to him—more important than our relationship, our future. Now, thinking about what might have been, I waited for tears that did not come. . . .

I knew the ravine where Geoff had died, could picture the exact spot, the base of a steep hill on the southeast edge of campus. We'd picnicked at the top among granite boulders and eucalyptus trees on warm spring days when the air smelled of orange blossoms. It was our spot . . . secluded, private. I could understand why it took so long to find his body. What I didn't know was whether he'd slipped or jumped into that arroyo. Or been pushed. I wondered if I'd ever know for sure.

If I don't hear from you by Monday, I'll fly up to scope out the situation, Jamie had written. He must have forgotten how long it took snail-mail to reach the outback. I had to assume he was already on his way. Damn. When he arrived in Pair-a-Dice, Isabel would tell him I'd gone to Elko. I vacillated. To leave now, or not to leave now. I decided to give it one more try this morning before tossing in the towel. Jamie couldn't reach Elko before late afternoon, which left me an adequate window of opportunity. . . .

The manila envelope contained Diane's notebook, half the green pages filled with scrawled sentences. I wouldn't have time to decipher it until evening. I wrapped it in the plastic bag and slid it back under the ice chest.

My traverse took me halfway down Red Mountain at a point south of the scarred slope where Killeen and I had worked yesterday. The narrow valley, breached only by the elevated Jeep track, lay far below the target outcrop. On my map, I'd approximately located the contact at the base of the outcrop, using a dotted line to indicate it was covered. Sweat ran between my breasts to soak the waistband of my jeans. Even my leather belt was damp. After drinking a quart of water, I sighted over to the outcrop that saved our lives the day before. I was about fifty feet higher, but roughly on strike.

The shovel and pickax were buried somewhere on the hillside—better them than me—so I hacked at the colluvium with my rock hammer, all the while fearing that the overhanging rocks would come crashing down on my head. I uncovered an area a meter square on the steep slope, but I was still too high in the section. I moved lower, cleared another barren interval. Closer. The number of silty lenses was increasing.

At the base of the next interval, I found it. The Rosetta stone. Sparry discoid shapes of countless ammonites lay frozen in a ground-mass of iron-stained limestone. Now I could get the hell out of Pair-a-Dice.

As quickly as possible, I mapped, measured, described, photo-graphed, and collected the rock sequence, anxious to get off the mountain as soon as possible. I had what I needed. I wouldn't push my luck by storming the last site.

Poor choice of words. The heavens opened as I stowed the samples in my pack. I climbed until I was sliding back two feet for every one I attempted. Only then did I seek shelter up against the cliff face. Below, under the onslaught of the rain, my route off the mountain was becoming narrower by the minute. Around me, the shrouded sky trailed rain like a widow's veil. I was truly on my own.

I huddled against a rough limestone cliff, the only shelter for at least a square mile. Horizontal rain and wind whirled around the corners, whistling like the airhorn on a Peterbilt. The Jeep was off to my left. The problem was, it was parked a thousand feet above me, and the route led up a knife-edged ridge. I settled down to wait out the storm with only my thoughts for company.

Hit-or-miss thunderstorms were the normal pattern in summer. This was different, a wall-to-wall carpet of clouds. The deluge showed no signs of abating. Water cascaded down the cliff face, blew at me from the sides, swirled up under my cheap plastic poncho. It hardly mattered—condensation had made the poncho nearly as wet inside as out. I crouched for thirty minutes. If the rain didn't let up soon, I'd have to crawl up that damned ridge. Otherwise, I'd never get my vehicle off the mountain.

I'd been in worse predicaments. One time, my old Willys Jeep broke down in the middle of nowhere. I had to hike seventeen miles across the Mojave Desert in June. When I reached the highway there was one sip of water left in my canteen. A trucker named Igor stopped and took me into Barstow. He had a doctorate in philosophy from Dartmouth. I'd always wondered what philosophers did for a living.

I waited for the rain to lessen, ate some trail mix, processed memories of Geoff. I tried to fit the pieces together, tried to make sense of our last few months. Suicide or accident? Planned or unplanned? The pieces didn't fit.

The storm's energy increased. The cliff face no longer sheltered me from the onslaught. The wind now blew straight at my face. The temperature had dropped at least twenty degrees, was still falling. Time to leave. Now or never.

My feet were asleep. When I stretched, they prickled as if struck by a thousand quilting needles. I rocked gently up on my tiptoes and down, up and down, all the while whispering encouraging words to my toes. After five minutes, I started slowly toward the ridge, testing each step before I put my full weight on the forward foot. It took forever.

A ravine separated my cliff-topped slope from the ridge. I maintained altitude, hugging the treeless hillside, clutching low-growing bushes for support. I slipped once, cracked my knee on a rock.

The rivulets that traversed the mountainside collected a thousand feet below into a torrent that ripped away chunks of the valley walls. Pieces of the hillside, loosened by yesterday's blast, broke free, tobogganing to meet the torrent below. The water was brown with mud, a debris-laden death trap rushing nonstop to spill out on the valley floor. The highway would be impassable where it crossed the washes. Whoever was in Pair-a-Dice, good or bad, would be stuck there.

I was breathing like a marathon runner when I reached the ridge. Now I had to find a way to the hilltop without being blown off. I wanted a cup of coffee so badly I could taste it, smell it. But there was no place to build a fire even if I had coffee. The supplies were in the Jeep. I let my mind drift into hyperspace, stayed off the skyline, started to work my way up the slippery ridge. I didn't look up, didn't look down. I focused on my hands. It would be a whole lot easier if I had gloves, I thought. Pulling my hands inside the poncho, I searched the pockets of my field vest: one projectile point; one work glove, recovered from a stranger's campsite. I left the point where it was and slipped the glove on my right hand.

I don't know how long it took—an hour, two. The sky was the same dull-gray color I associate with war. This was war. I fought the rain, the rocks, the wind, the bushes that kept snagging my poncho. I felt like Salieri in his great black cape, so I hummed Mozart's *Requiem,* then switched to Berlioz. Why, I wondered aloud while facing a particularly nasty stretch of slick rock, did I have such a wonderful memory for lugubrious choral works, even if they did suit the circumstances? The wind whisked away my voice without comment; the rock was mute. The requiems were for Geoff, I realized. Wherever he was, he'd found more peace than I had.

My earlier hollow agony turned to anger, anger that Geoff died before he could apologize, before he could restore order to my world, set things right. Wanting to cry, I instead jammed my fist into a crevice and pulled my body another meter up the ridge. And started humming another requiem. . . .

When I eased over the last layers of rock, I'd finally run out of dirges. But the anger was gone, as well, lost in waves of exhaustion. My hands and legs were shaking so badly I couldn't drive. I could barely walk. Whether it was safe to delay or not, I was going to have to rest a while and restore my energy supply.

My Jeep sat there, looking cleaner than it had all summer. I longed to slip inside, roll up in my sleeping bag, and take a nap. But I wanted coffee more. Grabbing the single-burner propane stove, a pot, and the coffee, I wobbled toward the rock shelter. While the coffee boiled, I changed clothes in the car, shivering as the cold air struck my damp skin. I was safer in there anyway. The rubber tires would help protect me from the lightning that glanced off nearby peaks. Luckily, I hadn't bothered to set up camp—my tent would have drifted into the Great Salt Lake.

I checked the Jeep trail off the mountain. The road seemed to be holding, but it was awash with runoff. It would be safer to wait for the storm to abate. A line of blue showed off to the south. I'd warm myself and feed my growling stomach before I attempted the descent.

I backed the Jeep as close to the shelter as I could, so I wouldn't get wet again crossing back and forth. The aroma of the boiling coffee was better than Fern's cinnamon rolls—well, almost. I fished out Diane's notebook and popped her "Priscilla" tape in the tape deck. This might be the only private time I had before I scraped the mud of Pair-a-Dice from my boots.

I set the coffee aside and put a package of noodle soup on to boil. While I sipped the thick brown liquid, I found the page Diane had been writing the evening I visited her home. I recognized the doodling on the margins, the Madonna and child. Working backwards, I located the end of the last section of manuscript that I'd read, finding her handwriting more legible than my own. She didn't have my habit of abbreviating half the words, a form of shorthand. Just after the doodled page, the tone of the text changed. So did the handwriting. Gone was the self-deprecating humor. Diane's alter ego took over the stark listing of facts, a narrative that bore witness to the truth. Either Diane was schizophrenic, or the change confirmed that more than one person wrote the novel.

Twelve years ago, rancher Von Boyle had raped and accidentally murdered a teenage girl from Easytown—Shelley Gates, Milo's sister. The author didn't even try to mask Shelley's identity. Von buried Shelley's body on the ranch, under the site of the helicopter pad. What Diane hinted at earlier in the novel, she now dissected like a corpse in an anatomy class, right down to the leveling of the concrete poured over Shelley's body. But Boyle didn't stop at Shelley: a year later, he attacked her best friend, Emmajean. She became pregnant, but refused to press charges. She told her boyfriend, Willy, that the baby was his. When he didn't marry her, she raised the boy with his support—and hush money from Boyle. Three years later, she married a man from Wells, but she periodically threatened to tell her story to the world. Boyle couldn't let that happen.

There were four pages torn from Diane's notebook, just before the end. The little green nubs still clung to the wire spiral. What was missing? Who tore out the pages, wrote the last entries, mailed the notebook?

I puzzled over the answers while I ate chicken soup and listened to the rain drumming on the metal roof. From the intimate knowledge of the facts, I suspected that the narrator was Ruth Bovey. Gabbie was too young to know the truth, while Lon wasn't the type to self-immolate. Milo was a possibility, but I suspected he would have given himself a bigger and more heroic role. Besides, the grammar was too clean to be Milo's. The writer of the last pages *had* to be Ruth. Or was I missing something?

It bothered me that there were inconsistencies in the plot. If Ruth wrote the last pages *and* collaborated on the rest of the book, how could she have found out about Shelley's murder? She hadn't been married to Lon at the time, and Lon certainly wouldn't confess. And why wasn't there any mention of the liaison that must have existed between Lon and Bill's mother for at least ten years, albeit before Ruth came on the scene? Lon's siring of three bastards would have been the final nail in his coffin. Finally, why, for God's sake, was Diane trying to hurt and discredit her lover? Why did Ruth give her the ammunition? To blackmail him? I doubted it. The book's allegations would be more apt to get him arrested, which wouldn't do Diane *or* Ruth any good.

I had no answers. So I approached the problem from another angle. Who would benefit from publication of Diane's book? Diane would receive notoriety, money—things she didn't seem to crave, unless she had her eye on another Harley-Davidson motorcycle. If she'd had a child and given her up for adoption, did Diane now want to provide for the child's education or future? The idea was so fanciful I wondered what was in the creamer I'd added to my coffee. Ruth and Gabbie would suffer humiliation, but would be protected from Lon's abuse if he were in jail. Maybe. But he was rich; the lawyers would get him off. He'd get even.

Bill Anderson could stop paying child support to Emmajean, but otherwise the Andersons weren't affected—as long as Lon was alive. If he died, they might have a claim against the estate. The same was true of Emmajean's child. Was that why Diane had left the Andersons out of the story? If Emmajean had helped craft the Pair-a-Dice chapters, then she might have wanted not only to blackmail Lon, but to insure her son's inheritance—which would be larger if Bill and Randy weren't factored into the equation. Was that why she was murdered? To shut her up?

I considered Milo. How long had he worked for the Boveys? Could he have supplied the necessary details for the novel? If so, then why had he been after the notebook last night? Second thoughts? To destroy it? To use it for blackmail? That was more Milo's style. If the allegations about Lon's murder of Shelley Gates were true, then Milo could want either revenge or money. Or both. With the rest of the manuscript destroyed, Milo would need the last chapters to hold over Lon. But if he'd been privy to Lon's secrets, why would he have shared them with Diane? He didn't need her help to blackmail Lon. On the other hand, Milo was definitely serious enough about this manuscript to threaten me and to have attacked Diane Monday night. As was Lon. And I couldn't discount the elusive I-80 killer.

Each question led to another, but Diane was the key. I wondered what Buddy was learning from her today.

For me, it was decision time. I'd completed my fieldwork. I could leave the mess behind and head for Tucson, or I could stay long enough to launch an investigation into a twelve-year-old murder. Of course, if I gave a list of questions to Buddy and then hightailed it home, I'd be out of the way when the shooting started. Listing questions was easy, I told myself. It was safe. I'd press the red handle, the dynamite would explode miles away.

I slipped into my still-damp vest, picked the field notebook from one pocket, mechanical pencil from another. All of the data I'd gathered over the past three summers lived in that five-by-seven yellow book—but only another geologist would be able to decipher the abbreviated symbols and language. If anything happened to me, I hoped my advisor, Sarah Barstead, or one of her other grad students, would be curious enough to check my notes. Geoff could have done it, but Geoff was gone. . . . I grabbed my thoughts before they started down that path.

The tape was finished. I turned it over. The music kept me company, lifted my spirits, made me feel less alone. It was odd how the words of Charlene's song paralleled the early part of Diane's novel: *"I've been to Paradise, but I've never been to me."* Had Diane plagiarized that, too? But why? What had she to gain? People would notice, would sue . . . unless she'd never meant to publish the book, had intended it only for my eyes. I felt manipulated. I rewound the song. Charlene, in a breathy voice, advised me to settle down, have the babies she'd never have, commit to one partner. Was Diane, consciously or unconsciously, focusing on children and monogamy in order to send a message that she was dissatisfied with her choices in life? Did she want to settle down with Lon and have children? Then why brand him a rapist and murderer in the book? Why imply he'd physically abused her? Was it all fiction designed to cause Ruth to divorce Lon? Then why give it to me? And if it wasn't true, why did Lon try to kill me? Or was it Ruth or Milo who'd flown that helicopter?

I couldn't answer the questions, just write them down for Buddy to solve. I opened my field notebook. Each locality description was numbered, the numbers and Brunton compass measurements located on the topographic map. I'd habitually left one or two lines between descriptions. Beginning with page four, I now tacked questions onto locality descriptions, skipping entries and pages at random. I let my subconscious go free, listing all the details and questions I'd pushed to the back of my mind since I'd written the note to Buddy last night, all the niggling problems I'd shoved aside so I could concentrate on finishing the field work.

Listing the questions and observations took another thirty minutes. I'd just locked the field notebook along with Diane's notebook in the glove compartment when lightning and thunder hit simultaneously, the strike so close the Cherokee jumped and quivered. So did I. Lost in the writing, I'd forgotten about the storm. It existed as a background beat, steady, hypnotic, changing direction with the buffeting wind. I rubbed a circle in the foggy windshield with my sleeve. The next flash illuminated a sheetwash-covered landscape. The hair on my arms stood up. I could smell scorched brush where lightning had touched off a brushfire.

The flames were doused almost instantly. But the danger didn't abate. Distracted by the troubles in Pair-a-Dice, and my own involvement, I'd ignored the narrowing of the one trail off Red Mountain.

I scrambled to get the Jeep in gear. If I didn't get off the mountain pronto, my transport would become a permanent landmark. And so might I.

Sixteen

I always felt safer driving uphill in a four-by-four than I did descending with the gears and brakes fighting the pull of gravity. But this was a nightmare. Even in lowest gear, I had to ride the brakes as the tires fought for traction on the saturated slope and I fought to keep a half-ton of steel from hydroplaning into the ravine below.

The beginning of the Jeep trail was devoid of banked curves. Even a washboard surface would have been preferable to the slick grass. I took it by inches, talking to the growling motor. I promised the Cherokee that I'd take him in for a tune-up as soon as we got home; promised I'd rotate the tires; promised I'd never sell him, but drive him till the body was solid rust and the engine begged for retirement. The vibrations in the steering wheel seemed like answering groans.

We lurched, we slipped, we skidded ten feet before one rear wheel caught on a small limestone outcrop. I gripped the wheel more tightly as knuckles turned white, then blue. Easing up, I watched the tanned flesh tones return while I dragged in three shuddering breaths. Inch, by inch, by inch . . . We were nearly at the bottom of the hill where the road straddled the ravine. I slid to a stop, trying to judge the narrow crossing that had been just wide enough for the Jeep before. Could I make it now? Did I have a choice?

Yes. There was always a choice. But I wasn't ready to abandon the vehicle and all my gear. I shouldered back into the clammy poncho, strapped on my field belt, slogged partway down the trail. Mini-landslides had left semicircular cuts in the roadbed, as if a giant had nibbled the edges. I was sure I could get around all but two. I stood there in the rain, watching more soil and rock carried by rill wash to join the torrent below. I needed to partially fill in those cuts with debris enough to support my vehicle for a second or two. I pulled out my puny rock hammer. I would have traded a year's pay for the pickax and shovel I left buried on the mountain. The hammer would have to do.

I rooted around in the back of the Jeep until I unearthed some burlap bags. In my book of useful inventions, burlap ranks right up there after duct tape. In the past, I'd used bags to plaster vertebrate fossils, provide traction in sandy washes, rig temporary shelters, and weave into rope. This time, I'd build a road.

I cut terraces across the tops of the worst spots, creating platforms for the dirt and rock-filled bags. I had only four bags. I'd have to fill them, put them in place, drive over them, drag them to the next spot, and place them again. How was I going to get them around the vehicle when it was parked on the isthmus between the two slides? *One step at a time, Frankie.* Great. Now I was talking to myself.

The work was slow, numbing. I used a flat rock and my hammer to shove sandy mud and stones into the bags, but when I tried to shift them, they wouldn't budge. What now? I loaded as many rocks as I could find into the back of the truck, added the half-empty bags, and drove out onto the narrow span. Far below, water flowed away from the trail in both directions, on one side carving a new path around yesterday's slide. I wished Killeen were here. He'd have lifted the bags, shifted boulders, reassured me that this was child's play. I wished my brothers were here taking bets on which side of the road I'd fall off. Misery loves even warped company.

The road surface was so clay-rich that friction was reduced to nothing. The Cherokee fishtailed through patches before one tire would catch on solid rock. When I tried to stop, momentum carried me another yard. I stopped three feet from the first cut, with six inches on one side of the Jeep, a foot on the other. The drop-off was about sixty feet. I opened the back, unloaded the rocks one by one, and inched around the side of the vehicle to lay the foundation. On the hill above me, lightning blossomed. I flinched as a small explosion rent the air. Crouching beside the Jeep, I searched the hillside for a gunman. Nothing moved but sheetwash and tendrils of smoke dissolving in the downpour. I guessed my little propane stove was history. Better it than me.

I work better to music. I tried to think of something cheerful, but my mind kept returning like a do-loop to the prisoner's lament:

155

"Breakin' up big rocks on the chain gang, breakin' rocks and servin' my time, oh, yeah." At least the rhythm fit the slinging of sandbags.

The finished product would not have passed an engineering inspection. I worried that my wheels would push the bags outward and they'd tumble down the hillside. With a couple of two-by-six planks, I'd have been across that track in a minute flat. If wishes were planks . . . I added a few more rocks to secure the bags. Now or never.

Because I'd studied the roadbed like a golfer studies the green, I knew where to guide the Jeep. Inhaling deeply, I forced myself to relax. I let out the clutch. The vehicle bumped and lurched across the makeshift road, nearly stalling when both right tires were on the bags. But with a final lurch, three tires gained relatively solid ground. I stopped within inches of the next cut-away.

The wind blew back the hood of my poncho, rain lashed my face, neck and arms. I wanted coffee and a bathroom—not necessarily in that order. But above all, I wanted to be off that span. So I carried rocks, and more rocks, to mix with the sand and gravel I scooped into coarsely woven bags. I felt a definite kinship with Jean Valjean, prisoner 24601.. . . .

I'd misjudged. The bags didn't span the gap. I was out in the middle of the isthmus, no loose rocks in sight, the trail only wide enough for me to stand flattened against the Jeep. I didn't dare whittle the trail down any further. I grabbed my sleeping bag from the back, and jammed it in the remaining space. Dragging my rock hammer perpendicular to the road, I dug a little trench that shed its debris between the bags.

The earth seemed to shiver. Ahead, I could see curvilinear cracks developing as the roadbed was undercut. I jumped in the Jeep, threw it into gear, inched over the fill when I wanted to drive like hell. The Jeep and I crawled at one mile per hour until I was past the cracks, past the end of the isthmus, on solid ground. Leaving the motor on, I ran back to the cut, dumped out the burlap bags, grabbed the sleeping bag, and hotfooted it to safety. Mission accomplished.

Wind gusted and rolled down Red Mountain carrying the stench of smoke, but the fire was already out. It was as if now that I had been forced off the mountain, had conquered that narrow trail, the elements could relax. Killeen was right. I *am* a closet romantic.

The water streaming down my face tasted salty. I did a little boogie by the Jeep, dropped to my knees, and kissed the ground. The adrenaline surge abated, my strained muscles ached, and my nose ran. I was sick of rain. Yet I smiled as I searched the pockets of the field vest for a dry tissue.

The projectile point jabbed my thumb. I'd meant to leave it with the matching chert flakes on top of the mountain—a symbolic gesture to whoever had made it there so long ago. Instead, I made a vow: if I got out of this safely, I'd return with the point—even if I had to walk up that damn mountain.

I took off my poncho and draped it over the passenger seat. Pulling out the topographic sheets I studied each possible route back to Pair-a-Dice. All the roads ran through canyons. The northern road followed higher ground with the best grading. Runoff would be shunted to the side until the road entered the coyote's valley. Then, the resistant cliff walls and bench would channel the water right down the middle of the road for half a mile. A definite problem. And getting to the northern canyon would require skirting the edge of yesterday's landslide. It gave me the heebie-jeebies just to think about it.

The central canyon was closest, just south of me. I wouldn't run into trouble until I reached the eastern flanks of the range where the older alluvium dipped toward Pair-a-Dice. There, the road crossed a steep-sided, sand-and-boulder-floored wash. Right now, that wash was probably running bank full. But if I stayed south of the wash and drove straight down the bajada surface until I neared the highway, I knew I'd be able to find some stable crossing onto the asphalt. Barring that, I could park, hoof it to the highway, and hike back to Pair-a-Dice.

Option three was a much longer route. I had to drive south, then dogleg west before heading south again, circling the range until I intersected the most southerly cross-cutting canyon—the road I'd taken with Killeen yesterday past Easy Thomasson's cabin. The roughest part would be a section of road crossing the argillaceous Tertiary tuffs that flanked the western side of the range. There, the road banked steeply toward a tributary wash about eighty feet deep. I'd traveled that section in rainstorms twice before. Both times, I'd had to fight to keep the heavy vehicle on the road. I'd probably be okay, as long as I didn't hit the brakes.

Option four: I could find a place nearby, gather enough dry wood for a cook-fire, and hole up for a wretched night in a wet, muddy sleeping bag. A dismal proposition.

I selected Door Number Two.

Hunched over the wheel, driving like a centenarian at midnight, I munched an apple, trying to make believe it was five-alarm chili, hot-and-sour soup, steaming tamales—anything warm and spicy . . . It didn't work. To this scientist, an apple is always an apple.

I was about a mile down the central canyon road, feeling complacent because I'd made it so far, when I lost the road. I slammed on the brakes. Water coursing on either side coalesced into a pond that grew by inches as I watched. At the other side of the pond, a tremendous jumble of rocks had dammed the road. I hadn't felt or heard the rockslide. The tires must have absorbed the vibrations.

If this were television, I'd drive straight through the pond, up and over the pile of rubble, and into the yard of a magnificent estate. Unfortunately, this was real life. God alone knew what was on the other side of that slide—certainly not an estate. I backed half a mile until I found a wider spot in the road. Back, crank wheel, turn. The outside mirror was too foggy to use. I got out to check how close the rear tires were to the edge of the road. Too close. The California driving test didn't cover this one. The maneuver took seven minutes and left me with another decision to make . . .

Option one would be impassable. Option four was still my last choice. Time for option three.

There was a momentary lull in the storm when I reached the western side of the range. Looking back, I could see the mountain peaks dressed in soft gray skirts. Then the clouds moved together, obliterating everything. I couldn't wait for Opal's fried food and my lumpy bed in Room 6.

There was a sense of unreality about the day. I felt as if I were a player in a full-scale game of Dungeons & Dragons, with an omnipotent Dungeon Master directing my adventures. I'd been driven from the mountain by smoke and lightning, blocked by rockfall and water. What next? Gray ooze? Wandering monsters? Invisible stalkers?

Before me lay the western foothills of the range under a cloud bank that seemed to stretch to the Pacific. Rain fell again from one horizon to the other, streaming down slopes and in washes, erosion in action. Far away, water collected in a huge shallow lake that merged with the leaden sky. . . . No exit that way. The Jeep would mire to the axles.

White volcanic tuff layers peeked from beneath their alluvial masks. No buildings lay among the undulating brown landscape, no fences. This sight had changed little since the Boveys first settled in the area, since Killeen's great-grandparents had been murdered. In fact, except for a decrease in rainfall and vegetation, the land looked much as it had when an ancient hunter had created a perfect point on top of Red Mountain.

I turned south, curved in and out among the pine and juniper, and forded shallow washes. At each ford, I got out to check the water depth, the firmness of the channel bottom. I encouraged the Jeep to hug the center of the slick road. The engine fought the gray ooze that seemed to push us off the road and down into the adjacent ravine now coursing with eight feet of thrashing, mud-charged, boulder-punching water. Rain drummed, windshield wipers brushed furiously at the constant stream.

I never heard him coming.

There was no shadow as the helicopter flew above me thirty feet off the deck. It made a small, arcing turn, then hovered for a moment. A gust of wind caught it, tilted the rotors. I could see Lon's face, smiling, as he fought for stability. He was insane to fly in this weather. Maybe he was insane anyway. Unconsciously, clutching the steering wheel, I willed him success. The Jeep crawled slowly forward. As the helicopter veered up and over the Jeep, I let out the breath I'd been holding a lifetime. Or so it seemed.

And then he was back. This time, he didn't hover, but flew straight down the road scant feet above the surface. I jammed on the brakes. Shit. A sign on the visor told me exactly what would happen: *If you make sudden sharp turns or abrupt maneuvers, you may cause this vehicle to go out of control and roll over or crash . . .*

The Jeep fishtailed for a lifetime before gravity grabbed the rear end. Front tires spinning ruts in the ooze, the Jeep hung there for a moment as, in slow motion, my camping gear shifted to the back. That did it. Lon flew by, in front of my face. The Jeep slid down the bank toward the rushing water.

The Dungeon Master was toying with me. The Jeep came to rest, rear bumper against a thick-boled piñon, ten feet down the bank. My mouth hung open, voice choked in mid-scream. The truck tilted precariously. I couldn't climb into the back to get my daypack because that might send the Jeep the rest of the way into the stream. With shaking fingers, I fumbled to turn off the engines, lights and wipers. I automatically switched on the emergency blinkers—why, I didn't know. Who, besides Lon, would be out in this storm?

I had on my field vest with snacks in one pocket, my belt with rock hammer, compass, and knife. My wet poncho still draped the passenger seat. I turned my head to check what other necessities were close. The canteen was on the passenger seat floor; everything else was jumbled against the rear hatch. The ice chest lay open. Water had soaked everything. Damn Lon Bovey.

The good news was that I was alive and unharmed, my Jeep wasn't under water, and Lon hadn't come back to check his work. Twice now, he'd tried to kill me. Twice now, he'd failed. He'd make a terrible congressman.

With excruciating slowness, I lifted the poncho from the seat. The canteen was just out of reach. I didn't want to chance upsetting the apple cart. I wasn't worried about water anyway—there was plenty of water coming down from above. I grabbed my empty coffee cup from the dashboard before shoving open the door just enough to allow my body to ease out. The vehicle lurched away from me until it caught on some unseen obstacle. I hoped the obstacle was big enough to hold the Jeep until I could get back with a tow truck.

Out of habit, I tried to lock the driver's door. But my trembling fingers dropped the keys. I gave up. Wrapping myself in the poncho, I crawled through the mud and brush back up to the road, an insane mimicry of my fight with the ridge a few hours ago. Hours? It seemed more like years.

Which way to go? The maps were in the Jeep, and my exhausted brain functioned on two cylinders. The wind whistled at my back, pounding rain drove me forward. My world-view consisted of mud-caked boots that led me down the road toward Easy Thomasson's place. Good choice, I informed them, conscious that I was talking to my feet. It seemed like the most natural thing in the world to talk to my feet. Maybe there was a dry corner at Easy's where I could build a fire while waiting out the fierceness of the storm. I was down to option four—minus the damp sleeping bag. Pair-a-Dice was just too far away. . . .

This time I heard him coming. He was above me, in front of me, circling again to face me. I stared stupidly at the intent face, refusing to believe he'd come back. Too late, I dashed toward the slope on my left, aiming for the trees that stood just above the rushing water. I never made it. As he came at my head with the struts, I dove for the road bed, protecting my head with my arms. If I hugged the mud, he couldn't get me. Unless he had a gun.

The rotor noise grew louder. When I lifted my head, he was bearing down inches above the slick ground. I rolled right, onto my back, and watched the struts slide past on either side of my body. Too close: only three inches between my shoulder and the left strut.

I shoved myself to my feet, dragging at my rock hammer. When he came at me again, I heaved it at the bubble. He pulled up in time. The hammer fell short, bounced off a rock in the road, slithered over the edge of the bank.

He circled for another pass. I headed for the uphill slope, knowing I wouldn't make the trees, knowing he could pick me off the nearly vertical road cut I had to climb to reach the upper hillside with its screen of vegetation. Wind gusts tore at my poncho, lifted it to flap around my face. My arms tangled in the plastic folds. I jerked it over my head, and the wind carried it up the hillside, plastered it against a sagebrush. No time to climb. I flattened myself against the cut. My vest flapped open. Something in the pocket slapped against my hip.

The helicopter was twenty feet away, approaching carefully. I was exhausted beyond the point of caring. He could see it on my face. He smiled once more, the teeth beautiful, white, and straight. I was the hare, standing still, mesmerized by the headlights.

He was so close he couldn't miss.

Neither could I. I flung the projectile point at that perfect smile. It bounced harmlessly off the Plexiglas, but Lon's hands flinched instinctively. The craft jerked to port, the tail rotor grazed the hillside. When Lon tried to correct, he turned too sharply. The main rotor clipped the top of a tree and the craft flipped over, tumbling into the ravine. I waited, muscles slack, for an explosion, the ball of flame shown in all the movies. It never came.

I stumbled over to the edge, refusing to believe that my nemesis was gone. My legs gave way and I sank to the ground. Arms wrapped tightly around my knees for support, I willed my brain and muscles to regain control of my body. . . . And I waited, staring down into the ravine.

Nothing was left of the helicopter but twisted metal and Plexiglas, rapidly being ripped apart by the rushing water. I didn't go down to check for a survivor. No body parts littered the slopes. Lon hadn't had time to bail out.

I felt robbed of my fitting ending. I threw a rock at the only piece of Plexiglas large enough to support an air pocket, and felt a fierce delight when I hit it squarely. Plunk. The rock bounced into the water, the bubble shifted, rolled onto one side. The corpse of Lon Bovey was strapped to a seat staring with sightless eyes from a watery coffin.

Seventeen

I did not feel diminished by Lon's death. I felt empty. Maybe that's what diminished means: the nothingness left behind when all emotions have drained away.

How long I sat hunched over at the ravine edge, staring at the wreckage, I don't know. But when the shaking and hiccups finally stopped, the sluicing rain had eroded a semicircular channel around my rear end. Water flowed out of the channel mouths into my boots. I sloshed when I stood up.

What next? My natural inclination to cooperate with the law conflicted with an innate desire for self-preservation. I needed the security of home, the unfailing support of family. Did I owe anything to the Boveys? No. They could find and bury Lon without my help.

To hide my presence, sever my involvement, I would remove all traces of my presence at the crash site. The rock hammer lay caught in some brush a few feet down the slope. I clambered down, retrieved the evidence, and used it to grapple my way back to the road. I climbed higher to rescue my torn poncho, the only other evidence that I had been at the scene.

Back on the road, I picked up the projectile point, kissed it reverently before snapping it into my vest pocket. I still had a vow to keep. Rain or shine, I should have kept it right then. . . . By such small decisions are our lives irrevocably changed.

It was roughly two more miles east to Easy's cabin, an equal distance south to the Bovey line shack I'd used earlier in the summer. I hadn't considered the shack before because the route took me farther away from town, and subconsciously, I'd wanted nothing more to do with Lon Bovey. With Lon dead, the shack offered shelter, warmth, a fireplace—things I wouldn't find in Easy's tumble-down cabin. Since I wasn't going to make it to Pair-a-Dice tonight anyway, I might as well be comfortable.

My feet turned south. If I were lucky, I'd reach the shack before dark.

I'd walked a mile when I heard a truck, which meant that somewhere, someplace, the road was open. Hallelujah. I wanted a ride back to Pair-a-Dice, but first I wanted to make sure who was driving. I didn't trust Lon not to have Milo scouring the roads in case I slipped by the helicopter. So I stepped into the brush at the side of the road and crouched beside a fence post. In my camouflage-patterned poncho, I'm sure I resembled a lichen-covered rock. If I didn't move, they'd never see me—one of the lessons I'd learned from playing hide-and-seek with my godfather's half-Apache children.

Killeen stopped almost beside me. Climbing out of the truck, he scanned the hillsides with his binoculars, taking his time. He didn't even glance at the foreground. The rain had stopped at last, but clouds hovered still among the mountaintops and drifted in the canyons.

To move, or not to move? I stayed hidden. It wasn't because of the gun at his hip. I was used to seeing it there. It wasn't the fact that I'd already been wrong once today. Lon had come back to make sure I was dead. I froze because a second truck pulled up behind Killeen. Milo Gates hopped out. Reaching back into the cab, he lifted down the rifle he'd used to kill the jackrabbit and strolled over to confer with Killeen. Their voices were so soft I couldn't make out the words. A minute later, Milo turned his back on Killeen, put the rifle to his shoulder, and scoped out the opposite hillside. His finger rested on the trigger.

I did my best to imitate a fence post while I tried to make sense out of the scene. Killeen was supposed to be in town guarding Sylvie and Tommy. Why were he and Milo scanning the hills for signs of intelligent life? If they wanted to rescue me, then why weren't they calling my name? Last night, Milo had been interested in only one thing, Diane's notebook. I couldn't believe the situation had changed in eighteen hours.

The arrival of the baby-blue pickup brought a sigh of relief. I wanted to stand up and wave my arms when Bill Anderson stepped out to greet the others. But I waited. In the clear air, the crunch of his boots on gravel sounded like pistol shots from the gun at his waist.

Milo ignored him. The rifle's telescopic sight swung in a broad arc, and I remembered Nora Bovey's words: *"Had I known that in one desolate canyon Henry's quarry was human . . . "* My heart lurched.

Bill was out of jail, which meant either that the sheriff had caught the real killer, or there wasn't enough evidence to hold Bill. He leaned against the front of Killeen's truck, hands tucked in pockets of worn Levis. He looked leaner, moved easily. My eyes lingered for only a second before I closed them, afraid he'd sense me watching. . . . I jumped as a shot reverberated off the mountain walls.

"Damn it, Milo, the whole county'll hear you coming." Bill had Milo's rifle pointed at the sky.

"So?" Milo shrugged. "Figured I'd flush her out with the grouse." The grouse in question lay dead in the middle of the road. Milo started towards the headless corpse.

"What you did was make our job a whole lot harder, Gates." Killeen's voice stayed calm, but I saw his hands clench. "She'll probably run when she sees us."

The prospect didn't seem to bother Milo, who carried the dripping grouse by the feet. "So? I can track her. Just give me back the gun."

Bill hesitated, but at a nod from Killeen, he transferred the rifle. "Let's cut the bullshit and get moving," he said. "If she's not at the line shack, we can split up and cover more ground."

As the trucks took off down the road, I reconsidered my options. It was an unlikely trio, Killeen with Milo and Bill. Maybe I'd jumped off the proverbial fence a little too soon. At that moment, the only person in Nevada I trusted—the only one I could afford to trust—was Frankie MacFarlane. That's what Buddy had said the first night in town. Better to be suspicious and alive, than trusting and dead. . . .

I was jumpy now, leery of staying with the road. What if I didn't hear them coming next time? What if I were caught out in the open? I opted to strike across country, the route shorter, but more difficult. I'd need to ford a few intermittent creeks, but since the rain had stopped, the main flooding would be over. And by the time I reached the line shack, they'd be long gone.

Hunger clawed at my belly. I found jerky in one pocket, two Power Bars in another. I'd save the bars for later. While I gnawed the leathery beef, I dreamed of something hot—coffee, tea, soup. . . .

Damn. I'd dropped my coffee cup at the crash site. I tried to remember if it had my name on the bottom, but my mind drew a blank. Maybe the investigators would think it had come from the helicopter.

I crossed low ridges, one after the other, staying in the trees as much as possible. My boots and jeans couldn't get any wetter, so I splashed through the dwindling runoff without bothering to search out fords. I was almost across the third stream, deeper than the others, when I tripped and fell, face upstream. I swallowed a bellyful of muddy water before I crawled onto the bank. There I lay sobbing among the pine needles, unable to take a breath that didn't catch. It seemed as if I'd spent my entire day fighting water, mud, fear, and exhaustion. . . .

Exhaustion won.

The sun was low enough that the rays flooded beneath the clouds, touching my eyelids. I awoke slowly, as if my body was reluctant to let go of the safety of sleep. It was the first warmth I'd felt since the coffee and soup so many hours ago. The surface of the distant playa lake gleamed like a worn gold coin. Steam rose from the hillsides as evaporation sucked the runoff back toward the clouds. There was probably an hour's worth of light left. If I hurried, I'd make the cabin before night-cooled air dropped a new load of rain. Even now, lightning do-se-doed with the mountain peaks where thunderheads still dueled.

Overcoming inertia was the toughest thing I'd done all day. My body wanted to assume the fetal position and rest for at least a week. When I stretched, my body reacted as if I'd been used as a punching bag. Every single inch screamed when I sat up. It seemed like ages before I was upright, leaning against a half-dead pine. What a pair we made.

The sun dipped below the horizon. I'd never make the cabin before dark. I figured my dangerous trio would be long gone, so I headed for the road, where I'd be able to see or feel the graded roadbed even in the dark. I'd also stand less chance of breaking a leg in some rabbit hole.

I trudged along, feeling like one of those sculptures on the bow of a ship: woman with sea-soaked garb and flowing tresses, bravely broaching the wind and spray. My own mud-encrusted tresses had come loose from their braid and now hung lankly to my hips. If I'd had scissors right then, I would have chopped them off at the shoulders . . .

At the last curve in the road, I paused, testing the night. The line shack sat in the middle of an intramontane valley dotted with trees. But it was fully dark now. I couldn't see the trees, much less the shack.

No lights shone in the rectangular windows. I couldn't tell if there were fresh tire tracks in the yard. The breeze smelled of damp sage and pine resin. No smoke. No cooked food. I heard only the wind in the trees and a coyote on a nearby ridge.

It seemed safe enough. But just to make sure, I watched for another five minutes. I didn't dare sit—I wasn't sure I'd be able to get up again. Everything seemed quiet. Straightening, I followed the barb-wire fence beside the road until I reached the gate. The wire loop that held the gate closed was stretched taut, biting into the swollen cedar. I couldn't force the wire up and over the post. To climb or to wriggle? I'd had enough of crawling for the day . . . for a lifetime. I swung my leg over, snagging my pants on the wire. My fingers fumbled trying to unhook the coarse material. Giving up, I dropped into the yard. Casualties: a rip across my bumper, as Randy would have said, and a savage scratch. I hardly felt it.

Although I'd win no awards for stealth, the shack remained silent. I passed the well, passed the barbecue pit, left tracks even a two-year-old could follow. I didn't care. I could smell the rain coming. My tracks would be erased.

The front steps creaked under my tiptoeing boots. The door was unlocked, as I expected, for there was nothing of value inside. Or so I thought. Considering my track record for the day, I should have stopped thinking altogether.

An ancient Coleman lantern glowed faintly in the middle of the table. I hadn't seen the light because black cloth had been tacked over the windows. The old, gray metal-legged Formica table stood just as I'd left it last week. But carrots were piled on one side, next to a can of beef stew—*my* beef stew. The smell lingered in the air like yesterday's baking. A pile of ashes lay in the fireplace . . . I was sure Lon's round-up crew would have cleaned it out before they left.

My senses processed the information in record time. *Go*, a voice screamed inside my head. I wheeled toward the door, but stopped when I spotted the body, stretched out on the bunk bed under the window.

Alive or dead, I couldn't tell in the half-light. Adrenaline kicked in. I stumbled back outside, dragging the covering off the window next to the door as I went. I molded my body to the unpainted wall of the shack, listening. The breeze had died. Reassuring silence pushed at me from all sides.

My skin tightened, raising the fine hair on my arms. I peered in the window, needing that transparent barrier between the body and me: a woman's shape, oddly contorted, with pale hair. Her eyes were wide, startled.

Sylvie didn't seem to recognize me. But then, my own parents wouldn't have recognized me. I smiled reassuringly, as I tapped the glass, scaring her witless. Through the pane, I could hear her garbled cry through the gag. I assumed her hands and feet were tied, as well. I sensed there wasn't much time. I ran back inside, prying open the blade of my pocket knife on the way.

"Where's Tommy?" I asked, yanking down the gag. The knife sliced through the clothesline that bound her limbs. The rope seemed to be knotted in a million different places, forming a web.

"I left him with Bill and Randy this evening while I went home to get his night things. Eddie was still out looking for you. But Raef was there, waiting for me. Oh God, Frankie." It sounded like a prayer. "Hurry. He's just gone after firewood. He'll be back any second."

The last of the ropes parted. She swung her legs over the side of the bed. "I can't feel my feet."

Arm wrapped around her waist, I half-carried her to the door. We tried to be quiet, but we needn't have worried—all sound of our stumbling exit was lost in the hammering of rain on the tin roof. Pitch-black night enveloped us as we ran, thunder rumbled nearby.

Sylvie regained the strength in her legs, but developed a worse problem.

"I can't—" She doubled over, clutching her side. "Stitch. I'll have to slow down."

I slackened my pace.

"Where are we going?" she asked.

I could barely hear her. "There's an adit . . . across the valley."

"Adit?"

"Mine opening." I smiled. "We might have to kick out a snake or two, but it'll be dry."

She stopped, clutching a cottonwood for support. "No. His truck's—" The rest of the sentence was lost as thunder and lightning erupted simultaneously.

Too late. The flash outlined a tall, muscular figure holding wood like a sword above his head. I had a strobe-light impression of fierce beauty and strength, poised not five feet away.

In the darkness, I pivoted, and reached for Sylvie. She wasn't there. Pain exploded at the base of my neck. Then nothing.

———

167

I didn't know where I was, or how long I'd been unconscious. It was dark, the total darkness of an underground mine. Night or day? I couldn't tell.

I knew my eyes were open because I blinked, but my limbs seemed paralyzed. My brain sent signals to my fingers and toes: wiggle, twitch, *do* something. But the messages weren't delivered. Maybe I was dead, my spirit sticking around until my body grew cold.

Sound—a curious, atonal humming, coming closer. I wasn't alone, then. I almost recognized the melody. My mind grasped at the music as at a lifeline . . . "Amazing Grace," sung by a voice with no relative pitch. It definitely wasn't Sylvie. Nor Killeen. What was his name again, that form revealed by lightning?

Rape? No, stupid. Raef. Raef Kingsley. He was real. He was here, squatting next to my head. I could smell his skin, sweat mixed with wood smoke. I closed my eyes and held my breath. Light flared briefly, glowing red through the curtain of my eyelids. Then it was dark again. The humming was nearly drowned out by the rustling of dried brush being pushed against the opening of my narrow space. My mind automatically filled in the words. I couldn't be dead. Not if I could remember the words to a song that didn't get much airtime.

I heard pounding coming from above my head. The vibrations thumped my right cheek, which pressed against wet sand. Something gave way and sand trickled down on my face.

Raef was burying me alive.

I tried to scream, but my neck muscles refused to respond. I was lucky to be breathing. I had been wrong. The darkness before was high noon compared to the darkness of the grave.

Air. Was there enough trapped among the brush to support me until the paralysis left? Would it leave? Or would I lie here and slowly suffocate?

I felt the vibrations as he walked away. When the humming receded, I was more alone than I'd ever been in my life.

Was Sylvie dead? Buried nearby? No. If Raef had wanted to kill her, he'd have done it earlier.

Unable to move, I retreated into my head, waiting for the paralysis to leave. No one but Raef knew where I was. I cursed my stupidity. I should have taken my chances with Killeen and Bill. Surely Bill wouldn't have let Milo hurt me. We'd known each other too long. Hot-wiring my Jeep was one thing—a childish act to get my attention. But I was positive he wouldn't harm me. So why hadn't I trusted him? Because of Geoff, who'd lied to me, and stolen from me . . . and paid a higher price than anyone asked. Would I pay a similar price for refusing to trust my friends? Would it be three long months before my body was found?

I refused to panic, because that would use up air. Air was precious. I forced myself to breathe slowly, calmly.

How long did I lie there? I don't know. A second is a lifetime; an hour, eternity. In my head, I recited the geologic time scale, created a class syllabus, and composed poetry—each image more morbid than the last. That wouldn't help. I changed tactics, searching for uplifting verse, but my brain was sluggish now, as the air grew thinner. I passed out, slept, I don't know which. . . .

A scrabbling sound roused me. He was back, the bastard. Checking on me?

More earth shifted down, cutting off my air supply. Then there was silence. I didn't know how long it would be before I used up the available oxygen. I closed my eyes and tried desperately to wiggle a finger. My right foot twitched. The wires were crossed, but something was happening. I tried again. My left index finger poked my thigh. Progress. A deep breath? No good. My chest muscles refused to respond.

More scrabbling accompanied by snuffling. Not Raef . . . Raef wouldn't be digging me out. I hoped to God that it wasn't a starving mountain lion. Please don't let it be a mountain lion. The digging caused sand to collapse on my head, clog my nose, eyes, ears. I sneezed, and found I was able to lift my head slightly. The eerie barking yelp of a coyote accompanied frenzied pawing. A section of the thin, brush-and-dirt wall fell away; sweet air flowed in on my face.

I could breathe. Finally, the rain had stopped. The moon was up, shining with the stars between lenses of cloud pushed ahead of the wind. And it was cold. The temperature had fallen as the low swept through. Beside my head, the coyote stood, front feet splayed, watching. She stayed motionless, alert, as I moved my head again and grunted. The pale eyes caught starlight as she turned and loped away, back legs limping.

With hope, energy began to flow through my veins. I concentrated on movement. Slowly, painfully, my body began to respond. I ignored the ache in my neck and head, the scraped hands and bruised body. Ignored my thirst. I moved, lurched, wriggled my way out of the grave, like a snake shedding its worn-out skin.

On my knees, I stared at the moon, trying to figure out where I was. I found the North Star, made out the large cottonwood in the center of the valley. I was due west of the cabin, at the very edge of the valley.

Raef had dumped me where water had undercut old valley fill. He'd shoved me under the cut, piled brush across the opening, and then caved in the bank over me. I was grateful he'd taken time to collect the brush . . . otherwise, I'd be ant food. It was odd to feel grateful to a murderer.

What next? It would be useless to storm the cabin again, assuming Sylvie was still there. I was no match for Raef. Hell, at this point, I'd be no match for a newborn. I needed help. I started walking again, which triggered waves of gnawing hunger.

I couldn't remember my last full meal. I pulled the Power Bars from the back pocket of my vest. The foil wrapping had kept out the sand and water. I ate one as I trudged along. It tasted like a Tootsie Roll left over from last Halloween. I wondered how long it would take to convert the sugar to energy.

I wasn't dressed for cold weather. Damp work shirt, damp jeans, damp vest—my clothes sucked the heat from my body, to be replaced by wave after wave of chills. I walked quickly, hoping that movement would warm my blood and stave off hypothermia. Fighting the wind and cold sapped my reserves. For the first time, I doubted that I had the strength to go the distance.

Pain. I'd played sports with broken fingers, a cracked rib, torn muscles. I'd left patches of skin on various mountainsides. But this was different. I couldn't seem to disassociate my mind from the parts that hurt. With each step, the wet clothes rubbed every square inch of my body, the silt-saturated fabric acting like sandpaper. *Buff* took on a whole new meaning. But I kept stumbling along.

There was the faintest hint of light in the eastern sky when I stopped to eat the second bar. I'd traveled two miles, maybe three. It was hard to tell. My legs were on autopilot, my mind lost somewhere in the ether.

The truck came out of nowhere, pinning me in its headlights. A door slammed.

"Frankie?" Killeen's voice. He sounded as if he'd seen a ghost. Maybe he had.

I started to run, back up the road, but he moved like a blur. His leg swept the back of my knees, and I collapsed. He caught me before I landed in a graceless heap at his feet. I struggled, but he wrapped my hair around his fist. I wasn't going anywhere.

Eighteen

"Stand still," Killeen said.

"I have a choice?"

"No. Why'd you run? I wouldn't hurt you."

"Milo."

He paused, as if trying to make sense of the name. "Milo's not here."

"He was with you . . . with you and Bill."

When he let go of my hair, I sank to the ground. "Where?" he asked, as if it were the most important question in the world.

"Near Easy's cabin. You stopped. I hid near the road."

He just stood there, silently staring at the damage revealed by the growing light. I refused to meet his eyes. For some reason, I felt ashamed for not trusting him.

"Anderson and I were looking for you. Gates tagged along." he said.

"Milo threatened me the night before."

"I didn't know. . . . You look like a prisoner of war."

"You don't know the half of it." I started to shake again, in waves that wracked my whole body. I could feel tears cutting miniature gullies through the dirt on my face, but I made no attempt to brush them away. The last of my energy drained away with the tears.

"It'll wait." He took a blanket from behind the seat, and wrapped it around me. It was blessedly warm from lying on the drive train. He lifted me into the truck before pressing a cup of coffee into my hands. "Sorry. No cream."

"It's all right," I whispered, sipping the bitter brew. "Killeen, Raef has Sylvie."

"I know. He got her yesterday, while I was out lookin' for you."

"They're here."

"Not a chance. They were sighted in Pocatello."

"They're here. At the line shack."

"You're sure?"

"I found her . . . last night. But we couldn't get away. Raef knocked me out. I assume he got her back. I was heading to town for help."

He put the truck into reverse. "I'll drive you to Pair-a-Dice, then round up the others."

"I don't think there's time. It's almost sun-up. They might disappear before you get back. I'd never forgive myself."

He shifted back to neutral and leaned on the steering wheel, thinking. "You sure?"

"Yes. Do you have your gun?"

He lifted his hat from the seat. The gun and holster coiled there next to my thigh like a rattlesnake ready to strike. Coffee sloshed out onto my lap as another wave shook me. Killeen dabbed at the wet spot with a corner of the blanket.

"Is there more coffee?" The caffeine felt wonderful. I could take on the world.

He uncorked a battered steel thermos and poured, while my fingers curved gratefully around the warmth. The cup felt familiar. "My mug . . . "

"Found it beside the road. Bovey's helicopter was at the bottom of the canyon." He started the truck due west, toward the line shack.

"Did Milo see it?" I asked.

"The helicopter? Yeah."

"The cup."

"Nope. I slipped it into the truck while he was checkin' the crash site. Your name's on the bottom. I figured I'd ask you before I showed it to anybody."

"Lon ran me off the road—"

"I found your Jeep. Nowhere near the helicopter . . . "

"He came back to finish the job. I'd rather keep that between us."

"I don't have a problem with that. Want to tell me about it?"

The world seemed to fragment for a moment. I'd tucked yesterday's horrors into a little compartment in my brain. They refused to come out. Perhaps it was better that way—at least for now.

"Later," I said. "When this is over. The shack's just ahead, in the valley on the left. We should walk from here. Do you have a rubber band?" I'd braided my hair, and sat holding the end so it wouldn't unravel.

He pulled one off the radio knob. Eyebrow raised, he offered the dirty pink treasure.

"Don't tell me—I wouldn't win any beauty contests."

He grinned. "I know better than to touch that line."

We leaned against the cherty limestone cliff that marked the entrance to the valley. Killeen had wanted me to stay in the truck, but I'd refused. Two against one seemed like better odds, especially when the one was crazy.

Cottonwoods seemed to float in the fog shrouding the valley floor. The morning star winked out, overtaken by golden light. To the north, a coyote bayed, another answered. I wondered if one was *my* coyote. The smells of sage and wet earth mingled with wood smoke. In this bucolic dawn-time, it seemed impossible that dark minds stirred below the flame-tipped clouds clinging to southern peaks. Impossible until I glanced at my hands, saw the lacerated skin, bruised knuckles, scored nails. Yesterday was real. Last night was real.

"What's the layout?" Killeen's lips hardly moved.

I drew in the dirt with a stick: outhouse, well, shack, fence. Smoke spiraled lazily up from the chimney. The wind, reduced to a whisper, wouldn't cover our advance.

We moved together from one bush or tree to the next. Limp, pause; limp, pause—a new kind of dance. I wasn't the best dancer in the world. My attempts to imitate Killeen's silent, economic movements proved unsuccessful because I ran like a wounded giraffe. If we arrived at the side window unobserved, it was a credit to Killeen.

We knelt under the windowsill. Slowly, he raised his head to peer through the glass. He touched my shoulder. "Stay here."

Without waiting for an answer, he dashed for the front door, pushing it open so softly it made no noise. I watched through the window. Nothing moved in the shadows. The room was empty. We were too late.

I crept around to the front. Pine and cottonwood logs still smoldered in the rock fireplace. Congealed remains of Dinty Moore beef stew decorated two paper plates on the table. The ropes and gag were gone. Sylvie must be alive . . . and with Raef. I'd hoped, somehow, that she'd gotten away last night.

"Looks like he means to come back," said Killeen.

"He's probably gone after Tommy. We should check the adit across the valley. Just before Raef hit me, Sylvie said something about his truck. He might have hidden it there. He might have left her there, too."

The adit was perhaps a quarter of a mile away. We could have driven, but if Raef were still around, he'd hear the noise. We skulked again. I seemed to be improving.

The adit was a rectangular reinforced tunnel heading straight back into the limestone. I had no idea what the miner had been after—not phosphate, for this was too high in the section. I saw no surface alteration, and the limestone wasn't pure enough for cement. Killeen waved me to one side of the entrance, while he took the other, gun drawn. I tossed a rock into the tunnel, but heard only the *clunk* of it landing. No scurrying of creatures big or little. No rattling, either.

Killeen pulled a pen-sized flashlight from his pocket. A truck's tire tracks showed clearly on the dusty floor. I followed so close on his heels I almost tripped him. A small wooden ramp lay about twenty feet in, between Diane's cherry-red Harley and a mountain bike. A shotgun lay on the rocky floor. Killeen used a clean white handkerchief to pick it up and examine it.

"Bert Hogue was shot twice with his own shotgun," Killeen said, as he automatically checked the barrels. They were empty. "I guess Kingsley didn't take the extra shells."

I could almost hear the cogs turning in Killeen's brain as he stared at the booty. "He could go anywhere . . . ditch a vehicle in Utah, and have an easy downhill bike ride back to Pair-a-Dice. Could pedal around town at night, give his boy a ride—no one would hear him. And there isn't a road in this region he couldn't take with that motorcycle. . . . I underestimated him." He admitted it as if it were a mortal sin. Maybe it was. "You didn't hear or see a truck last night?" he asked me.

"No. But the wind might have covered it. Or he could have left as soon as he buried me." I spoke without thinking, forgetting I hadn't told him about last night. My breathing was loud in the silence that followed. Turning, I hobbled outside, escaping nightmare images evoked by the darkness of the tunnel. He followed more slowly toward the soft gray of dawn. I felt his hand on my shoulder.

"Don't say anything," I said. "Please. I'm feeling rather fragile. And we still have to find Sylvie."

He squeezed my shoulder. "When the time comes, I'll handle him, Frankie." I wasn't sure what he meant; wasn't sure I *wanted* to know. But it must be nice, I thought, to feel that confident.

We walked side-by-side toward the truck, eyes scouring the ground for Sylvie's footprints. Behind the house, I stopped. Killeen was so deep in thought, he didn't notice for a few steps.

"What's the matter?"

"The coffee," I said. "I need to use the outhouse."

The outhouse door was wedged shut with a log. I assumed the round-up crew had left it that way—until I heard a moaning sound from within.

"Killeen!" I kicked the log aside and pulled open the door. Sylvie tumbled out into my arms, knocking us both to the ground. Killeen cut loose with a string of epithets as he sliced the ropes. I untied the gag, the same black sash she'd worn yesterday. We half-carried her to the side of the house, away from the stench of the place.

Killeen held her fragile form against his chest. She didn't cry, just dragged in deep, shuddering breaths. With an angry flick of the wrist, Killeen brushed a black widow from her hair, then ground it under his heel. His face was bleak as he stroked the fine strands, murmured soothing words.

"He put me in there because I tried to escape." Sylvie's whispered. "That's what they did when he tried to run away from the orphanage—locked him in a shed every night for a week . . . with the spiders."

She pushed herself away from Killeen. "Raef went after Tommy. He left hours ago. I had to describe Randy's house, but I told him it was on the other side of town. He'll come back when he doesn't find it. If we hurry—"

"Too late, love."

I was too slow. By the time Killeen had drawn his gun and stepped in front of Sylvie, I was yanked back against Raef's chest, with a knife at my throat. He twisted my braid between his fingers. I should have chopped it off yesterday, when I'd felt the urge.

Stalemate.

"You're dead," he said in my ear. There was an odd note in his voice.

"Apparently not."

"But I made sure you weren't breathing."

I kept my tone matter-of-fact. "My great-grandmother said once that I'd live to be one hundred and two." She'd said nothing of the kind.

"Mebbe so. We'll see."

Not the response I wanted. Each person waited for the other to move. Killeen had inched to his left, giving him a better shot at Raef.

"You kill me, you'll never find my boy."

Sylvie stumbled forward, put a restraining hand on Killeen's forearm. "Wait, Eddie. You've got Tommy?" she asked Raef.

"Sure as death."

"Is he okay?"

"For now."

"What do you want?" Killeen's voice was resigned. He couldn't take the chance that Raef was bluffing.

"What's mine."

"She's not a horse. She doesn't *belong* to you. She doesn't belong to anyone."

"As long as she's alive, Sylvie belongs to me. Two halves of a whole. She knows it—see? She's still wearing my ring." All eyes focused on the plain gold band. Sylvie twisted it off and flung it at the outhouse door. It ricocheted off into the weeds. "Don't change nothin', Sylvie. I'll just buy you another. Now, drop the gun, man."

Killeen's face remained impassive, but his hands moved more swiftly than my eyes could track. He ejected the clip, threw it over our heads, tossed the gun at my feet.

"Smart," Raef said. "Now, give Sylvie the back-up clip."

"Don't have one."

Raef pressed the knife harder. I expected to feel a trickle of blood slide down my throat, but the mud caked on my neck must have protected my skin. I stared straight ahead, willing my face not to show fear. Inside, there was turmoil. Killeen didn't even blink.

Raef was becoming impatient. He tightened his hold on my hair, pressing the swollen patch where he'd hit me last night. I slumped against him as the world turned foggy.

"Don't pass out on me, girl. We got a long way to go. Come on, Sylvie."

"Why take Frankie?" Killeen asked. "She'll just weigh you down."

"One less behind me. I'll turn her loose down the road a piece."

"Like you did those Canadian women? Like you did Emmajean Rogers?"

"I didn't kill that Wells girl. The others deserved what they got. Sylvie?"

She didn't hesitate—turned on a dime and started for the truck. Killeen met her eyes briefly before he stepped aside to let us pass.

"If I see you in my mirror, one dies. I won't tell you which one."

I had to distract Raef, keep him from disabling Killeen's truck. When we were near the valley wall, I started to weave, nearly tripping Raef who walked just behind me, still holding my braid like a halter. My shoulder blades twitched as if the knife were homing in on the shortest path to my heart.

"What's wrong?"

"I feel dizzy." I put a hand to my forehead.

"Walk, or I'll cut your throat."

How could I argue with that approach? I walked, but I bumped into Sylvie, who put her right arm around my waist for support. When I stumbled into the side of Killeen's truck, Raef slapped the back of my head. I doubled over with nausea—for real, this time.

"Leave her alone, Raef. She's hurt," said Sylvie. "You have me. You don't need her anymore."

He stood in front of me, like judge and jury. I had a good look at him for the first time. The sun rose above the eastern horizon, shining straight into the canyon. He was a couple of inches taller than I, with a beautifully shaped head, high cheekbones, heavily muscled neck and torso. He stood there, relaxed, smiling, in a white sweatshirt with the sleeves ripped off, olive cotton work pants about three inches too short, rubber-soled sandals on surprisingly small feet. He looked like an athlete in peak condition. Not a killer.

"No, love." His teeth were perfect except for one gray, dead canine. "She's my good-luck charm, my shield. I bury her—she rises. I cut her—she doesn't bleed."

Without being told, I started for the pick-up parked close behind Killeen's. Maybe he'd forget—

"Wait," said Raef. He leaned down and stabbed Killeen's rear tire. The air whooshing out described a fan in the damp sand. "Smart—but not smart enough."

He found my angry glare very funny. Laughter echoed off the cliffs, scaring a peregrine falcon off her nest. I lifted my hand to brush back the hair that had come loose. The laughter stopped abruptly. He let go of my hair, grabbed my right wrist, staring at the soft ventral surface.

"The mark of the Spider." His voice held fear, or perhaps awe. He rubbed the dull edge of the knife over the nickel-size scar on my wrist. I'd tripped while running with a glass when I was four and needed thirty stitches to close the jagged wound. I looked to Sylvie for explanation.

"In Jamaica, *Anancy*, the Spider, is a hero. He fooled Death," said Sylvie.

Raef pointed at the back of his hand with the knife. There was a scarred pit in the center with eight white lines radiating out. I knew of only one spider bite with that result: the brown recluse. I looked at my own scar, trying to see it through Raef's eyes. It did resemble a spider, albeit a dead one with curled-up legs. But then, we all see what we want to see.

Raef dragged me forward. Another *whoosh* sounded as he slashed Killeen's right front tire. Damn. Killeen had only one spare. I looked back at the line shack. Killeen was out of sight. I had to trust that somehow he'd find a way to follow us.

"Where did you hide Tommy?" Sylvie asked.

Raef regained his sense of humor. "I lied. Couldn't find the house. You'll take me to him, or I'll do something worse than kill your friend."

So that was the real reason he'd brought me along—to hold as a sword over Sylvie's head once she learned he didn't have Tommy. I kicked my mind into gear. If Sylvie and I escaped in different directions, Raef would lose his sword, and Tommy would remain safely hidden away.

Raef read my thoughts. Dropping my wrist, he backhanded me across the face. When I could focus again, Sylvie knelt beside me. Plastic handcuffs joined my left wrist to her right.

NINETEEN

"Get up," Raef said.

"I'm sorry, Frankie," Sylvie said, helping me to Raef's truck.

Not half as sorry as I was. But I didn't say it. What would be the point?

"Shall I drive?" I asked.

He hesitated, looking for the flaw in the offer. I prayed they didn't practice reverse psychology in Jamaica.

"No. You'd run us into a ditch. Sylvie will drive."

"But you know I don't drive a stick-shift, Raef."

Exasperated, he opened the passenger door and shoved us inside. He hadn't left the keys in the ignition. . . . Nothing was going my way today. While he walked around the truck, I slid the army knife from the case on my belt and into my left hand. He'd never thought to check me for weapons. If he were distracted, I might have a moment to open it.

My feet knocked over something on the floor—a gallon-size pickle jar with air holes punched in the lid. I bent closer to take a look, accidentally yanking Sylvie with me. Inside the homemade collecting jar, cardboard partitions divided the space into six segments, each containing an asymmetrical web . . . *Anancy* . . . black widows and brown recluses inhabited Raef's spider motel. I backed up so quickly I banged the back of my head on the rear window. My vision blurred for a moment, and the pain grew more intense. I think I whimpered.

179

Raef grinned. "Ever been locked in a small, dark space—like the boot of an automobile? I have. It's bad, man. No room to turn around . . . hot . . . not much air. These things you don't forget."

I swore I heard scrabbling sounds from the jar. I prayed the lid was screwed on tight.

"Those women, now. I tied them nice and tight. Let the spiders crawl *all* over. Up and down, in and out. One was so scared, she almost died right off. What's the fun in that, I ask you? Other one . . . well, she took longer. Sometimes I opened the trunk and prodded 'em a bit. The spiders, I mean. A bite here, a nip there. Slow." Raef's black eyes held mine, as if to will a reaction. "They screamed. Over and over. I didn't scream. A little boy like that should've screamed, don't you think? But I didn't. I was strong, stronger than those women. . . . You'd scream. I can tell. But out here, who'd hear you?"

I turned, stared out the window, swallowing to control the nausea. Beside me, Sylvie was sobbing. I squeezed her hand. After a moment, Raef started driving. He drove a lot faster than I did on these dirt roads. My head hit the roof at each bump. So did his, but he didn't seem to notice. I felt miserable. I'd never used the outhouse, and now each jolt was agony. In more ways than one: my head ached so badly I wanted to scream; my cheek was swelling; I'd probably have a black eye. I felt anger surge and spread throughout my body, heightening my awareness. I would not go meekly with Raef Kingsley.

"Sylvie, love, stop crying now. Believe me, those women were sent to me. Being locked away in prison brought all the memories back. That's where I started my spider collection. I found them everywhere. A sign from God. A sign the wrongs would be made right. And when I got out, God put those women in my path. They had *her* voice, *her* eyes, *her* way of talking down to me. Amazing how God works with you, and for you, if you just give yourself to Him." He stopped speaking to concentrate on a deeply rutted section of road.

"Amazing," I agreed.

"At the end, I gave them a friendship necklace—get it? A friendship necklace?" His laugh was rich music in a minor key. It sounded so normal, so sane. "They were hurting so bad they even thanked me when I twisted it around their necks."

If I'd been through what they had, I'd have welcomed death, too. I picked up the pickle jar and threw it out the window. It shattered on a black chert boulder. Welcome to Nevada.

"I wish you hadn't done that," Raef said, staring at the rearview mirror. "It wasn't right."

A knotted length of doubled-over rope hung from the mirror. The necklace swung to and fro with a hypnotic movement. I imagined it tightening around the necks of two women, as it might soon twist around mine. Or Sylvie's. And then what would happen to Tommy? . . . Tommy—just a little boy caught in a web of hatred and revenge. It was up to Randy and Bill to protect him now.

We left the canyon, started across the sloping alluvium, paralleling the face of the mountains. I felt the truck slow as Raef saw dust in the distance, but he stuck with the road. When we arrived at the edge of the next canyon, part of the road was washed away, and boulders littered the sandy bottom. The truck lurched left, then right, as Raef fought for control. . . . I opened the knife, hiding it, blade down, beneath my hand.

We climbed out of the canyon. The dust was closer now, and I thought I could make out four large vehicles. Fate had sent the thumper crew to survey this section of the range first.

Raef's face was fierce with concentration. Skin stretched tautly over cheekbones, forehead furrowed, his eyes never left the road. It was as if he'd forgotten about Sylvie and me. I slid the blade between my skin and the plastic bond. The next bump severed the handcuffs.

The creak of the truck jolting back on the road covered Sylvie's gasp. I pressed her hand, hoping she'd shut up. The knife slid back into its leather holder. I waited, poised, right hand on the window ledge, just above the door handle.

The geophysical crew saw us coming. They pulled as far off the one-vehicle track as they could, but Raef had to slow down to go around them. As we reached the last truck, I opened the door, executed a diving roll over my right shoulder, and came up in a crouch. I heard Sylvie scream. Door flapping at each rut, the truck continued down the road, gaining speed.

The driver of the last thumper truck came running. "You all right?" she asked.

I nodded, trying to pull breath back into my lungs. The look on her face said she wasn't convinced. There was a buzzing sound, growing louder, that seemed to be in my head. The rest of the crew gathered around, a babble of voices talking at once.

"Why didn't he stop?"

"What the hell was he trying—"

"Lunatic ought to—"

I interrupted them with a raised hand. They gently lifted me to my feet, and dusted me off. It didn't help much. I still looked as if I'd spent the night in a mud-wrestling tournament.

"Can you call for help?" I croaked.

"Better," the first woman said. "I'll drive you to town."

"Call the sheriff first. The driver of that truck killed two women in Utah. Now he's going after his son, the boy that was missing two days ago. Tommy Kingsley. Tell the police that Raef Kingsley's heading for the Anderson place."

The woman was already moving toward her truck when a motorcycle appeared over the rise. Killeen, on Diane's stolen motorcycle, pulled up next to us in a cloud of dust.

"We're late," he said.

The White Rabbit couldn't have made a more startling entrance. I mounted behind him, careful of my abused body. When I wrapped my arms about his bulky waist, I felt the gun resting again in its holster. The liars' club added one new member—either that, or he'd found his clip.

"You are the most welcome sight in the world," I shouted in his ear. I could feel the vibrations as he grunted.

He did not return the compliment.

———

The only change in the Anderson shack since the last time I'd visited was that Randy wasn't stretched out on the sofa watching the mountains. He was lying on the ground, unconscious.

I touched his neck. The jugular pulse felt steady, strong. Raef must have been more interested in grabbing Tommy and getting away than in killing. I wondered where Bill was.

Killeen checked the cabin while I tried to revive Randy. We needed whatever information he had.

"Was Tommy still here?" I asked Killeen.

"Can't say for sure. I didn't see a child's footprints. . . . Raef parked the truck by the side of the shack. He must have sent Sylvie to talk to Randy, then clobbered him from behind. Wouldn't have taken more than a few seconds. They're maybe five minutes ahead of us right now."

Perhaps they'd carried Tommy. Perhaps he hadn't been here after all. Randy groaned. When his eyelids fluttered open, the dilated pupils made his eyes look black. I moved so the sun struck his face. The pupils contracted. I hoped that meant he didn't have a concussion. "How do you feel?" I asked.

"Like I been kicked by a bull. What happened?"

"Raef came for the boy," Killeen said. "Where is he?"

"With Freda." Randy sat up, swayed, then let his head rest on his upraised knees. There was a lump right at the base of his skull. We were twins. "She promised him a ride in her wheelchair." He lifted his head again, focused on me for the first time. "What the devil happened to you?"

"It's a long story. Where's Bill?"

"Out looking for you. Wanted to get an early start 'cause he was gonna climb Red Mountain. I was just writing a note for Killeen, when Sylvie arrived."

"Can you drive?" Killeen asked him.

"I think so."

"Then get Pete and whoever else you can find, and meet us at Freda's."

I was already running to the motorcycle. "Tell Isabel to call Buddy," I yelled over my shoulder.

"Step careful," he called back. "Freda's got a sawed-off shotgun under the bar." He yelled something else, but the sound was lost in the roar of the motorcycle. I hoped it wasn't important.

We took the shortest route. Maybe we should have waited for Buddy, but it honestly didn't occur to me that we'd need help. Killeen seemed determined enough to take on the world. And he had a gun.

I should have known it wouldn't be that easy.

We parked out of sight, not wanting to alarm Raef. His truck was parked on the windowless side of the bar, under a huge cottonwood. We paused there for a moment, listening, looking. We were at the edge of town, only the mountains and bajada lay behind. No voices lanced the morning stillness, an unnatural stillness broken only by a killdeer, calling from the underbrush. Smashed beer bottles, remnants of the dance two nights ago, littered the ground, but the tire tracks had been washed away.

Killeen circled toward the front door while I took the rear. I crept as silently as possible around the corner of the building. The loading dock was a concrete slab stretching the width of the back of the building. Heavy metal doors opened out, as inviting as a crypt. Flattened bales of corrugated cardboard boxes, stamped with brands of liquor and frozen pizza, formed a pile to the right. Empty milk crates were stacked on the left. A dolly lay like a body, toes up, in the dirt. Beside it, a line of drops trailed up onto the slab where they soaked into the porous surface. The saturated ground couldn't absorb the blood droplets. The larger ones reflected the flood-lamps above the door. I found it odd that the lamps were still on, an hour after sunrise.

My mind processed the information in an instant. Cold air rushed like a wave from the black hole of the doorway. There had been no shots, no sounds of struggle. As I hesitated, the flood lights flickered once, went out, came back on. The sequence was repeated. Again. SOS? From Freda? Killeen? I heard a thud, like a body falling.

I couldn't do it—couldn't force my boots to step up on the concrete, couldn't enter that black square. I was entombed again, night air blocked by sand and brush. The blood drops glowed on the hard-packed dirt, turned brown on the gray cement. I fought panic. For the first time in my life, my body refused a direct order from my mind. Or maybe my mind was sending the wrong signals. Maybe I should listen.

Fear. I'd never, truly, feared a man before. I was tall, strong, intelligent, and in better physical shape than the average male. And for much of my life, I'd had family at my back. No sane person tangled with a woman whose brothers topped them by half a foot and outweighed them by thirty pounds. But my family wasn't here, I was hurt . . . and Raef wasn't sane.

Insanity scared the hell out of me. I couldn't predict how he'd act, much less react. I hadn't the faintest idea how to proceed in a world where disorder ruled. I stood paralyzed by indecision.

One step at a time, I thought. Make a plan. . . . Any action is better than inaction. No it's not. Action could get someone killed—could get *me* killed. I hadn't survived the last twenty-four hours just to die on a beautiful, sunlit morning when the sky reflected deep blue in the mud puddles and the air smelled of sage. Furthermore, I flat-out refused to die in an obscure corner of Nevada apart from my family and friends.

Where the hell were Randy and Pete? How long did it take to drive from the shack to the restaurant? One minute? Three? Unless Bill had the truck, and Randy had to walk. Damn. Was that what Randy had yelled after us? Was he lying unconscious in the middle of Not So Easy Street?

I focused on the blood. Whose blood? We'd heard no shots, so it couldn't be Raef's or Sylvie's. Inside that building, someone needed help, but Killeen didn't know. Killeen *had* to know.

I stepped up onto the slab. The movement seemed to break the spellbound morning. The dirt-charged denim molding my inner thighs brushed together, loud as a swarm of cicadas devouring a pear tree. I heard a dragging sound from the black hole of the doorway, then Raef's voice, muffled, but the cadence clear. Killeen's quiet rumble. A female scream was amplified by a child's—Sylvie and Tommy. I had no choice. I plunged into the dark.

Of course I tripped, sprawled headlong over a man's body, and hit my chin on his head. I felt and heard the breath explode from his lungs—an effective Heimlich maneuver, except he hadn't been choking. My eyes adjusted to the dim light. I rolled him over, raised his arms to force air into his lungs. His eyes opened, reflecting squares of sunlight from the open door. After a moment, he recognized me.

"I'm sorry, Walker," I whispered. "Where are you hurt?" Stupid question. He probably hurt all over after that body slam.

He looked confused, eyebrows nearly meeting to make a line across his forehead. When he touched the side of his head, his hand came away covered in blood. My chin felt wet and sticky with the stuff. But under my hand, his heartbeat was strong.

"I have to help Freda," I said, pushing him down as he started to sit up. "Stay still. I'll come back for you." I hoped it was true. I refused to think of the alternatives.

His eyelids drooped, hiding the reflected light. I patted his chest, stepped over him, and put my ear to the inner door. Its wood smelled faintly of varnish and stale beer. I looked around for anything I could use as a weapon. Crates of liquor were stacked on one side of the room; a commercial refrigerator-freezer, surrounded by empty silver beer kegs, dominated the other side. I spotted a crowbar hanging between two nails on the wall. Reaching for it, my hand brushed a square of dark cloth tacked to the door at eye level. It felt like a spider's web. Shuddering, I lifted it and peered through a small diamond-shaped window at a motionless tableau in the main room.

Killeen stood, arms slightly away from his sides, backlit by the open front door. A Budweiser clock on the left wall showed six-thirty. Lights behind the bar reflected from the inset glass and polished surface. Sylvie stood to the right, clutching Tommy in her arms, his head pressed against her neck. I couldn't see Freda.

Killeen and Sylvie's attention focused on a point to my left. I shifted, pressed my right eye to the glass. Raef, towering above the bar from his stance on Freda's wheelchair ramp, smiled jovially. His hand held a sawed-off shotgun. The barrel gleamed dully in the minimal light.

If I barged in, Raef might use the gun, or he might not. I'd either be dead or a hostage again. If I did nothing, Raef might shoot Killeen or Freda. At the very least, he'd take Sylvie and Tommy. Once they were in the truck, I doubted he'd let them go—alive, at any rate. Hearing Killeen's voice, I pushed open the door a crack, praying the hinges were freshly oiled.

"Now?" Raef answered. "Now, *we* leave. *You* stay."

"The police will follow you."

"So? It's a big country. I'll disappear—poof!—into the air. Just like I did before."

I couldn't tell from his tone if he meant that literally or figuratively.

"They'll find you. You killed one of theirs." Killeen was playing for time, waiting for a diversion. Me. His eyes flickered to the little window that framed my face. Almost imperceptibly he shifted his body an inch, two inches. . . . He was going to put himself between Sylvie and Raef.

There wasn't time for me to run outside, disable Raef's truck, and get back before Raef dragged Sylvie and Tommy out the door. Where the hell were Pete and Randy?

"Sylvie and Tommy could be hurt," Killeen continued.

"Don't scare the boy. He knows I'll take care of him." The smile flickered out. "Time to go. You—move over there." Raef pointed with the shotgun at the barstool farthest from the door.

I shoved the swinging door and launched myself through the opening. At the same time, Freda flicked on the black lights, turning Raef's sweatshirt an eerie purple-white. Startled, Raef pivoted on the balls of his feet. I brought the crowbar up, knocking his wrist toward the ceiling. The shotgun's discharge was deafening in the cavernous room. A Tiffany-style lamp shattered into a thousand fragments. Tommy screamed. I swung the crowbar again, this time at his shins. Raef teetered, then fell backwards off the ramp, landing like a cat on all fours at my feet. The impact triggered the second blast. Chunks of wood flew from the wall near the end of the bar. Damn, that was close. The stench of gunpowder filled the air. I thought I heard a truck engine sputter to life.

I had no room to maneuver. I stepped back, raised my weapon to strike his head. Too slow . . . always too slow. Transferring the gun to his left hand, Raef hit the back of my knees. I crumpled. The crowbar glanced harmlessly off his shoulder as he dropped the useless gun and vaulted the bar. Even without the use of his right arm, he looked graceful.

"You don't kill worth a damn, girl," he said, landing lightly.

I wasn't quite sure which way he meant it, but I didn't care as long as he left me alone. It was up to Killeen, now.

In the distance, I heard running steps . . . then nothing.

TWENTY

I tried to pull myself up, but my lower right leg was numb. There was a whirring in the shadows behind me at the left end of the bar. I flinched, clutched the crowbar more tightly, and struggled to turn my body. Freda was on the ramp above me, hand extended.

"I'm not sure I can stand," I said.

"I was after the gun."

"Oh." I felt foolish. First things first. There were extra shells in a box under the counter. Raef hadn't thought to look, or had been too distracted. I passed up the gun and watched her feed shells into the twin chambers before placing it in a tooled-leather holster attached to the right side of the wheelchair.

"Where's Killeen?" I asked.

"He got Tommy and the girl out. Raef went after them." She surveyed her domain, controlled anger showing on the square, Germanic face. "What a mess. Hope the insurance will cover it. Want some help?" She offered her hand.

I took it gratefully. Freda pulled me upright as easily as if I'd been a featherweight, dismissing my thanks with a wave of her hand. While I leaned on the bar, testing my legs to see if they'd carry me as far as the restroom, Freda wheeled to the phone on the end of the counter.

"Line's been cut," she said a moment later. "I'll have to use the CB in the van."

"Just give me a minute." I slowly crossed the floor, turned at the restroom door. "Oh, damn. Freda? Walker's hurt. He's on the floor in the back room. I'll help you—"

But I was talking to a swinging door.

I sat in that bathroom for ten years—at least it seemed that way. It couldn't have been more than a minute or two, but my body refused to be hurried. After washing my hands and face, I gathered the curtain of hair that had come loose again, twisted it into a coil and stuffed it down the neck of my shirt. Not much of an improvement, according to the mirror. My eyes were red-veined pewter chips in a bronze face sharpened by fatigue. One cheek was puffy where Raef had struck me, and I'd lost one of my great-grandmother's silver earrings. Black hair was streaked with clay, speckled with sand and bits of brush. Boris Karloff and I had a lot in common.

The dirt from my adventures now littered the sink. I wiped it clean with a paper towel. My hands, scraped raw on palms and knuckles, ended in broken fingernails. My legs shook so badly I had to clutch the sink for support.

The loud drone of the overhead fan provided a white noise. A terrorist could have destroyed the bar and I wouldn't have known. But I couldn't hide in here forever. Freda needed me. Walker needed me. I was tired of people depending on me. I just wanted to go home.

I opened the door. The room was empty. I was beside the pool tables by the time my eyes adjusted to the shadows. Colored glass crackled underfoot. I heard an engine start up, and then the crunch of gravel as Freda drove past the front door. Amazing woman. Somehow she must have maneuvered Walker into the big blue van and was taking him to the clinic. She hadn't waited for me. She must have figured I'd already gone to find another phone.

For the last two days I'd felt like clever Sisyphus, condemned for eternity to push the boulder up the mountain in Hades, only to have it slide down again as he reached the brink of the summit. If Raef were to come back now, I wouldn't have the strength to fight him. I didn't have the strength to shift a pebble.

Adrenaline gone, I limped on jelly-legs as far as the bar, collapsing on a stool. I was too tired to drink, too tired to eat, too tired to walk back to the motel. Even my lumpy bed in a trashed room sounded wonderful. A shower would be heaven. I'd crouch under the spray until the hot water ran out. But I couldn't walk that far, not till my limbs stopped shaking. I'd given up on Randy and Pete coming to the rescue. The final push was up to me. I rested my head on my arms and drifted.

I must have dozed off, because I dreamed of dark shapes surging down a long green valley at dusk. Then I was running, running for the safety of a cave, hide cloak tossed back by the breeze, brown chert point clutched in my hand. I heard the heavy footsteps behind me, heard the hoarse breathing of a runner, felt my heart pumping with fear and the need to escape. I left the safety of the trail. One stranger followed. Only one. I glanced back. Across the ages another hand reached for me. . . .

I nearly jumped out of my skin when the hand touched my neck. I didn't know where I was. Lifting my head, I saw Raef's reflection in the mirror behind the bar, smelled the sweat and dust on his skin. Or was that my own? He must have mistaken my trembling for fear—until his eyes met mine in the mirror and he saw the stubborn set of my mouth. His grim smile of triumph drained away. I felt no fear now, only exhaustion such as I'd never before experienced. It filled every cell in my body, until even the neurons in my brain sparked in slow motion.

"Where did he take her?" Raef was breathing hard, as if he'd been running.

"I have no idea," I said, enunciating carefully. But still the words were slurred.

"Then come. I need you."

Back to square one. "No."

"Yes. Now get up." He grabbed a handful of my field vest, twisted, pulling me to my feet. "If it weren't for you, I'd have my wife and boy back."

I let myself hang by the vest, a dead weight. "Face it, Raef. They don't want you."

"Of course they do. They're mine. I'll make a trade—you, for them."

"No. I've had enough."

"Then I'll kill you."

I just looked at him, waiting for the knife. Unfortunately, the shotgun was with Freda, somewhere between here and Elko . . . a lifetime away.

The anger that seemed to bubble like carbonation just below the surface exploded. He threw me to the floor and followed me down, straddling my body, one sinewy hand gripping my throat. My left hand was caught up in my vest, the right wrist clamped under his against the smooth cool wood. I jerked my head once, trying to escape, and his thick black brows drew together in a frown as the hand tightened on my neck. I couldn't move, couldn't scream. I fastened my eyes on his face, waiting . . . wondering, in a detached way, what death would feel like. The beautiful, flat black eyes, windows to a soul long departed, stared down without expression. His nostrils flared. The thick dark mists started to descend.

My mind retreated and I looked down on our two bodies, one taut with purpose, one unresisting as a dead carp. My mind screamed at me to kick, strike, anything but this passive acceptance. And instinctively, as the need for air became desperate, my left hand searched for some way, any way to hurt him, stop him. Through the heavy cotton, my fingers felt the hard contours of the projectile point. I struggled to pull it out of my pocket while my lungs ached for air and the room darkened around me.

I aimed for his neck, but caught his cheek. He jerked back with surprise at the pain. When he lifted his hand to check my second jab, I sucked in the wonderful dry air. My mind was back in my body; the mists cleared a little, enough that I could see his face. The smile had disappeared. Blood ran down the glistening cheek to drip on my chest. And while he struggled to rip the point from my hand, I bucked and twisted, trying to dislodge him. The point flew out of my hand, bouncing harmlessly off the bar and down onto Freda's ramp. But then he had both my hands in one of his, and cursing, he backhanded me across the face. I think I whimpered once as the hand tightened again on my neck. . . .

"Let her go."

The blood pounding in my ears almost drowned out the voice that seemed to come from another galaxy. But the hand on my throat stilled, loosened, slowly withdrew. Forgotten or disregarded—I didn't care which—I gasped for air. When I could see again, I turned my swollen, throbbing neck, following Raef's gaze.

Killeen's bulk blocked the doorway. The light glared behind him, bouncing off the dusty road. I couldn't see his face. He leaned forward, weight on the balls of his feet, arms slightly out from his sides, relaxed. But his massive shoulders lifted and fell, and I knew he'd been running. He took two slow paces forward. I saw his ugliness as Raef must see it, as I had seen it for the first time six days ago: heavy, squat body; blunt face; wide-lipped mouth; slightly protuberant eyes; twice-broken, bulbous nose. At that moment, he was the most beautiful person I'd ever seen.

"The police are right behind me," he said.

I couldn't tell whether he was lying. I listened for sounds of the cavalry approaching, but my ears still roared with pulsing blood. It didn't matter. Raef believed.

"Let me pass, man." Raef rose lightly to his feet and stepped away from me in one fluid movement.

"No!" The thought of Raef free, lurking in the shadows, waiting to bury me again, was more than I could bear. It took me a moment to realize the sound had died in my throat. Neither man glanced my way.

"No," Killeen said. And I started to breathe again.

I saw thoughts chase themselves across Raef's mobile face. One eyebrow went up in disbelief and white teeth showed in a smile that curled down at the edges. "Sylvie . . . you think she'll have *you* when I'm back in prison?"

Killeen's voice was so soft I could barely make out the words. "She already has—*man.*"

Raef launched himself across the intervening distance, head down like a battering ram, arms out, hands tightened into claws. I felt, heard, the bodies collide, the impact shaking the plank floor, momentum carrying them out into the dusty street.

I watched in horror, fixated on the writhing forms. I had never seen men fight to kill. I was a pacifist. I'd never enjoyed boxing or professional wrestling, never been able to stomach the sight of people inflicting pain on one another. I'd reveled in team sports, in individual contests of skill. But this fight came from some ancient time and place. I felt sickened. I felt helpless. I felt an overwhelming urge to end the violence.

A weapon. I needed a weapon. I dragged my eyes away from the fight. My body trembled like an old woman with palsy, while my stomach threatened to force its meager contents past my throat. Even my legs betrayed me. So I dragged my body around the end of the bar through a mile of glass shards. Freda's ramp taunted me with its height. I pulled myself along the floor looking for the stone point, not knowing what good the puny weapon would do me now. But it had helped me twice before. It was something.

The point perched on the edge of the ramp above me, the tip coated with a blackening crust of blood . . . Raef's blood. I couldn't convince my hand to touch the tainted stone. A shudder started at my shoulders and worked its way down my body. Someone groaned outside. . . . It sounded like Killeen. Fumbling, I pulled out the crumpled red handkerchief, used it to grasp and wrap the point before sliding them into my vest pocket.

I was lying next to the storeroom door. Pushing my body into a sitting position, I searched the shadows with my eyes. The crowbar should be somewhere on the floor nearby. It lay six feet further along, against the base of the ramp. I scooted the remaining distance, feeling strength seep back into my legs as I reached the crowbar. Now I had two weapons—no, three. My knife was still in the leather pouch at my belt. A switchblade would have been heaven, I thought, as I pried open the blade with my teeth. Crowbar in right hand, knife in left, I crawled out to engage the enemy.

I paused near the doorway to catch my breath. The fight continued out of sight to my right, the soundtrack consisting of grunts and thuds, scrapes and ominous silences. Obviously, the cavalry hadn't arrived. Killeen had lied again. I shouldn't have been surprised—*everyone* in Pair-a-Dice lied: Diane about her novel; Killeen about sleeping with Sylvie; me about having Diane's manuscript; Lon about the rockslide; Raef about having Tommy. . . . Pair-a-Dice was going to hell.

I don't know how I expected to stop the fight—a baby could have taken away my weapons. Dragging myself to the threshold, I tried my voice, but managed nothing louder than a wheeze. The wrestlers didn't pause.

I remembered, as a child, watching a Greco-style wrestling demonstration on television: the pit of fine sand, dust coating glistening skin. There was an element of sport to that contest. Even in professional wrestling, a pause for dramatic effect follows a brutal hit. This was different. Organized sports, our culture's metaphors for war, paled against this fight with teeth, knees, head butts. Fingers reached to gouge out eyes . . . failed.

They broke apart for a moment, circled, neither speaking. Raef laughed. Killeen's face was carved basalt. And then they closed again, bending, twisting, stomping together in a frenzied dance, feet pounding out a furious rhythm, like the tarantella I saw once in an old documentary.

The furious tempo stopped suddenly. Through the screen of dust, I saw two bodies that looked like one huge animal with eight legs. Raef lay belly down in the dirt, right arm bent cruelly back, his body covered by Killeen's black-clad bulk. Raef's teeth showed in a rictus-like grimace as he tried to buck Killeen from his back. Killeen, chest heaving, facial muscles set, refused to be thrown. Raef rested his cheek on the ground. Little puffs of dust rose at each breath.

I started to relax. In the heavy silence, a truck roared to a stop at the corner of the building. Even Sylvie had lied—she drove a stick shift.

"Don't kill him," she yelled at Killeen, her voice high and shrill.

Killeen took his eyes off Raef. I saw Raef's fingers clutch a handful of dirt and fling it back and up. Blinded, Killeen put his left hand automatically to his eyes. He momentarily relaxed his grip and I saw Raef's muscles bunch. Killeen toppled to the side in slow motion. Raef, first on his feet, launched a vicious kick at Killeen's head. I heard a dull thud, and Killeen lay still.

Then Sylvie was standing, Killeen's gun pointed at the pair. I don't to this day know which man was the target.

And the gun went off.

The bullet kicked dust, missing Killeen's head by inches, the report splintering the quiet morning. Raef's head swiveled in Sylvie's direction. Laying down my crowbar and knife, I used the doorframe to pull myself upright. The acrid smell of gunpowder hung in the soft air.

Sylvie stared down at the gun as if it were a scorpion poised to strike. "I didn't mean to," she said. "Really. I didn't mean to."

Raef started towards her, hand outstretched. He'd taken two steps when she looked up.

"Don't make me shoot you, too, Raef." Sylvie must have thought she'd hit Killeen. The gun wobbled in her hand . . . and she dropped it.

I reacted instinctively. Two strides of my long legs brought me to within kicking distance. As Raef's hand reached for the gun, I booted it in a low arc into the sagebrush across the road. Bless my steel-toed leather.

Raef, already striding toward the truck, checked when he saw Sylvie's arm move. Sunlight glinted off keys as they traveled the path of the gun. In an instant, Raef's hands fastened around her neck. Sylvie fixed her eyes on his. I flinched. It might as well have been my neck back in his grasp.

I hadn't heard Killeen move, but as I hobbled in search of the gun, he passed me, blood dripping from a cut above his ear. He grabbed Raef from behind, wrapped huge arms around his chest, locked fingers together . . . and squeezed. They stood there, like some frozen *ménage à trois:* Raef's hands still at Sylvie's throat, Killeen's arms crushing her husband's chest. Time seemed to stand still. When Raef exhaled, Killeen's grasp tightened, mimicking a boa constrictor killing its prey. Dark muscles bulged in Killeen's arms; I thought I heard bones crack. Sylvie's face was turning blue, but her look never wavered. If I didn't find that gun quickly, she'd be dead.

The seconds seemed like eternity as I scrabbled among the sagebrush, the pungent scent filling my nostrils. I spotted the dusty handle in the middle of a tiny clearing, barrel pointing down into a rabbit hole. Clutching the heavy gun, I turned to face the trio. Raef's hands fell; his head lolled forward. When Killeen loosened his grip, Raef crumpled at his feet. Sylvie swayed, dropped to Raef's side, half-kneeling, half-leaning against him, golden hair brushing his chest. I watched her hand reach out tentatively, pause, then touch his uncut cheek. Killeen didn't say anything, just stood spraddle-legged looking down at her with a bleak expression.

"I'll go call an ambulance," I whispered.

"Not for him." The words seemed forced out of Killeen. He'd taken a risk, made a choice. In order to save Sylvie, he'd taken her husband's life.

Sylvie uttered a choking cry. Wrapping her arms around Killeen's leg, she buried her face against his massive thigh. I saw her shake, silent sobs tearing through her body. I felt like a voyeur. As I turned away to give them privacy, I saw one dark hand slip down to stroke the shining hair.

The vast sky, devoid now of clouds, covered us like an inverted glazed bowl. One buzzard glided on the air currents above us, then two, circling, eternally patient. On the ground, Raef's body seemed to shrink. One by one, the flies arrived, alighting on smooth skin and stained clothes. The air smelled of death.

The heat of the morning sun prickled my skin, and I felt the salty sting of sweat in the cuts on my hands and face. I was not needed here. The darkness of the barroom door beckoned. My feet were lead weights that dragged through the dust. I plucked the truck keys from a saltbush as I passed, paused on the threshold to pocket the knife and pick up the crowbar. I dropped the latter in the shadows behind the bar—I didn't want to try to explain to Buddy why I'd allowed Killeen to kill Raef when I had a crowbar handy. I didn't know the answer myself.

The fractured glass of the fluorescent-mineral display distorted the glowing colors inside. The mirror behind the bar reflected a Halloween mask where my face should be—hollowed eyes, red and green streaks on purple shadows. Sirens wailed in the distance, coming closer. My head pounded and the colors wavered as I walked around the bar. I reached for the light switch, heard a crunch as a figure blocked the light from the doorway. Jamie?

"You're a little late," I told my brother, before dancing black dots fused into a blob that shut out the world.

Twenty-One

I awoke to a hospital room decorated in shades of beige, except for the pastel swirls on the window curtains. Clint Black's voice sang softly from the small black boombox that perched on a peach-colored chair beyond the foot of the bed. Slowly, my senses awakened. If there is a heaven, I decided, it has cotton sheets worn smooth by years of use, like those that swaddled my body. I became aware of hospital sounds, muted voices that seemed to ebb and flow from a different dimension. From somewhere nearby came steady breathing, the creak and rustle of someone moving restlessly. The antiseptic smells of cleansers and the sharp odor of broccoli pricked my nostrils. I felt the intravenous tube at my wrist, one discomfort among many. But I was alive.

There was a slight scraping sound, the sound a swinging door makes when it doesn't quite clear the vinyl flooring. Quiet footsteps. When I turned my head, waves of colored light flashed in front of my eyes. I decided to lie still. Warm fingers felt for a pulse; a tiny flashlight checked my pupils.

"You'll live," said my brother, the pediatrician, who needed some work on his bedside manner. I hoped he was better with children. "How's the pain, G. I. Jane?"

"Stupid question." I couldn't manage more than a ragged whisper.

"That bad, huh? You look like you went a few rounds with Holyfield—in a sandstorm." He pressed a button attached to the I.V. tube. "This should make you feel better in a few minutes. Did you get my letter?"

Letter . . . letter . . . I tried to think, but the synapses misfired.

"About Geoff?" he prompted.

Oh, God—that letter. "I got it."

"I'm sorry, Frankie. I wanted to tell you in person, but I couldn't get away from the hospital until yesterday."

"It's all right. I'm all right. At least I know what happened."

The bed creaked as he sat down. Bless his heart, he didn't say I'd botched things up, made stupid choices, nearly gotten myself killed. His long fingers traced the surface of something in his left hand, like a blind man feeling the image on a coin. The projectile point. The blade was clean; the remnants of Raef's blood washed away. "Isabel found it when she did your laundry."

"It seems like you've met the denizens of Pair-a-Dice."

"Quite a few." He handed me the point.

The chert felt warm in my palm. "This saved my life," I said. "More than once." Speaking in a whisper, I told him of ancient murders; of landslide, cave, coyote pups, and helicopters; of my own emergence from the grave; and finally, of Killeen's arrival and the dance with death.

Jamie took the blade and ran the edge lightly across the back of his wrist, leaving behind a white streak of dead skin. "It should be in a museum."

"Probably. But I have something else in mind." The words slurred. The painkiller was taking effect. I felt myself sliding into that nether world between sleep and wakefulness, where pain doesn't exist.

Faceless beasts chased me through endless corridors. Their frigid breath touched my neck, claws clicked on dry limestone walls. I searched for a doorway, a window, any exit from the labyrinth. There were no helpful green signs to point the way. I sped faster, hampered by the wheelchair I pushed across a floor littered with human bones and fossil shells. Sylvie sat unblinking in the chair, Tommy on her lap. I couldn't desert them, couldn't save them.

One beast grabbed my shoulder, jerking me to a stop. I turned to see a butter knife raised in its paw . . . Butter knife? I laughed. This couldn't be hell—the Devil's minions don't carry butter knives. Which meant that I probably wasn't dead, either.

Desperation drained away as I struggled to push aside the heavy velvet layers of sleep. I felt a kiss, soft as the brush of a butterfly's wing, touch my forehead, then my lips. I awoke to laughing blue eyes in a healthy, weather-beaten face. Gone were the stale odors of cigarettes and alcohol. He smelled of soap and herbal shampoo and shaving cream. . . . He smelled a lot better than I did, actually.

"Figured it was safe," said Bill. "You're in no position to fight back."

"Where's Jamie?" I asked, my voice a raspy thread of sound. It hurt to breathe, let alone talk. "Or did I imagine him?"

"Getting a bite to eat. He'll be back in a few minutes." He trailed a hand across my cheek—a light touch where Raef's hand had left deep ache. "The rest of your family's been calling."

My family. I'd have a lot of explaining to do, but it could wait. "How's Randy?"

"He'll be okay. Found him in the middle of Easy Street—he blacked out on the way to Isabel's. I just had a hunch all of a sudden that there was trouble in town, so I came back early. Too late to help you, though."

The story of my life. "Killeen—" My voice petered out as images of the fight crawled off a dusty street and into my mind.

"I know. Sylvie's in the room across the hall." He took my hand, gently rubbing his thumb over the bandages.

"What happened . . . after?" I asked.

"Killeen won't be charged with anything. It was self-defense. Sylvie'll be okay—Killeen's keeping an eye on her and Tommy. Raef's autopsy's done. He'll be buried on Monday."

"What's today?" I asked.

"Thursday."

"Still?"

He looked at his watch. "Only for another hour or so."

"Ruth?"

"Is in seclusion at the ranch. Diane's moved in to keep her company." There was an odd note in his voice, and his eyes flickered towards the door as he said it.

Something niggled at the back of my mind, something I needed to clear up with Diane and Ruth. But I couldn't focus. Maybe it was shock, maybe the drugs that slid down the I.V. It didn't matter. . . . Diane could wait. I started to drift off again.

"Frankie?"

"Umm?"

"I pulled out your Jeep and fixed it up."

"Atonement?" I was only half-listening.

"Something like that. I brought your notebook and maps. They're in the drawer—along with some papers Isabel gave me." He pointed to the bedside table. "I . . . I read them."

So he knew at least part of the story. "I'm sorry," I whispered.

"Me, too," he said. "You should never have gotten involved in our troubles." Bill used tissues from the bedside box to dab ineffectually at the tears that slid from the corners of my eyes to soak my hair and pillow. When he couldn't stem the flow, he gave up and tossed the pile of tissues in a nearby trash can. "I also stopped by the school library and took Ma's copy of the Bovey genealogy before Diane could destroy it. Walker gave it to me. He's fine, by the way—his head's as hard as Freda's bar."

"Your black-light boxes came in pretty handy."

"Glad I did *something* right. I'll fix them up before I leave."

"Where to?"

"Reno. Mackay's said they'd take me back into the mining program—on probation. I'll have to prove myself all over again. Randy'll go the U, and we can live together—at least till he can scrape up enough money to live on his own.

"Jail was good for me. I went to AA. Had time to sit and think—"

"Novel idea."

"Oh, shut up. Anyway, I talked to Father Vincent. I knew him a long time ago . . . before Ma died, before . . . well, I started taking my anger out on everyone around me. That's one reason Emmajean and I broke up. And because I realized Bobby couldn't be mine. I was still at MacKay when he was conceived."

"You know who the father was?"

"I figured it out early on. He looked enough like me to be a blood relative. That meant Lon. So I helped support him. I didn't want to see my half-brother fall through the cracks like Randy and I did." He read my look. "Yeah, I know the story. Lon's first wife, Ann, had polio. She was in an iron lung for years. Lon and Ma were going to marry when Ann died, but Ma died first. I found letters from Lon among her things. I burned them."

"Why? They proved who your father was."

"Lon changed after Ma died. Oh, he went through the motions—married Ruth, had kids. But inside he was twisted. Or maybe he was always that way, only he kept it hidden. Anyway, I decided it was better for Randy and me to make our own way. There's just one thing. . . . " Bill fished something out of the coin pocket of his jeans. Turning my hand over, he placed a small silver bell in the palm—my missing earring. In his eyes I saw a pain as deep as my own. "I found this on the road above the crash site. I didn't show it to anyone. I wanted to talk to you first."

I didn't say anything. My throat constricted; my mind resurrected the helicopter, the rain-slick road, the thud of rock on Plexiglas.

"Frankie, what was Lon . . . er, did Lon . . . shit, this is hard. I mean, I just need to know what he was doing out there in the storm." Bill was expecting the worst, was braced for the worst. But at the same time he wanted desperately to have me tell him his father wasn't as sick as he believed.

What good would it do to tell the truth now? Only the living would bleed—the seven Bovey offspring, Ruth, and Gabbie. Lon could no longer be hurt. . . . My moral compass swung two more degrees off magnetic north. "I'm not sure, Bill. But he flew way too low and clipped the hillside. It happened quickly."

Tears welled in his eyes. He got up and walked over to the window. There was a soft knock on the door, and Randy peeked in before closing it again. I don't think Bill noticed. Footsteps crunched in the gravel outside. I heard Randy say something, then Jamie's baritone. Bill took a couple of deep breaths and turned around, rubbing his cheeks. "Life's a bitch," he said.

"And then you die," I said.

———

Buddy arrived in the wee hours, looking tired but satisfied. His questioning was a straightforward affair. He concentrated on my interactions with Raef, and he seemed satisfied with the answers. He asked a few questions about the helicopter crash, just for the record. He assumed Lon was out chasing strays when he was caught by the storm. I let him assume. But I couldn't just ignore Lon's involvement with Shelley Gates's disappearance. I suggested Buddy have a talk with Milo. I wondered what story Milo would make up for knowing where his sister's body was buried all this time, yet never reporting her murder.

"You'll be okay?" Buddy closed his notebook with a snap of the wrist.

"So Jamie tells me." Jamie was deep in slumberland on top of the adjacent bed.

"I don't mean physically."

"I expect it'll fade in time, along with the bruises."

"Talking helps," he said, touching my hand. "I've been there."

A few minutes after he left, Killeen tiptoed in. There was a bandage behind his ear, but he moved with silent grace and looked content. He was holding a sleeping Tommy in his arms. Hospital rules about visiting hours wouldn't faze Killeen. "You're awake," he said, sotto voce, and smiled.

"My internal clock's all screwed up. How's Sylvie?"

"About the same as you, I'd wager. Fragile. Fighting nightmares. She feels thankful it's over, yet guilty that she's thankful. It'll sort itself out."

"Promise?" I'd tried to reassure Buddy; now I needed Killeen's reassurance. I watched him shift Tommy from right shoulder to left. I envied Tommy that shoulder.

"Yes. Just don't rush it."

We weren't talking about Sylvie's mental health any more. "Geoff's dead," I said. The words sounded bald even to my ears.

"I'm sorry. What happened?"

"They don't really know. He fell, or was pushed, off a cliff."

"Another mystery. And speaking of mysteries, Buddy gave me Bessie's tooth and button," Killeen said, patting a box-shaped outline in his breast pocket. "Tomorrow I'm going to bury them . . . with John."

"You found the grave?"

"I always knew where it was. More or less. Once I found Thomasson's cabin it was no sweat. I'd like you to be there tomorrow afternoon—if you're able."

"I'll be there . . . come hell or high water."

"The forecast is for clear skies," he said, and took his precious bundle back across the hall to Sylvie's room.

Twenty-Two

The geologist in me hated loose ends. I finally remembered why I had to talk to Diane and Ruth, so I checked myself out of the clinic at dawn and had Jamie drive me to Paradise Ranch. I dreaded the confrontation to come, yet wanted to get it over with as quickly as possible.

Milo walked out to meet us as we rumbled over the cattle guard and pulled to a stop in front of the stone ranch house. He stood next to the passenger window, hands in pockets, looking uneasy.

"I'm not sorry about anything I did," Milo said. "But if it makes you feel better, I've been sacked."

He deserved it, but it didn't make me feel better. I'd never been able to hold grudges. Hate destroys. "Why?"

"Had a dust-up with Diane. She's livin' here now."

The obnoxious sound of a jackhammer came from an area in back of the house where the helicopter pad stood. "Is that Buddy?" I asked.

"Yeah. He came nosin' around. Asked about Shelley." Milo looked at the dust cloud raised by the jackhammer. If I hadn't known him, I'd have suspected he was hurting inside. Maybe he'd loved his sister. "I told him, and I'll tell you: Lon had rough sex with my sister. Too rough, but he never meant for it to go that far. Lon said he'd tell Buddy *I* killed her, if I didn't keep quiet. Now, who d'ya think they'd believe? So I helped him build that helicopter pad over her grave. . . ."

Shelley's under the center mark. From up there," he pointed to the sky, "it looks like a cross."

"Is that why you wanted the last chapters of Diane's book? As proof to take to Buddy?"

"Hell, no. Goddamn, you're retarded, Frankie. Those pages meant I'd keep my job till I was so old I had to crawl the fuckin' fence line. That's all I ever wanted, to be foreman of this spread." And now he'd lost the one thing that mattered. "In spite of that I miss him, ya know? I really miss him. This country lost a great man. He shoulda been fuckin' *president.* "

God forbid. "I have a feeling you two'll share a bunkhouse someday, " I said, as he walked to his truck. But I was talking to dust.

"You go ahead. I'll stretch my legs," Jamie said.

I watched him wander off toward the corrals before I knocked at the door. Gabbie let me into the flagstone foyer. She looked immeasurably older somehow, but happier. Definitely happier.

"It's awfully quiet around here," I said. "Where are the boys?"

"Gram and Gramps took them down to Salt Lake for a few days."

"And you miss them already."

"How'd you know?" She smiled that beautiful smile, Diane's smile minus the cynicism.

"Because I have brothers, too. One of them's outside. Want to show him around for me?"

"Sure!" And she was out the door like quicksilver. "Mom's in the kitchen," she called over her shoulder.

Diane and Ruth were sitting at a large oak table in the breakfast nook, hands clasped around mugs of steaming coffee. They didn't bother to get up, just poured me a cup and waved me to a chair.

Ruth was wearing black. I noticed that the bruises on her face had nearly faded away. A jungle-print scarf tucked into the neck of a conventional khaki shirtwaist covered Diane's bruises. The pigtail was gone; her roots were showing. Defensively, she brushed a hand across the neatly trimmed ends. "I'm growing it out," she said.

I dropped a manila envelope, the one that had been taped to the underside of Diane's filing cabinet, on the table. They women seemed to draw closer together, although their chairs didn't move.

"We're alone," I said. "I sent Gabbie outside to show my brother around. There's no reason she should hear this—at least, from me."

"Thanks," Diane said. The chip still rested squarely on her shoulder. "Do you want to start, or shall I?"

"By all means, counselor, take the floor." Diane picked up the envelope, undid the clasp, pulled out the papers and the audiotape.

"Bill has Nora Bovey's genealogy. He took it from the library." I spoke to Diane, but I watched Ruth out of the corner of my eye. She was the more vulnerable of the two. "I've pieced together most of the story, including Lon's abuse and Ruth's fear that she'd lose custody of the children. I know that she asked you for help because you're Gabbie's birth mother. I know you moved to Pair-a-Dice to be near her."

"How—" Ruth started.

"Shush," Diane said. "I want to hear this."

I switched my attention to Ruth. "To protect you and Gabbie, Diane started an affair with Lon—if he were focused on her, he wouldn't be hurting you. She started her novel, a masterpiece of fiction that contained just enough fact to make me believe it was autobiographical. But a few things didn't fit. Diane was raised a Mormon in Provo, not a Catholic in California. Bill confirmed that she got the tattoo after she came to Pair-a-Dice, not in the Middle East. She plagiarized whole passages from Nora Bovey's book. And she lifted the story line from Charlene's song, right down to the clergyman. 'I've been to paradise, but I've never been to me'? As puns go, it wasn't bad."

"We were pressed for time," Diane said.

"What was on the last four pages that Ruth tore out of your notebook?"

"Only the—"

"Ruth—" But Diane was too late. I already knew who had mailed me the notebook. It no longer mattered what the pages held. "Look, Frankie, in order to put Lon away, without involving Ruth or me directly, we had to release the information about Shelley through someone else. But before you could read the manuscript, Lon killed Emmajean. That would have been the end of it if Raef Kingsley hadn't come along and taken the blame for her murder. Lon was off the hook. Again. The Teflon Lon. So we had to improvise. We gave you the rest of the manuscript and staged my attack."

"You both risked a hell of a lot, Diane. If I'd been one minute later, you wouldn't be sitting here."

"Ruth was wearing gloves. She didn't realize how far she'd gone until it was too late." Diane ran a hand across her throat. "Luckily, you arrived—in the nick of time, so to speak."

204

"It never occurred to you that by giving me that manuscript you were making *me* a target?"

"You're angry."

"That's an understatement. For Christ's sake, Diane! Lon sent a *mountain* down on my head, on Killeen's head. And when that didn't work, he came after me in the helicopter. All because of that manuscript. Indirectly, you and Ruth could have been responsible for four deaths."

"Four?" said Ruth.

"Emmajean's, Killeen's, Lon's—and mine."

"Lon killed Emmajean because she tried to blackmail him, Frankie. Diane and I had nothing to do with it. We honestly didn't think you and Killeen were in any danger."

"I wish I could believe that."

"Nothing that Ruth said could convince you now. But with Lon dead and the manuscript destroyed, there's also nothing linking us to what happened."

"Except for the last two chapters. I gave the notebook to Buddy. That's why he's out there digging up the landing pad."

Diane laughed. "He can't hurt us, Frankie. Shelley's body will prove the truth of what's in those last two chapters. Buddy will find that they're in Emmajean's handwriting. She wrote them long before she died."

"But I saw—"

"You saw me doodling in a notebook that was written weeks ago when Emmajean decided she wanted more money from Lon. I offered to help, that's all."

"But why involve me, Diane?"

"Because you were from the outside. Because you were honest and available."

"And expendable?"

"No, never that. You were just a vehicle to get the word out. None of the rest of it would have happened if Raef hadn't followed Sylvie to Pair-a-Dice and been blamed for my attack. The whole thing was a comedy of errors."

"I'm not laughing."

"You don't understand. We were desperate," Ruth said, shifting closer to Diane, who smoothed her hand over the chestnut hair. "With Lon in jail, Gabbie and the boys would be safe . . . I'd be safe. We could get on with our lives."

I pushed back my chair. My coffee sat untouched on the table. I didn't trust them enough to drink it. That was one of the legacies they'd left me. Mistrust and unanswered questions. I'd always wonder if Lon killed Emmajean because one of them revealed what Emmajean had written in that green notebook. I'd always wonder if they knew what Lon would do to her and didn't give a damn. I'd always wonder if it was about money rather than survival. "Thank God, Randy will never know he's related to the Bovey family," I said at last.

"We wouldn't have let Billy stand trial," Ruth said.

"Wouldn't you?"

"I had to think of the children—"

"*Bobby's* a child, for God's sake. And now he has no mother."

Ruth's face crumbled. The more she scrubbed at the tears, the blotchier and more miserable she looked. Diane pulled her gently into her arms, giving me a fierce look. "Let it go, Frankie. Leave us alone. Whatever you may think of us, we did what we thought was best. It's over."

"I wish you joy in each other," I said, staring at them for a moment before I made my way to the front door. I shut it firmly behind me.

———

Killeen, Sylvie, and Tommy were waiting in the dusty front yard of Easy Thomasson's cabin. Tommy had collected a pile of pebbles and was sculpting them into a mountain. Every time he exceeded the angle of repose, the sides trickled down. Jamie hunkered down beside him, keeping him company, giving me the space to say my farewells.

From the ground beside the front door, Killeen picked up an irregular piece of sandstone crudely carved with John's name. It had been protected through the years by the rosebushes that flowered still in the August heat—a nicer tribute than the cold headstone Lon would have. I'd rather be fodder for a rosebush than crowded into a graveyard with all the Boveys and their sins.

Killeen consigned Bessie's tooth, the wind-worn green button, and a small cloth bag holding who knew what to the hole he'd dug under the thorns. Sylvie read the traditional Biblical verses, and Killeen finished with something I'd never heard.

"And we are put on earth a little space," he said, "That we may learn to bear the beams of love, And these black bodies and this sunburnt face Is but a cloud, and like a shady grove." Then he answered the question in my eyes. "It's from a poem by William Blake."

Killeen covered the makeshift graves with John's marker and a new sandstone block carved with Bessie's name. A peregrine falcon screamed high among the canyon cliffs. Killeen glanced up, tracking the sound.

We walked slowly to the trucks. "What next?" I asked him.

"I'll keep moving, looking for a place to settle. This isn't it."

"What about you, Sylvie?" Her face had lost the haunted, hunted look; her eyes had lost their innocence. Pain had etched grooves in her forehead and cheeks. She'd danced with Death, and some piece of her had died with Raef, just as her dreams had died. Her already slim body looked as if it wouldn't stand up to a modest gust of wind, yet she wore serenity like a mantle.

I knew I looked similarly changed. When I'd dressed that morning in a pair of loose cotton pants and soft red tee shirt, everything seemed a size too big—even the sandals I slipped on my feet. And mottled cheekbones and huge gray eyes dominated my reflection in the mirror.

"We're going with Eddie," Sylvie said. "It will be lovely to choose a place just because I like it, for a change."

"If you get to Tucson, you're welcome to stay with us until you get on your feet. There's plenty of room at my parents' place."

"We just might do that," she said, giving me a hug.

I hunkered down in front of Tommy. The pebble mountain had been redeposited as a gravel bed.

"I'm sorry about your father, Tommy."

"Is he an angel, now?"

Chilling thought. But even Lucifer was an angel. "Could be, Tommy."

I kissed Killeen's cheek. I was too sore to hug him. Besides, the last person I'd seen him hug had stopped breathing. He walked with me to where Jamie waited patiently by the Jeep. "Tell me something, Killeen?" I asked as I opened the door.

"Maybe."

"What was the second reason you came to Pair-a-Dice?"

"I was in the Middle East with Isabel's husband. I got food poisoning, and Ted took a mission—alone. Something went wrong. If I'd been there . . . Well, anyway, it's still classified, so I couldn't write or call Isabel. I shouldn't even have contacted her. But I had to. I owed it to them both."

In my mind, the death assemblage extended on beyond the horizon.

The late afternoon sky held clouds like frozen ripples in Triassic sandstone. Jamie and I parked where Milo had parked the day he checked his coyote trap. I led the way toward the split-boled juniper. The air was so still we could hear the musical plink of water in the cave. Jamie held the branches apart for me to crawl through, then followed me inside. The sun wasn't high enough to dispel the gloom, so I turned on my flashlight.

Jamie silently picked up the bone disc, running his fingers lightly over the grooves. Someone had been here since my visit—a jackrabbit's foot, carefully preserved, lay next to the quartz crystal. I took the chert point from my pocket and placed it next to the disc on the small limestone shelf. Turning my back, I put my hand where the braid touched the base of my neck. "Cut it for me, Jamie. Right here." I held out my pocketknife.

"You can't be serious. You'll regret it tomorrow."

"No I won't. It's caused me no end of trouble."

I felt a tug as he sawed through the thick braid, heard him say, "Jesus." My head felt wonderfully light. Jamie handed me what looked like a lariat. I coiled the silken rope and placed it next to the projectile point. "Animal, vegetable and mineral," Jamie said.

"What?"

"The offerings—water, minerals, leather, bone, seeds. I was trying to figure out what gods they served here."

"This is a woman's place, I think . . . Mother Earth, Gaea, Ishtar, Isis, Ceres—she's been given so many names."

After one last look, I turned to the entrance. From the corner of my eye, I saw Jamie place the knife across the braid before rinsing his hands in the basin and drying them on his jeans. The need for symbolic gestures appeared to be contagious.

Walker was sitting next to the Jeep, spearing pieces of pineapple straight from the can he held between thumb and little finger. Only stubs remained where the other three fingers should be. A riflescope was fixed to his belt with crude leather thongs.

"Hi, Walker. You're looking better," I said. "The jackrabbit foot was a nice touch."

He kept his eyes fixed on the pineapple.

"I think this belongs to you. I found it a few days ago." I pulled a torn glove from my pocket. "A little the worse for wear, I'm afraid. I had to use it on the mountain." I held it out where he could see it without lifting his eyes. When still he didn't move, I placed it on his knee and kissed his cheek. He started to his feet, like a buck surprised on a twilight meadow. "That's for helping me find Nora Bovey's genealogy. And for giving it to Bill. Good-bye, Walker. Keep watch over Pair-a-Dice."

Before the words were out of my mouth, he was striding away on gangly legs, pineapple can clutched in one hand. The other hand touched his cheek.

SATURDAY, AUGUST 12

At first light, the Jeep was packed and filled with gas. Jamie and I drove by Pete's to fill my thermos with coffee and grab four cinnamon rolls. As I paid Fern, I heard scrabbling sounds from the lot next door where Bill and Randy were hard at work. Although it was early, both men were stripped to the waist. They were mixing mortar in a rusty blue wheelbarrow. The front wall was as high as my head. I didn't stop to visit. We'd said our good-byes at the hospital.

"You don't suppose there are more bodies entombed in those foundations and walls, do you?" my brother asked.

"Don't go there, Jamie. Don't even *think* about going there. Just honk and wave and drive as fast as you dare. You can tell me boring hospital stories all the way home."

So we turned our backs on Pair-a-Dice, pointed the Jeep in the direction of Tucson, and followed the blue highway south.

Acknowledgments

Although Frankie MacFarlane, Pair-a-Dice, Nevada, and its denizens are my inventions, the geology portrayed here—including the rocks and fossils, faults and folds—is true to the northern Great Basin. Therefore, I would like to thank all of the geologists who climbed the mountains with me and who helped me collect, decipher, and interpret the geologic clues contained in the rocks. And to those who long ago suggested that I might be creating structural fairy tales in the field, I say: perhaps you were right—about the fairy tales, if not the structure.

Novels are not written in a vacuum. A supportive community of fellow writers, scientists, friends, and family members offered invaluable comments on the manuscript-in-progress and roped me in when I ventured too far down tangential pathways. In particular, I would like to thank Maura Baker, Lynda Gibson, Leesa Jacobson, Jan Mike, the Miller and Chapman families, Steven Moore, Lisa Cher-nin Newman, Carol Nowotny-Young, Davis Palmer, Barbara Porter, Robert Powers, Jim Sullivan, John Weston, and Allen Woodman. For their careful reading of and suggestions regarding the final version, I am indebted to Drs. Douglas M. Morton, Lou H. Rodenberger, and Carole Young. And for their humor and patience during the book's gestation period, I am grateful to Jonathan, Jordan, and Logan Matti.

Lastly, my thanks go to Judith Keeling for her act of faith, to copyeditor Sr. Kilian Metcalf for her attention to detail, and to the staff of Texas Tech University Press for their help in bringing this book to completion.

Don't Miss

DETACHMENT FAULT

NEXT IN THE **FRANKIE MACFARLANE** MYSTERIES

We were off Cholla Bay, seventeen miles out in the Sea of Cortez, when our fishing lines became tangled with a rope-bound package. During the previous night, someone else had gone fishing. He'd used Jorge as bait.

My younger brother Jamie, his girlfriend Carla, and I shared the boat with a family of three from St. Paul. Our skipper, Chuy Desierto, a Seri Indian with leathery skin, mischievous black eyes, and compact body, had been guiding our family fishing trips since I was a child. He remembered me, he said, though I'd been away twelve years.

The sea was calm, the swells as gentle as an unbaffled waterbed. High-altitude haze created a halo around the sun. Throughout the morning, there had been just enough breeze to keep us cool, not enough to make big waves. For five hours, Chuy had led us from fishing hole to fishing hole, using small squid to coax triggerfish, rockfish, and flounder onto our hooks. Our final stop was his favorite fishing hole, marked by an old buoy—and by Jorge.

Shock, dismay, and anger flashed across Chuy's face as he looked from the water to me. "*Mi hermano* . . . Jorge," he said.

Oh God, I thought. I felt helpless—and nauseous. I shouldn't have been able to identify the body. I'd seen Jorge only twice before, and there wasn't much left of the man in the water: a portion of his bloodless torso and upper arms, partially covered by a tattered, plaid shirt. But I remembered the shirt.

Jorge's coarse black hair drifted back and forth with the waves. His face was gone. Somehow, a heavy gold chain with its sunburst medallion still clung to his neck—a most effective lure.

The St. Paul family promptly lost their lunch over the side of the flat-bottomed skiff. I chewed furiously on my cinnamon-flavored gum. Carla Zorya dropped her pole, moaned something unintelligible, and curled up in the bow of the boat. I covered her with my jacket.

Chuy cut the weighted line that held the body just under the surface. Then, with Jamie's help, he gingerly hauled what was left of Jorge aboard. Jamie, who'd explored his share of cadavers in medical school, returned to his seat in silence, his wind-burned face a study in control.

Chuy opened the throttle with shaky fingers. The skiff had a big, fast motor, but it still took forty-five minutes to get back to Puerto Peñasco. When we reached the beach, a crowd gathered around the boat. Two boys ran off to get the police as Jamie lifted Carla out.

"I want to go home," said Carla.

We were on the road in thirty minutes, some kind of record, even for MacFarlanes. It never occurred to us that our departure might be misinterpreted. It took us seventy-five minutes, driving the speed limit, to reach the border at Sonoyta. Three lanes were open. The car in front of us was waved through. A border guard in khaki uniform, automatic rifle over his shoulder, tapped at Jamie's window. He rolled it down. The guard ordered us to pull off to the right and park. He looked all of seventeen. Two other guards closed in, one at Carla's window, one at the back. My stomach plummeted through the floorboards.

— **DETACHMENT FAULT** *coming in 2004* —

from Texas Tech University Press

SUSAN CUMMINS MILLER was born and reared in Southern California, where she studied history, anthropology, and geology. She worked as a field geologist with the U.S. Geological Survey and taught geology and oceanography before becoming a writer of fiction, nonfiction, and poetry. She now lives in Tucson, Arizona.